A DAGGER BEFORE ME

A Selection of Recent Titles by Jeanne M. Dams
from Severn House

A DAGGER
BEFORE ME

Jeanne M. Dams

This first world edition published 2019
in Great Britain and the USA by
SEVERN HOUSE PUBLISHERS LTD of
Eardley House, 4 Uxbridge Street, London W8 7SY.
Trade paperback edition first published
in Great Britain and the USA 2019 by
SEVERN HOUSE PUBLISHERS LTD.

British Library Cataloguing in Publication Data
A CIP catalogue record for this title is available from the British Library.

ISBN-13: 978-0-7278-8870-9 (cased)
ISBN-13: 978-1-84751-995-5 (trade paper)
ISBN-13: 978-1-4483-0208-6 (e-book)

This is a work of fiction. Names, characters, places and incidents
are either the product of the author's imagination or are used fictitiously.
Except where actual historical events and characters are being described
for the storyline of this novel, all situations in this publication are
fictitious and any resemblance to actual persons, living or dead,
business establishments, events or locales is purely coincidental.

All Severn House titles are printed on acid-free paper.

Severn House Publishers support the Forest Stewardship Council™ [FSC™],
the leading international forest certification organisation.
All our titles that are printed on FSC certified paper carry the FSC logo.

Typeset by Palimpsest Book Production Ltd.,
Falkirk, Stirlingshire, Scotland.
Printed and bound in Great Britain by
TJ International, Padstow, Cornwall.

'Is this a dagger which I see before me . . .?'

William Shakespeare
Macbeth, Act II, Scene 1

AUTHOR'S NOTE

The inspiration for this book was the book *Keepers of the Kingdom* by Alastair Bruce, Julian Calder, and Mark Cator. I had forgotten I owned it, and when I came across it while cleaning out bookshelves I was immediately entranced. My copy was published in the United States in 1999; I'm sure there are more recent editions, and I heartily recommend it to anyone interested in Britain, her history and her traditions.

Many of my books are almost as much travelogue as mystery, and this one has perhaps more of that element than most. If you have no interest in eccentric English ceremonies, you can skip to chapter nine without missing too much of the plot.

The most recent State Opening of Parliament, as of this writing, involved less ceremonial than usual, because an unexpected election changed the date of the Opening and the Queen had insufficient time to rehearse. The date change also required the cancellation of the Garter Ceremony at Windsor Castle. In writing this book, I have made the assumption that all will proceed normally in my fictional time frame (which is somewhat altered from the likely real-life dates).

A note about settings: many of the ceremonies and incidents described in the book are real, and I have used the real settings. Otley Hall is real, and was really where that historic journey was planned, and the Beaumonts are as delightful as I have portrayed them. However, the Montcalm family of Suffolk is entirely fictitious, as are their home, the town of Grantham, and its inhabitants.

I owe thanks to several people: Pat and Roy Littlewood, who took me to Otley Hall years ago; Jaime Owen, who read the manuscript and made valuable suggestions; Thomas Gresik,

who advised me about financial matters; and Edwina
Kintner, who made sure I didn't write something stupid
concerning the profession of financier, about which I am as
ignorant as any three-year-old.

PROLOGUE

At last! The match wasn't perfect, but it was close enough for the purpose. The antiques dealer happily took the cash (about five times what the thing was worth, the purchaser thought bitterly) and handed the customer a well-wrapped parcel. 'Mind you're careful, now,' he said. 'I've used plenty of tissue, but it's sharp, you know. Lovely little thing. Going to use it as a paper knife, I think you said?'

The customer coughed, nodded, and walked out the door.

ONE

D oes everyone get wanderlust in the spring, or is it just me? When Browning wrote his poem swooning about April in England, he was in southern Italy, not exactly a desolate desert. Yet he was homesick for the remembered joys of an English spring.

Well, on an April day that would have made Browning swoon all over again, with a blue sky and puffy white clouds and green shoots poking through the sweet-smelling moist earth, I didn't have to yearn to be in England. I *was* in England, in a lovely small city that was now home to this transplanted Hoosier.

My first husband and I, both avid Anglophiles, had planned to move to Sherebury, in the south-east county of Belleshire, as soon as he retired. When a heart attack felled him a few months before the planned move, I was too numb to change plans, so I came to the cathedral city that welcomed me and made me feel at home. I've lived here for so long now that I never want to move again. There's the place, a lovely small city full of the kind of houses and shops that only England seems to possess. And then I've made good friends here, among them my neighbour Jane Langland, and the Endicotts, proprietors of the Rose and Crown, the old pub and inn in the Cathedral Close. And the Cathedral itself lives in my heart. These make up the essential fabric of my life.

And I wanted to be elsewhere. 'Alan!'

'Mmm?'

'Let's go someplace. I've got spring fever, or something. I'm going to jump out of my skin if I have to stay in this house one more minute. Just look at it out there!'

He looked at me instead, wresting his attention from the book in his lap. 'You know, somehow I had an idea you were about to get restless. Happens every year around this time. Come sit down by me and look at this.'

'I don't want to look at a book. I want to be up and doing.'

'Yes, dear. But indulge me for one moment.'

I love my husband. Having him turn up when I was newly widowed and wallowing in self-pity was the best thing that ever happened to me. Most of the time I remember that. At that particular moment I wanted to take that book, a large and heavy one, and throw it into the fire, to get him moving. But there was a tone in his voice that usually meant something pleasant, so in spite of the 'yes, dear' (a response I loathe), I shoved the cat out of my lap, pulled my feet from under the dog who was resting his considerable weight on them, and joined Alan on the couch.

'I think you might find a number of places to go in here.'

The title of the book was *Keepers of the Kingdom: The Ancient Offices of Britain,* which didn't raise any thrills. The cover photograph showed a man dressed in black, with lace at his throat and a fancy wig like the ones judges wear on this side of the pond. He was sitting against a background of huge black-and-white checks, and holding in one hand a beat-up horseshoe and in the other a clumsy-looking knife. I frowned.

Alan smiled. 'I borrowed this from the Endicotts. They keep it in the lounge to amuse the tourists. Most Americans seem to find our titles and ceremonies highly entertaining. As several of the ceremonies take place in the spring, I thought you might enjoy doing a sort of tour of some of our more obscure traditions. There's nothing special going on just now, though, so now why don't we drive out to that tea shop in Little Wimsey, the one you like. And then this evening you can pore over the book to your heart's content and we can plan an itinerary.'

Well, the drive to the tea shop was pleasant, and satisfied (temporarily) my need for new scenery. It wasn't really new, of course, but everything is new in spring, and the countryside was England at its best. I couldn't put a name to all the flowering shrubs, certainly not to the wildflowers in the hedgerows and pastures, but I could take them in greedily. The birds, even in the afternoon, were singing madly. I knew some of them, though by no means all. One of my first love affairs when I moved to England was with a pudgy, cheeky little robin in my back garden, the real thing after which the big American thrushes are named. I made the acquaintance of the blue tits, adorable little blue-and-yellow guys, and of course the magpies. Raucous bullies, they are not appreciated by a lot of English bird lovers, but I can't help but love their brilliant black-and-white suits, and their audacity.

Then there were the lambs. Something in me goes all soft and custardy at the sight of lambs, gambolling crazily over the pasture, then running back to their mothers for comfort and food. Okay, maybe they're not the brightest animals in the world, but they're sweet, and so very much a part of the English spring landscape that I would love them just for that, if nothing else.

By the time we reached the tea shop, I was stuffed so full of spring that I didn't think I was hungry. Of course the smell of freshly-baked scones took care of that illusion. We're a good long way, in the county of Belleshire, from the source of the West Country's famous clotted cream, but this particular shop always had a plentiful supply, along with the best strawberry jam I've ever tasted. I proceeded to make a pig of myself, as usual. I could make all my meals tea for the rest of my life, I think, and die happy. And probably a lot sooner. There's enough cholesterol in your average afternoon tea to clog every artery in the Western world.

Finally replete, I regretfully turned down yet another scone. 'If I eat or drink one more molecule of anything, I'm going to pop like a balloon. I feel like Christmas afternoon, too sated to move. *Why* do I let myself eat so much?'

'Because it tastes so good. Never mind. The new lettuce in our garden will be ready in a day or two; you can live on that for a while. Feeling better?'

'Aside from thinking I ought to be served up with an apple in my mouth? Much, thank you. But I've still got the itch to go someplace interesting. When I can move again, that is.'

'Right. As soon as we're home we'll plant ourselves in front of the fire and study the book. I promise you, you'll find so many interesting places to go, we'll need the next year or so to cover them all.'

Alan really is a dear. He'd treated me to an extravagant tea and was now prepared to spend hours working out a way to entertain me. After all the carbohydrates I'd just ingested, I was pretty sure that what I'd do in front of the fire was fall sound asleep, but I would try to show at least some interest in his ancient offices and ceremonies. He's a Brit, after all, and these things are a part of his DNA. And he's always polite when I wax nostalgic about the Fourth of July celebrations back home.

The book surprised me. After a page or two, I was learning more about English history than I'd known there was to learn. 'But . . . but some of this goes back to the thirteenth century! Before Magna Carta, even.'

'Oh, and much earlier than that. The Romans left in the early fifth century, and a few of the current practices date from the attempts to restore order among the warring factions. And then of course there's Stonehenge, and the Druids.'

'I thought the Druids had nothing to do with Stonehenge. I'm sure I read somewhere—'

'Nor did they, according to most archaeologists. But Neo-Druids have claimed it. As with most really ancient monuments, the history is interesting because there's so little of it.'

'Mmm.' I had gone on to accounts of more-recent Britain. 'Oh, here's the Archbishop of Canterbury. No, York. Hey, I know Canterbury goes back to the time of Becket. Twelfth century, he was, right?'

'Right. But the office predates that unfortunate incident by many centuries. Read on, dear heart. I'm going to make us some coffee.'

He took his time about it, and by the time he got back I was awash in the more obscure backwaters of English history. 'My head's spinning,' I complained. 'I could only make sense of this if I knew about all the monarchs and all the battles and all the feuds, and having never learned more of English history than a few important dates, I'm completely at sea!'

'Which dates?' asked Alan, setting a tray down in front of me. 'I'm curious about what bits of our vast chronicle American educators might think important.'

'1066 and 1215,' I responded promptly. 'Oh, and 1588 – I think. Wasn't that the defeat of the Spanish Armada?'

'It was.' Alan sounded a little surprised. 'I expected the Norman Conquest and Magna Carta, but you've intrigued me about the Armada. Why did you have that one drilled into you?'

'I didn't. I learned that one by myself, because I boned up on Elizabeth. She's always fascinated me: a strong, indeed headstrong woman in an age when women were chattels. Especially royal women, meant to be bartered off in marriage however it suited their lords and masters. Elizabeth never allowed that to happen.'

'You intrigue me. All right, what comes next in your selective memory?'

'Not much until the twentieth century. Oh, of course you know I've always been a fierce partisan of Richard the Third, but I'd have to look up his dates. And I remember the general outline of the civil war – yours, I mean – but again, not dates. Actually, I've never been great about dates, even in American history. I found history boring in school and studied enough only to pass the exams, and then deliberately forgot everything the next day.'

'History boring!' He had forgotten to sit down. 'My dear woman, history is the record of human beings, their triumphs and failures, their virtues and vileness. How *could* you find that boring?'

'I don't anymore. Now that I don't have to study it, I've become absolutely riveted by some aspects of history. But it was never taught, at least not where I went to school, as the story of people. We just had to memorize lists of events and dates. So, as I said, I crammed them into my head for the test and let them fly out as soon as I possibly could.' I picked up a cup of coffee, ignoring the plate of chocolate biscuits. I was still stuffed full of scones and cream.

Alan ran one hand down the back of his neck. 'But . . . but you've always said one thing you love about England is the way we preserve our history, our old buildings and our traditions and all that. I thought you loved history!'

'I do love living history. When I can see the very gate at the Tower where Anne Boleyn was led to her execution; when I can walk on the stone floor of the Abbey where your kings and queens have been crowned for centuries, and where hundreds of your famous men and women are buried; when I can bask in the garden that Shakespeare's wife loved – oh, then I can touch history and it's real and gripping and I can feel a part of it. But reading about it in books is too much like school. It doesn't, as they used to say back in the hippy era, hit me where I live.'

'Then it's high time you experienced more of it! Give me that book back, woman. I'll choose some things to see and do that will have you so steeped in your "living history" that you'll forget which century you actually live in.'

'Yes, dear.' I handed him the heavy tome. 'And while you're up, you could pour me a little bourbon. If I have any more caffeine I'll never get to sleep tonight.'

I was just as happy to let Alan choose a few places to visit. For one thing, he would know how to get to wherever it was. I've learned to drive around our small city, though because of its medieval street pattern I still occasionally get lost. I can shift gears with the wrong hand, I almost never turn down the wrong side of a street anymore, and it's been years since I tried to get into the driver's seat from the left. But once away from Sherebury, I much prefer to let Alan drive, even if he needs me to read a map, and since we got satnav I seldom have to do that.

So he spent the time until supper reading the book and making notes, while I thought about places in America I wished I could show him. Not historic sites. Our history, stretching back a mere 400 years or so, wouldn't impress him. No, I wanted him to see some quintessentially American sights. First on the list, of course, was the Grand Canyon. They no longer talk about the Seven Wonders of the World, but surely that was one of them – the top one in America, I think. Then I wanted to show him American farms, acres and acres of wheat, or corn, or soybeans, or even (in Kansas) sunflowers. Farms on a scale unimaginable in sweet, miniature England. And I wanted to take him to a county fair. Not one of the state fairs. They could be slick and professional, but I wanted him to see the heart of America: the 4-H kids proudly showing their animals, from rabbits up to prize cattle; the girls (and now some boys) displaying their sewing and baking skills; the honky-tonk of the midway, with rickety rides and every variety of unhealthy food known to man, from corn dogs and funnel cakes to deep-fried Snickers bars.

'. . . one of the best ones, but there is a sufficiency to choose from.'

'Sorry, I was daydreaming and didn't hear some of that.'

'I said we've missed one of the best events, Hocktide and Tutti-Day in Hungerford. We'll try to do that next year.'

'Where is Hungerford, and what on earth is Hock – whatever

you said? I must say Hungerford isn't a terribly appealing name. Reminds me of Gnaw Bone in Indiana.'

'Actually, it's quite an attractive little town in Berkshire, about thirty miles or so south of Oxford. I believe the name derives from something other than the idea of starvation, but I don't recall what. Hocktide is a period after Easter, in medieval times the Monday and Tuesday following Easter Sunday. Very long ago the days were holidays, even for farm labourers, one of the few times in the year when the working man didn't have to work. Now the whole idea has been forgotten, except in Hungerford, where it's been extended to a two-week festival of all sorts of revelry, much of it bucolic and somewhat bawdy. Tutti-Day is a part of the celebration, involving a parade and a long and quite alcoholic meal.'

'You've been there.' It wasn't posed as a question, so I was surprised at his sheepish grin.

'Truthfully, no. I've always wanted to see the goings-on, and the mention in the book reminded me.'

'You rat! You looked it up, and thought you'd impress me with your profound knowledge of obscure English history!'

He held up his hands in surrender. 'Guilty as charged! Next year we'll go and see for ourselves. Meanwhile, I've thought of a place that isn't in the book, but that you'll love. It's a beautiful house in Suffolk, the oldest part built around 500 years ago, and it's simply oozing with history.'

I sat back and prepared to look interested.

'And you'll like this,' he went on. 'A significant item in that history has to do with a renegade country called America.'

That did make me sit up and take notice. 'America! What on earth is American history doing living in a 500-year-old house in – where did you say?'

'Suffolk. East of Cambridge, along the North Sea. This time of year the gardens will be especially beautiful. And yes, before you ask, I have been there.'

'It's a stately home, I suppose, owned by the National Trust or some such.'

'No, it's actually in private hands, and I know the family, though we've lost touch. When I first visited, their children were young; now they must be grown and gone, and I don't know how much longer the Beaumonts are going to keep the place. It's ruinously expensive to maintain, of course, and as it's a Grade I listed building, all the work has to replicate the original.'

Well, I knew a little about that problem. Our seventeenth-century house is a listed building (which confers protection, like historic monuments in the US), though certainly not a Grade I. That's reserved for the really old, really exquisite structures of great historic importance. Even in our much lowlier status, though, I'd had to jump through all kinds of hoops years ago when the roof needed to be replaced. Alan and I weren't yet married, and I nearly went mad dealing with English bureaucracy. I could really feel for the owners of . . . 'What's the name of the place, Alan?'

'I'm not going to tell you. You'd look it up, and I want you to be surprised.'

'Meanie! Then we'd better go soon, or I'll worm it out of you, or Jane, or somebody.'

'How about tomorrow, if the weather holds?' He looked at his watch. 'I can phone right now to make sure they're not booked for the day. They don't have regular "open house" hours, and they do quite a good business as a venue for weddings and conferences, so one doesn't just drop in.'

We were in luck. The Beaumonts had nothing planned for the next day and professed themselves delighted to welcome us to their home. Alan punched off the call looking pleased with himself. 'They've asked us to tea. We'll plan to get there in the early afternoon, though, so we'll have time for a leisurely tour of the house first.'

Some people called the planner finicky. In the planner's mind, that simply meant an infinite capacity for attention to detail. It was often an overlooked detail that caused a plan to fail. 'For want of a nail . . .' Well, there would be no overlooked details in this plan. Carefully, carefully, it was all worked out on paper and then memorized, and the paper burned. Oh, not in a fireplace. No, indeed. Someone might wonder at a fire kindled on a warm day. No, a little thought and research found a May Day bonfire not far away. A sheet or two of paper carefully tucked in amongst the sticks while no one was looking, and the written plan was consigned to fiery perdition.

Appropriate, that, the planner thought with satisfaction. The plan consigned to fire. Aristotle, with his unities, would have approved: the play beginning as it was to end.

TWO

The morning dawned clear and lovely, if chilly. The kitchen, warmed by the always-on Aga, was pleasant, though later in the season it might become intolerable. We had a leisurely breakfast, fed the animals and took Watson for a walk, and then Alan said it was time to set out.

I looked at the clock on the mantel. 'But it's not even ten. How far away is this place, anyway?'

'About eighty miles as the crow flies, and yes, I know what you're about to say. In America that's less than an hour and a half. But we don't have the same kind of roads, as you well know. There is no very direct route to where we're going, and as Colchester is on the way, I thought perhaps you might like to stop for a bit.'

'Why? What's in Colchester?'

'It's said to be the oldest town in Britain, for one thing, dating back at least 2,000 years. There's a remarkably well-preserved Norman keep, and several bits of the Roman wall. The legends about Old King Cole, on the other hand, are almost certainly just that – legends.'

'Spoilsport. All right, let's be off. I'll just ask Jane to look after the beasts; it looks as though we'll be gone all day.'

My itchy feet of the day before had gone away, as often happens, and I would just as soon have stayed home and worked a little in the garden doing the few tasks which Bob Finch, our gardener, allowed me to tackle. He was of the opinion that I could do more damage in less time than even our animals could cause, and I have to admit he had some justification. I've always had a brown thumb. Jane, our next-door neighbour, had made me hire Bob after she saw me pulling up a flourishing delphinium under the impression that it was a weed.

But it was a lovely day, and I was off for a holiday with the man I adored, and if I was force-fed with English history along the way, well, I could always forget it as promptly as I had my history lessons back home.

Alan drove at a moderate pace, which eased the anxiety I still felt at every roundabout. If they'd been invented by the time Dante wrote the *Inferno*, I know he'd have used them to navigate the circles of Hell. I'm quite sure that diabolical assistance went into their development, and was extremely grateful that I didn't have to cope with them anymore. With Alan at the wheel, I could close my eyes and pray when we approached one.

It wouldn't have taken us all that long to reach Colchester, had it not been for the Thames. Going from Sherebury north, there is no way to avoid crossing the river, and the only way to do that, without going into London itself or detouring far to the west, is the Dartford Crossing. It consists of a tunnel and a bridge. Alan knew my claustrophobia wouldn't let me handle the tunnel, so we had to creep across the bridge amidst heavy traffic.

The train would have been much easier, and faster. I didn't say it out loud, but Alan often knows what I'm thinking. 'We could have travelled by rail, of course, but we would have had to change more than once and still hire a car in the end; the house is not in a city. So, maddening as this is, we'll still arrive quicker. Patience, dear heart.'

The traffic thinned out once we got over the bridge, and we got to Colchester in good time, after all. Alan was right; it is an interesting town. One of the things I find fascinating about England, even after living here for years, is the juxtaposition of ancient and ultra-modern. An electric car was parked a foot or so from a section of Roman wall. The Norman keep wasn't far from Starbucks. I find it odd and somewhat disconcerting. In America, of course, we have no such odd bedfellows, because we have no ancient monuments. Except for Native American sites like the cliff dwellings in the west, which date back only about a thousand years, our oldest buildings are seventeenth-century. In England, that's verging on middle-aged.

We found a pleasant pub and had a snack lunch. I wasn't sure what "tea" implied at the house we were visiting, and didn't want to be too full to enjoy it, in case it turned out to be a feast.

'Are you still going to keep me in the dark about where we're going?' I asked as the roads became narrower and narrower, and more winding. 'It feels like we're headed for the back of beyond.'

'Not quite. If you'll promise to put your mobile away and

refrain from consulting it, I'll tell you a bit. The name of the
house is Otley Hall. I won't describe it; you'll see for yourself
in a few minutes. It has I can't recall how many bedrooms,
but the Beaumonts haven't turned it into a B and B, probably
because there are so many priceless artefacts scattered about;
they need to be able to keep an eye on visitors. And that's absolutely all I'm going to tell you, because –' he swung around a
corner and pointed – 'here it is!'

I saw only tall brick chimneys at first. Then we turned another
corner and the house revealed itself in all its Tudor glory.

It was a home. That was my first impression. A beautiful home,
half-timbered, with bricks in decorative patterns between the oak
timbers, a home for the wealthy, but a home, not a palace. In
fact: 'I want it,' I said without a moment's hesitation. 'If your
friends do decide to sell, I want it.'

'Yes, dear. Just as soon as my rich uncle dies, we'll look
into it.'

'I didn't know you had a rich uncle.'

'I don't.' He brought the car to a stop on the gravel sweep.
'Look at the swan, darling. Laid on just for you. And here's Ian
come to greet us.'

I don't remember what I said to our host, if I said
anything. I was nearly dizzy with the effort to look everywhere
at once. The magnificent swan, lazing on a pond that looked very
much like part of an old moat. The incredible brickwork. The
diamond-paned windows. Those immense chimneys.

'Ignore her,' I heard Alan say. 'She'll come out of it
eventually.'

'But this – but I had no idea – I mean, I've seen other manor
houses, but . . . Alan, no wonder you didn't describe it. How
could anyone?'

Our host chuckled. 'You're American, aren't you?'

'By birth, yes. I've lived in England for quite a while now,
but I never seem to quite lose the accent.'

'It's not the accent so much as the attitude. Visitors do tend
to be appreciative, but it's usually the Americans who are
overwhelmed.'

'Gobsmacked is the word, I believe.'

'Ah, you are assimilating our vocabulary. Well done! Now, do you need a moment to recover your senses, or shall we see over the house?'

'Oh, I want to see the house! I won't be able to take it all in, I know, but I want to see it right now.'

I quickly lost my way. As with most old houses, this one sported odd angles here and there, a step or two going down to another room, then a step or two up. The floors were uneven; some of the doorways low enough that Alan had to duck. 'People were shorter then,' Alan murmured, and I gave him a Look. Of course I knew that.

I asked about dates; Ian laughed. 'There's no simple answer. There are remnants here and there of a late fifteenth-century house, but the complete structures range through the sixteenth, and one staircase dates from about 1600. But I want you to look at the linenfold panelling in this room. It is said to have belonged to Cardinal Wolsey at Hampton Court.'

'Good grief! How did it get here?'

'That's a long and complicated story, much of it unprovable, but the quality of the carving certainly justifies the notion that it might have been done by royal decree. Note that at the bottom of the "folds of linen" there are tiny holes, as of the stitching of a hem.'

Up more stairs. Bedrooms, beautifully furnished. Corridors, lined with pictures and amazing documents, royal grants and the like, that would in America be in a museum. Downstairs again, to spend a moment or two in the kitchen, a lovely but very practical room where our hostess was putting the final touches on the sort of tea I would serve to guests at home: pleasant but not elaborate. 'I thought you'd need something reviving after following Ian all over our house. We'll take it in the great hall, so darling, if you'll see to the table?'

He left to do so, and I commented, 'You know, Mrs Beaumont, your house is a real home. I don't know what I expected, but take this kitchen, for example. It's a place where a family could sit around with their elbows on the table, if you know what I'm trying to say.'

She laughed. 'It's Catherine, please. And you're quite right. When the children were young, we practically lived in here. They did their homework at the table, and watched the telly in that corner.'

'Just what I would have expected. A real home. I do love it! I've told my husband I want to buy it, if you ever decide to sell. It's just a pipe dream, of course, but I envy you more than I can say.'

'You wouldn't, if you knew about the maintenance problems we face daily. Ah, here's Ian to help you find your way back.'

On our way in we had passed through the room where Ian now sat us down in front of the fireplace. He had built a small fire, and the warmth was welcome. Although some twentieth-century occupant had installed central heating, the room was chilly, its many diamond-paned windows letting in a good deal of air as well as light.

Catherine put down the tea tray, poured our tea, and then sat back, a small grin on her face.

'All right, Ian,' said my husband, 'now's the time, I think. Dorothy, you may want to put down your cup.'

It was too hot to drink anyway. I set it down, puzzled.

'We didn't want you to drop it when Ian tells the story,' said Catherine, the grin growing broader.

'What? What are you all hinting?'

'I believe Alan told you that there was something about this house that appeals especially to Americans. Now, I won't go into the details just now, but the fact is that you are sitting in the very room, in front of the very fire, where two sea voyages were planned, in 1602 and 1607. Their destination was a remote part of the world; their purpose to establish a settlement on that remote shore. That settlement was duly founded, and was named Jamestown.'

I was glad I didn't have that teacup in my hand. 'You don't mean . . . our Jamestown? Virginia? Here?' I didn't seem able to form coherent sentences.

'Your Jamestown. Here. In a very real sense, your country began in front of this fire.'

I picked up my cup and sipped. I hoped the hot liquid would do something to dispel the lump in my throat. The others were smiling sympathetically.

'I'm sorry,' I said when I could speak without sniffling. 'This sort of thing gets me this way sometimes. Ask Alan. I'll stand and cry just looking at the Houses of Parliament, because our government really got its start there. But those aren't the same buildings. The idea that this really is the house . . .' I had to stop again.

'And this is the lady who will tell you she finds history boring,' said Alan.

'Not living history! And this is about as living as you can get!' His intent had been to make me indignant, to rid myself of embarrassing tears, and he succeeded. I was able to finish my tea and enjoy the goodies Catherine had prepared and listen intelligently while Ian explained the history of the Gosnold family, who had lived in the house for several generations, and one of whom had conceived the idea of the English colony in far-off America.

'It wasn't all roses, you know,' said our host. 'The family was wealthy and in consequence had important connections. The guidebook will give you some of the details, but the Gosnolds occasionally found themselves on the wrong side, politically. Queen Elizabeth did not care for the Gosnolds, and in 1601 she charged the Earls of Southampton and Essex, two of those connections, with rebellion. They were sentenced to death. Essex was beheaded. The reputation of the Gosnold family was tainted. Robert, the resident at the time, was for another infraction fined forty pounds, which at that time was an enormous sum.

'However, Southampton's sentence was commuted to imprisonment, and from the Tower he was able to arrange for the funding of the first voyage.'

He went on about the ups and downs of the family, and I listened, but my mind was still stuck on the single fact. Here. It happened here. I was sitting right where a group of men, over 400 years ago, had talked my nation into being.

'Of course it wasn't quite that simple, was it?' I remarked on the way home.

Alan has become used to the way my mind works. If he can't figure out what I'm talking about, he just quirks an eyebrow and waits.

'The founding of America, I mean. Okay, some people went over and settled at Jamestown, and most of them died in the first year or two, but eventually there were enough of them to make it a colony called Virginia. I'm not good at American history, but I'm pretty sure things weren't all sweetness and light in Virginia back then. So why do I go all marshmallowy when I think about the beginnings?'

Alan just smiled.

'Okay, I do know, really. It's because, despite everything, I'm still a sentimentalist. A cock-eyed optimist, in fact. Beginnings are full of promise. I keep thinking about the way things might have been, if nasty little things like slavery and privilege and greed hadn't got in the way.'

'If, in short, the Virginia Colony had been populated by angels instead of fallible human beings. You do, my dear, have a tendency to overlook the serpent in the garden. Look at the dark episodes in the history of Otley Hall.'

'Oh, well. On balance, I'm glad that group of men got together in front of that fire and sent out that ship – or ships, I suppose. The country that resulted is very far from perfect, but it was a noble experiment. And still is, I guess. Though there are times when I think Patrick Henry and his gang should have kept their mouths shut and let us remain with the Mother Country. Look at Canada.'

'Yes, dear,' said Alan with a grin. We'd been over this before. Whenever I'm particularly in love with something English, I go into Royalist mode. When, on the other hand, I balk at English bureaucracy that seems even more convoluted and frustrating than the American variety, I start singing 'Yankee Doodle'. Figuratively.

'Very well. I showed you a lovely place where you could go all misty-eyed about your country. Now you've got that out of your system, I suggest, as Monty Python would have said, something entirely different. You're a great fan of King's College and its choir. How would you like to attend a ceremony that very few members of the public have ever seen?'

'At King's? You know I would!'

'No, at the Tower of London. A tribute of commemoration to a king who died well over 500 years ago, Henry VI, founder of King's College and of Eton.'

'Goodness! You do remember your heroes on this side of the pond, don't you?'

'Especially after they've been dead and gone for a safe length of time. Poor Henry was murdered, you know.'

'No, I didn't know, and I don't want to know right now. I'm sated with history. I want to go home and have something to eat, preferably something thoroughly American.'

'In your seventeenth-century kitchen.'

I maintained a dignified silence as we drove through the fading light to Sherebury and a pizza place.

THREE

Our lives got busy for a while, and we took no more jaunts until May had begun to think about June. One hot afternoon as Alan and I were relaxing in the garden, I said, à propos of nothing, 'Do you know what day Sunday is?'

Alan looked up from his book. 'I imagine you're going to tell me.'

'It's the twentieth of May!'

Alan looked blank.

'"Next week, on the twentieth of May . . ."' I carolled, sounding nothing whatever like Julie Andrews.

'Ah! "I proclaim Liza Doolittle Day",' Alan responded. 'Yes, I believe there's a group that does celebrate the day. Let's look into it.'

The Internet told us that celebrations of the day had grown more and more limited as *My Fair Lady* fans grew older and disappeared from view. However, one of the big movie houses in London was presenting a special showing of the film, perhaps with an appearance by Julie Andrews herself.

'Though she wasn't in the movie,' Alan commented.

'No, but Audrey Hepburn is dead, and so is Marni Nixon, who sang the role for Hepburn. So the one and only original Eliza Doolittle is Julie Andrews, who was my favourite singer for years. Oh, let's go, Alan! I love that movie and I haven't seen it in ages.'

'Your wish is my command, dear heart. And it fits in very well with the next plan for an outing. You'll remember that I talked about King's and Eton and Henry VI?'

'Vaguely. Something about him being murdered.'

'At the Tower, right, on 21 May, 1471. So on that date a contingent from both institutions, including Eton scholars and King's choristers, holds a brief ceremony of remembrance in the Wakefield Tower, laying flowers in the very spot where tradition says the King was slain. It is a private event, but I happen to know one of the men involved, a Yeoman Warder, and he has arranged for the two of us to be admitted. Choral music and royal ceremonial: right up your street, my dear.'

'Do you mean to tell me this has been done for something like 550 years? I don't believe it.'

'And you're right. In fact the tradition dates back less than a century. Sometime in the 1920s a tile was placed in the floor where the murder supposedly took place, and Eton scholars laid lilies there once a year. Later they were joined by King's choristers with roses, and the present ceremony evolved. Everything about it is a bit iffy, in fact. Henry certainly died in the Tower on the date specified, but exactly where is uncertain, as is the manner of his death. Perhaps he was murdered, perhaps not.'

'I'd just as soon not talk about murder, thank you very much. This once, we are not going to find ourselves knee-deep in gore.'

'My dear woman, we've never intentionally waded into that sort of situation! And any gore involved here would have been shed centuries ago, so unruffle your feathers.'

'Hmm. Well, I won't go looking for trouble. I suppose I'll need to dress up?'

'That blue suit you bought for Easter would be just right, I'd think. But wear sensible shoes. We'll be walking through the Tower a bit, and high heels would be dangerous on the cobbles.'

Well, I haven't worn high heels for at least ten years, but I'd hunt out my most presentable flats. I didn't want to sprain an ankle. 'Hat?'

He smiled. 'If you wish, my dear. Though it's in the early evening.'

'I won't, then. But if it's in the evening, could we stay for the Ceremony of the Keys? I've heard about that all my life.'

Well, it turned out that one needed a ticket, and they were booked for months ahead, so I'd have to wait for that. Meanwhile we planned our jaunt to London.

Spring weather in England can be capricious. Well, spring weather almost anywhere, I suppose. Saturday night a roaring thunderstorm kept us awake – all of us, including the animals. Watson, who is terrified of thunder, tried to climb in bed with us. As he's a large dog, and as both cats were already there, burrowed down under the covers, we told him quite firmly that

the thunder wouldn't hurt him and he'd have to seek refuge
elsewhere. He managed to wriggle under the bed, and lay there
moaning every time there was an especially loud peal. The cats
reacted differently: Emmy extended her claws, doing battle with
the horrible demon (and incidentally with my ankle), while Sam,
who is half-Siamese, uttered her distress in piercing banshee
yowls.

Eventually the storm wore itself out and Sunday dawned, a
grey, drippy morning that made me want to pull the blankets
over my head and sleep until Monday. The Cathedral bells,
though, called us to worship. As we live just over the wall from
the Close, the bells are hard to ignore, and we usually enjoy the
services. This morning . . . 'Can't we pretend we're heathens?'
I moaned.

Alan muttered something and headed for the shower.

We fed the animals and cleaned the sandboxes and let Watson
out and in again, and managed to dry him off before he sprayed
water all over the kitchen. Coffee and toast made the world seem
a trifle brighter. Not a lot.

'When do we need to leave?' I asked, rather hoping Alan
would say we were calling off the outing.

'Not till after lunch,' he said glumly. 'We've plenty of time.
Are you wearing that to London?'

'No. Yes. I don't know. I'll dress for the evening when we
get to the hotel.'

'Not much dressing up required for a movie. If we're going
to church, we'd best get on our bikes.'

The British equivalent of 'get a move on' usually amused
me. This morning I was determined to cling to my snit.

The rain made the walk across the Close a penance. Although
the walkway was paved, the stones were somewhat irregular, and
in some places sunken enough to allow water to pool. My shoes
were sodden and squishy inside by the time we reached the door.
We were almost late, so there were no seats left in the choir; we
had to sit in the nave where the chairs were far less comfortable
than pews.

I would like to say that the beautiful service left me serene
and in possession of my right mind. I would be lying. The choir
was a trifle flat in spots; so was the organ. The dampness, no

doubt. A canon I didn't much care for presided; another preached a sermon which I found uninspiring. The tourists sitting next to us had two badly-behaved children who squirmed and whispered throughout; their mother's loud scolding just made matters worse.

'Alderney's?'

I turned to see our neighbour, Jane Langland. She had her head cocked to one side in inquiry and looked more than ever like one of her bulldogs.

'Rotten day,' she went on. 'Need comfort.'

I gave in. Comfort at a lovely teashop was exactly what I needed.

Tea and warmth and cinnamon goodies and good company nudged me gradually out of my mood, so, once home, I was able to pack cheerfully for a London break. The shoes I had planned to wear, however, were still sodden and trying to fall apart.

'I'm told one can buy shoes in London,' said Alan, carefully neutral.

'You're on,' I replied. 'They'll cost three times what they should, of course.'

'Never mind, love. You deserve it. Soup for lunch?'

'There's some chilli in the freezer. Just right for today.'

So we lunched, asked Jane to look after the animals for a couple of days, tossed our bags in the car and headed for the station and London.

The movie was as wonderful as I remembered, and the audience was enthusiastic, though disappointed that Julie didn't show up. I noted, when the lights went back up, that almost all the heads I could see were grey. What a pity that recent generations didn't seem to appreciate this wonderful music and acting and general glamour. Ah, well – their loss. 'You know,' I said as we waited for a taxi, 'most of the time I'm really glad I'm old. Just think of all the things I've seen and done, that the young don't even know they've missed.'

'And we lived, for a while, in a world of relative peace and tranquillity, that we may never see again this side of the great divide.'

'Yes, but we can remember.'

Monday morning. I awoke somewhat disoriented, wondering what had happened to Watson and the cats, and then remembered.

'Coffee, love?' Alan brandished the electric kettle.

'Mmm.' I'm never at my best first thing in the morning.

After coffee had brought my mind up to speed, we had a quick breakfast and sallied forth in search of new shoes. By some miracle, I was able to find a pair of flats that not only looked dressy, but were comfortable enough to deal with cobblestones.

Our morning, spent in glitzy commercial London, got me thinking about contrasts. As we trudged back down Piccadilly toward the Green Park underground station, I looked more closely at my surroundings. Just down the street was the Royal Academy, dating from the eighteenth century sometime. Next to it, the Burlington Arcade, early nineteenth century, looked down its aristocratic nose at the peons (like us) who couldn't afford to shop there. All the shops were in beautiful, venerable buildings (not a concrete high-rise in the lot), and all featured extremely expensive wares, many imported from far-distant lands.

I knew that a few streets away, near our hotel, the homeless crouched, their sleeping bags rolled up around their few pitiful possessions, their dogs resting by their sides. They all seemed to have dogs, perhaps for protection, perhaps to garner more handouts from the dog-loving population.

The old and the new. The rich and the poor. I suppose all big cities are like that, but in America most of those buildings would have been torn down long ago and replaced with something new and probably (to my eyes) ugly. Cleaner, though. Safer, with elevators and ramps to replace or supplement stairs. Probably better suited to their purpose.

And the beggars? Would they be any different? Did reverence for history preclude compassion for present-day suffering? Or did the comfortable in all ages and all places simply prefer to look the other way? 'The poor you will have always with you.' Unfortunately.

It was an age-old problem, and one I couldn't solve.

FOUR

I t felt a little odd going to the Tower after it had closed to the public. Durward, Alan's Yeoman Warder friend, was waiting for us at the gate. He escorted us to the small group of spectators, and introduced us. Very conscious of the favour being granted to us, and a bit intimidated, I smiled and shook a hand or two and retired to the back, hoping to be invisible.

We filed in with the rest, at the very end of the procession led by an elaborate cross and then the Chief Yeoman Warder carrying his impressive mace (topped by a silver finial in the shape of the Tower). Taking our places in a small alcove in the high, vaulted room, we listened as the King's choristers intoned Anglican chant. The stone walls echoed and multiplied their voices. I could easily have imagined angels joining in. Or perhaps it wasn't my imagination.

We prayed, led by the chaplain. We listened as the choir chanted psalms. We stood in silence as boys from Eton and King's laid their lilies and roses on the place where Henry VI was killed so long ago. The sun sent its late-afternoon rays through one window, illuminating the scene like a benison.

It was a brief ceremony. 'Did you enjoy it, Mrs Martin?' asked Durward (I never did hear his last name properly) as he showed us out.

'Very much indeed, thank you.' I had recovered from my diffidence and was back to my usual enthusiasm over English ceremonial. 'You do these things so well. I mean, not just you personally – though the Yeoman Warders are always impressive – but Brits in general. In America, our ceremonies have the feeling of having been invented on the spot, and most of them are a bit embarrassing. People have a tendency to shuffle their feet and wonder what they ought to do.'

'Not always, Dorothy,' Alan put in. 'I once saw a funeral at Arlington Cemetery, when I was in Washington for a conference. That was a military ceremony, of course, but it was carried off with precision, and was very moving, especially when the bugler played the Last Post.'

'Yes,' I conceded, 'the military does ceremony well. It's Taps on our side of the pond, by the way, not Last Post, and I cry every time I hear it.' In fact just thinking about it had brought tears to my eyes. 'I remember Kennedy's funeral. There was so much that touched the emotions that day: the riderless horse, and little John saluting his daddy . . . oh, dear.' I had to fumble in my purse for a tissue, and Alan smiled.

'Durward, thank you so much for letting us see this. We'll never forget it.'

The sun would be bright for at least another hour, and the Underground station wasn't far away, but my feet, in new shoes, were complaining, so we found a cab and went back to the Grosvenor, where I changed shoes and we walked to a favourite Italian restaurant nearby.

'You're feeling better, aren't you?' said Alan as we sipped dry sherry by way of aperitif.

'Much. I think it was the simplicity of the ceremony. That, and the fact that it was private, not rigged up as a show for tourists. It was real, and sobering. Just the fact that they would go to all that trouble to remember a king who died almost 550 years ago – it's mind-boggling.'

'You wouldn't do that in America?'

'No, for the simple fact that we have no heroes dating back that far. And even our recent heroes don't get that kind of recognition. I have no idea if there is any sort of annual memorial of JFK in Dallas on November 22. Even in 2013, fifty years after his assassination, I suppose there was a ceremony, but I don't remember reading about it. I think we have a general tendency to forget history. We tear down buildings when they get to be about fifty years old, and memories too.'

'You remember your war heroes.'

'Well, sort of. Memorial Day, which used to be set aside to honour veterans of our civil war, has become just another holiday, and Veterans' Day is barely observed at all, except that government offices close and an honour guard visits cemeteries in some places. It's no big deal. And that's why—'

'You love England so much. Our sense of history.'

'One reason. The English aren't so bad, either.' I raised my glass in salute, and we ate our dinner in amiable complacency.

But on the way back to the hotel we passed a few of those hunched-up sleeping bags. I stopped to drop a few coins in the hats guarded by the dogs, and my sense of unease returned. Where was the balance? Honour to the dead versus care of the living?

Back home in Sherebury, June came in with trumpets. There were so many flowers in my garden, and all over town, that I could hardly get anything done for stopping to look at them and enjoy their fragrance. I even cut a few of my own roses for the Cathedral. I'm not on the regular rota of ladies doing the flowers, but this year I had such a lot of fine specimens that I thought they might be acceptable.

The first person I ran into was Mrs Williamson, who manages the Cathedral Gift Shop. I knew her well, as I had done volunteer work in the shop a while back. She was working at the font, trying to persuade a stalk of fine lilies to lean at just the angle she wanted. She waved at me.

'Hi, Willie. Do you suppose anyone could use some roses?' I held out my little bunch of red and pink and white glory.

'Oh, how lovely! I don't know about the pink ones, but I can do with all the red and white flowers I can get; we're going all patriotic this month, what with the Queen's birthday and the opening of Parliament. You're going to watch it, I suppose? Parliament, I mean.'

'Oh, I didn't know visitors were allowed for that.'

'On the telly, dear! Everyone can see it. The speech is some- times a bit – well – but you'd like the pageantry, I think.'

More English ceremonial. Oh, yes, I was up for that. I gave Willie all the roses, the pink ones for her own use, and went home to ask Alan about the opening.

Instead of launching into a lecture he handed me the book he'd borrowed from the Endicotts. 'Look up "Black Rod",' he commanded. 'You'll love it.'

I learned that the phrase refers not only to an object but also to the person who carries it, whose official title is Gentleman Usher of the Black Rod, Secretary to the Lord Great Chamberlain, and Sergeant-at-Arms of the House of Lords.

That mouthful almost stopped me, but I persevered. It seemed that this office was one of the few of the ancient ones that still carried more than ceremonial responsibility. He was, in fact, a senior administrator of the House of Lords, in his capacity of Sergeant-at-Arms. But his familiar title came from the first duties assigned to the official, who served as doorkeeper to the early Knights of the Garter at Windsor and carried a black rod, presumably to smite anyone who tried to enter without due permission. This was back in the fourteenth century. As the centuries passed, other duties were added to the original ones, and the holder of the title occasionally met with a dire fate; Henry VIII had one executed for infractions having to do with Anne Boleyn.

'Goodness,' I said to Alan when I reached that point in the story. 'These titles sound so silly, some of them, to American ears, anyway. But the history is sometimes a bit gory, isn't it?'

'Most history is, love. What will historians make of our own era?'

I went back to the book, not caring to dwell on the horrors in the daily news. It seemed that Black Rod's most visible responsibilities nowadays amounted to two, at the State Opening of Parliament and the Garter Ceremony at Windsor Castle. Black Rod leads that procession, thus returning to the original duties.

I read on. 'Alan, this sounds like fun! The guy actually has to bang on the door of the House of Commons to be allowed in?'

'Yes, it's traditional.'

Of course.

'The point is,' Alan went on, 'that the Commons needs to assert its hard-won independence from the Crown. The Monarch can't just command the Members' attendance willy-nilly. So when Black Rod goes to summon them to come over to the Peers, he gets the door slammed in his face – whilst the Queen sits on her throne and watches – and Black Rod has to knock his ebony staff on the door three times before they'll respond and let him deliver his summons. Except – you'll love this part – now it is she who will deliver her summons. For the first time in history, Black Rod is a woman.'

'Yippee! Gosh, it's only taken them six or seven hundred years!'

'So you see, we Brits are capable of moving with the times.'

'Not exactly at warp speed, but yes, I'll give you points for that. So when is this all happening?'

He consulted the *Radio Times*, lying on the table close at hand. 'Next Tuesday morning.'

When the day came Alan kindly refrained from damping my spirits with lack of enthusiasm. He named the carriage in which the Queen and Prince Philip rode to the Palace of Westminster, and made sure I noticed the close-up of the Black Rod (the staff) when it was pounded on the door of the Commons.

The speech, I admitted, was humdrum. 'She can't get political, you know,' said Alan when I complained. 'The speech is written for her by members of the government and is meant to set out an agenda for the coming session. Like most government efforts, it's often less than riveting.'

'Much less.' I yawned. 'But I love her Christmas addresses to the nation.'

'Ah, well, she writes those herself, doesn't she? And they come from the heart.'

'It's a good heart.' I sighed, got up and turned off the television. 'I guess it's time I did something useful. Lunch?'

FIVE

Afew days later we watched the Garter Day procession at Windsor Castle, also on television. Alan said it was possible to get tickets to attend in person, but not at the last minute. I had read about that one anyway, in a work of fiction that was pretty accurate about details of real events, so I was content to sit comfortably at home and watch. I'm a confirmed royalist, but not fanatic enough to stand in the blazing sun in the hope of a momentary glimpse of Her Majesty and the others in elaborate velvet robes that must have been stifling.

Parades almost always make me cry, but this one left me unmoved. Alan, sitting in his favourite chair with Samantha on his lap, noticed my attitude. 'Getting tired of ceremonial, are you, love?'

'I think maybe it's just that they're playing music I don't know. Stirring, no doubt, and patriotic, but it isn't John Philip Sousa. Or maybe I'm just getting old and crabby.'

'Never! Crabby, perhaps, but as for old—'

I tossed a cushion at him. He ducked and it hit Sam instead. She reacted predictably, uttering a Siamese yowl that threatened to shatter the window glass and running out of the room, pausing at the door to spit out some feline profanity.

'Next time you are taken with the impulse to chuck things at me, mind there isn't a cat on my lap, my dear,' said Alan mildly. 'Sam has very sharp claws.'

'Next time you are taken with the impulse to insult me, perhaps you'll remember that.'

He came over and kissed my cheek. 'Where would you like to go for lunch? My treat, by way of making up.'

June continued hot. Alan and I spent a lot of time sitting under the oak tree in the garden sipping lemonade and watching the squirrels and the birds fight at the feeders. The magpies tried to drive the other birds away, but my beloved robins just flew to a safe height (laughing, I'd swear) and then returned for more food.

'I know you're supposed to hate magpies,' I said idly. 'They're loud and aggressive and all that. But I can't help admiring them. They're so beautiful, and so smart. Sort of like our big blue jays back home.'

'We don't have blue jays here,' Alan commented, 'but I remember them from that trip to America you and I took. Fierce birds but, as you say, beautiful. Rather like swans, actually,' said Alan. 'Especially the cobs. When there are eggs or cygnets nearby, both the pen and the cob are protective, but the cob will attack anything or anyone he perceives as a risk. And he's big enough to do some damage.'

I shivered. 'I certainly wouldn't want to get on the wrong side of one. But what made you think of swans?'

'Beautiful, fierce birds, I suppose. But I was also thinking of swan-upping.'

'What's that? Sounds like some trendy kind of water sport. One-upping the swans in a swimming contest, or something.'

'Actually, it does have some aspects of a water sport, I suppose. It's done mostly in boats, and there is some risk of attack. It's the next English peculiarity I'd like to show you.' He handed me the book we'd been browsing since spring. 'I brought this out to show you, because it's almost time for another little outing. Have a look.'

The picture showed a serious-looking man in a scarlet jacket trimmed with gold braid. There was a patch on his sleeve with 'ER' on it, and his cap had, literally, a feather in it. He was holding something that looked like a rather alarming shepherd's crook, and from the proximity of the water in the background I thought he might be standing in a boat.

It was too warm and pleasant in the garden to read a great deal, but I skimmed. Apparently all swans on England's water-ways used to belong by right to the Crown, a tradition dating back many years, but some of them have been ceded to two groups, the Worshipful Companies of Vintners and Dyers. I couldn't make out exactly who these people were or what they did, but apparently at some point in the fifteenth century they provided some service to the King, who in turn gave them the ownership of a certain percentage of the swans – presumably for food. I grimaced at that and looked up at Alan, who understands me very well.

'They're not eaten anymore, of course. But they still catch them every year – that's what the hook is for – and ring them to signify ownership. That chap in red is the Queen's Swan Marker.'

I managed to keep a straight face. 'He's very splendid, isn't he? But if they're not rounded up for food, I admit I can't quite see the point.'

'It's a conservation exercise these days. They count the cygnets to see if the population is rising or falling, and use the occasion of the spectacle to educate the public about things like keeping dogs under control, so they don't savage the nests, and making sure fishing line isn't left trapped in the water. Swans die every year from swallowing it or getting it wrapped around feet or necks.'

I sobered. 'Oh well, then. I'm in favour of anything to preserve those magnificent birds, even if they can be mean. So this swan-upping is something you can watch?'

'Indeed, and thousands of people do. It goes on for nearly a week, every July, along quite a long stretch of the Thames. I thought we might go and watch at Henley. That's not the nearest spot, but it's one of the prettiest. You've never seen the Henley Regatta, have you?'

'No. I've heard of it, of course, but a boat race is not on my top ten list.'

'Well, it's quite interesting, actually, but rather expensive, if you want to get into one of the enclosures where they serve champagne and so on. But watching the swan-upping is free, and good fun into the bargain. Shall we?'

So it was that, early on a lovely morning in the middle of July, we set out for Oxfordshire and Henley-on-Thames. Alan had elected to drive, telling me we would be going through some beautiful country. And indeed, once we left the London sprawl behind, the countryside was indeed beautiful. 'He maketh me to lie down in green pastures; he leadeth me beside the still waters; he restoreth my soul,' I murmured, almost under my breath.

Alan heard me. 'It does have that effect, doesn't it?'

'This is England, Alan, right here. Not London, not the other cities, not the castles and palaces and tourist attractions. This green, green land – "this other Eden, demi-paradise . . . this blessed plot, this earth, this realm—"'

A tractor, pulling into the road on a blind curve, brought the car to a quivering stop inches from collision, and brought me rudely out of my rhapsody.

'That's England, too,' said Alan, only a few degrees short of fury. 'Roads and hedges designed with no thought to safety.' He took a deep breath and started the car again. 'One second later and we'd have ploughed into that chap. And I was only doing fifty.'

'Fifty! On a road like this . . . oh. Kilometres.'

'I'm trying to live in this century, love. Are you all right? Not too shaken?'

'I think as soon as my heart starts beating and I can breathe again, I'll be fine. But would there be a pub . . .?'

'Two hearts that beat as one. We're not far at all, and we've plenty of time. We'll stop at the next pleasant-looking establishment.'

A few more corners and we found ourselves in a tiny village: a few cottages, a church, and two pubs. The convenient one on our left rejoiced in the popular name, The Silent Woman, with the typical sign showing a headless lady. I made a face at the stale joke, but the place was clean and had pots of flowers by its front door, and a notice proclaiming it a 'Free House', meaning it wasn't owned by a brewery but could serve any beer it liked, including, I hoped, home brew.

'Looks good. Let's do it.'

We were both beginning to get hungry, too, so we ordered our pints (they did in fact have their own brew on offer) and a couple of roast beef sandwiches, and were happy to find both beer and food to be of superior quality.

'Here for the swan-upping, are you, then?' asked the barman, who turned out to be the publican.

'Yes, we're pushing on to Henley when we've finished our excellent meal,' said Alan with a smile. 'Will you have one with us?' He held up his pint, now nearly empty.

'Very kind of you, sir,' he said, and proceeded to draw himself a half. 'Good to have a bit of a break now. The place will be busy later, when the skiffs arrive. No need to go up to Henley, you know. There's not a huge crowd here, but we've seen a good few cygnets hereabouts, so there should be plenty of action. You could have another beer or two out on the terrace while you're waiting. Nice out there on a fine day.'

We didn't even need to consult each other with glances. Alan held out his glass for a refill, while I asked for plain tonic. It doesn't take much beer to put me to sleep, and I wanted to see the 'action' our host had promised. We repaired to the terrace at the back, which was only a few feet from the river.

'That's the Thames?' I said dubiously.

'As ever was. Doesn't look a lot like the river at London, does it?'

I nodded. The Thames at this point was more like the gentle rivers we had back in Indiana, lined with trees and grass, and moving slowly and easily. 'Oh, but look, Alan. There's a swan – no, two. And three, four, five babies. Except they're not cute little fluff balls anymore – more like half-grown, and not very pretty.'

'Ugly ducklings, in fact?' Alan grinned and finished his beer. 'We're getting some company,' he added, as a white-haired pair on a tandem bike wobbled to a stop on the river path and climbed up to the terrace. 'Afternoon,' the man said, nodding pleasantly in our direction. His wife smiled at us. They introduced themselves as David and Joan Spencer, and I couldn't help hearing it as Darby and Joan. White-haired, pink-cheeked, they were precisely my idea of a contented couple, growing old together. And then, with a start, I realized that the description might fit Alan and me, even though we didn't look the part. I smiled at him and he smiled back with that touch of amusement that told me he knew exactly what I was thinking – as he so often does.

'Won't you join us?' he asked the couple. 'You might be able to tell us what's going to happen. We've never watched swan-upping before.'

'Oh, it's great fun on a fine day. Colourful, you know, with the different liveries, and a bit noisy. The swans aren't always delighted about being caught.' That was Joan, her white curls dancing, her hands fluttering a bit with excitement and laughter. Darby – no, David, I mustn't forget – nodded and smiled.

'But what do they actually do?' I asked. 'I have only the vaguest idea.'

'Well, you'll see, but it can get a bit confusing. When all the boats arrive, they start circling the swans, trying to trap them between the boats, so they can pull them in.'

'I imagine that can get a bit tricky.'

'Queen's chap fell in one year,' said David. 'Fancy dress and all. Cob didn't want to be caught.' He chuckled and took a quaff of his ale.

'And once they've caught them?'

'They tie their feet and wings, so they can pick them up, and then they check them over, see they're healthy and that, and ring them according as who they belong to, and weigh them, and then let them go.'

'Swear a bit, they do, when they're free,' David said.

'They don't hurt them, do they?' I asked anxiously. 'Tying them up like that.'

'No, if anybody gets hurt, it's the handlers.' That was our host, come to escort some more customers to the terrace. 'Powerful necks those chaps have, and powerful wings.'

'I've heard they can break a man's arm,' said my husband.

'That's just a tale. Mostly they're just out to scare a bloke – and that they do, I'm here to tell you. And look, here they come.'

And to the accompaniment of ragged cheers and applause, here they came, one at a time, six low boats carrying crews of four and sporting banners. And the festivities began.

SIX

The crews were obviously well-trained. 'They've done this once or twice before, haven't they?' I murmured to Alan. Deftly they brought three of the boats, belonging to the three interested parties, in to shore to form a wall enclosing two parent swans and their three cygnets. As the boats drew nearer and nearer, the swans became more and more indignant, calling their protests and frantically trying to find a way out. 'Why don't they just fly away?' I asked, but nobody seemed to know. Maybe, I thought, the cygnets can't fly yet, and the parents won't leave them.

In any case, it wasn't long before all five of the birds were caught, restrained, and set down on the grassy riverbank, where they squirmed and fussed. The babies cried, setting off sympathetic murmurs from the crowd.

After the birds had been quickly but thoroughly checked, weighed, and banded – 'ringed', they called it – the children were encouraged to come up close to look at and gently pet the cygnets. I slipped out of my seat and down to the river, and timidly asked if I might pet one, as well.

'Is this one of the Queen's, or one of the others?' I asked.

'This one's parents both belonged to the Vintners, so this little chap does, too. If his parents had worn different rings, it would have been my job to allot the cygnets.'

'I have to ask: does anyone really care who owns them?'

He laughed. 'American, are you?'

I admitted it, with a sigh.

'I could just answer that it's a matter of tradition, preserving ancient rights.'

'And I'd understand that. I admire English tradition, and wish my native country respected the past a lot more than it does. But the question stands. In practical terms, does it matter?'

'Yes, in fact, it does. Let's move a bit. I want the children to hear this, too.' He handed the cygnet to a helper and raised his voice so it would reach to the children, who had begun to drift away. 'This lady wanted to know if it mattered who owned the swans. I wanted to tell you all why it matters a good deal. In return for the privilege of owning some of the swans, the Vintners and Dyers help every year with this, our annual census of the swans. Who knows what a census is?'

A shy little girl at the back whispered, 'Counting people?'

'That's right, counting people, or in this case swans. We've been very worried over the past few years because swans were dying so fast there might soon be none left, and we thought that would be terrible.'

A little boy nodded vigorously. 'Because they're so pretty. And they do tricks, like.'

'Ah, you're thinking of the Bishop's swans at Wells, who ring a bell when they're hungry. Yes, they're famous all over the world. So people all over the world would be sad if there were no more swans in England. And I've told you some of the reasons swans were dying. They would swallow lead weights used by fishermen, and die of lead poisoning. Or dogs might attack their nests. Well, lead weights are no longer allowed to be used, and most people have learned to keep their dogs under control, and gradually, swans are coming back. But there is one other thing that kills or injures many swans, and that's fishing line and fish hooks.'

'Ooh! They swallow those, too? That would really hurt!' The same little boy.

'Sometimes the line gets tangled in their beaks, and they could starve to death. When a human sees that, they can be cut loose and all is well. But sometimes they actually swallow a hook, and unless they are taken to a vet, they will die. And it is the Vintners and Dyers who take them to the vet and pay for their treatment, which can be very expensive.'

'Do they take the Queen's swans, too?' asked a little girl with red pigtails, who sounded combative.

'Indeed they do. They look after all the swans on this stretch of the Thames, and do it all as charity, because they love the birds.'

The little girl was satisfied with that answer, and all the children clapped. I did, too. And the Queen's Swan Marker smiled and went back to his boat, and the tangle of boats and birds untangled itself and rowed off up the river to the next stop, where they'd do it all again.

'That,' I said to Alan as we drove home through the long summer twilight, 'was a day well spent, and it's resolved some of my problems about the old ceremonies. This swan round-up, or a version of it, has been going on for centuries. Are there any horrid stories in its history?'

'Not that I know of, love.'

'Well, I'm certainly happy to hear that. Makes a nice change. And I'm happy that the process has been adapted to the needs of the twenty-first century without losing the charm or violating tradition.'

'Ah.'

That was all Alan said, but I could clearly hear the sentiment behind the expression. If he'd been less the perfect gentleman, he would have said, 'Isn't that what I've been trying to tell you?'

She was not the sort of woman that men often approach in pubs. Middle-aged, at best, with a pleasant but unmemorable face and a shapeless figure, she sat near the fire, her frugal supper and a modest half-pint before her. She was eating a bit late; it had been a long drive and a long day, and she planned to have her meal and go straight to bed.

The room was crowded. She wasn't particularly surprised when the stranger stopped and spoke to her.

'Do you mind if I join you? I assure you I . . . er . . . I'm perfectly respectable. I wouldn't ask, but this is the only table that doesn't seem to be full, or occupied by . . . er . . . louts, so to speak.'

He certainly looked and sounded respectable – coat and tie, clean-shaven, posh accent – but it paid to be careful. 'I've nearly finished. You're welcome, if you wish.' She gestured to the empty chair.

'You're very kind.' He put his pint on the table and sipped while he waited for his food.

She waited for him to start the usual lines – are you a regular here, I'm a banker (or whatever), what is your line of work, may I buy you another – but he said very little. He seemed a bit nervous, kept dropping things, his napkin, his fork. He pulled out a cigarette. She frowned, and he put it back, unlit.

'Sorry. I keep forgetting.'

Well, it had been over ten years since smoking had been allowed in pubs, but perhaps the man had been out of the country. Or something.

The last time he dropped something and picked it up he jarred the table, and her glass fell to the floor and broke.

'Oh, my word, how clumsy of me! I'm so sorry. What were you drinking?'

'Newcastle, but really, I was nearly finished – there's no need—'

'*Please! I hope nothing spilled on your clothing?*'

'*No, I'm fine, but—*'

He had gone to the bar. She sighed, too polite not to stay for the refill she didn't want. She would accept, and drink some of it, and then go up to bed. She was far too old, and too tired and discouraged, to play even one round of the mating game tonight.

He brought her beer, handed it to her with another apology, and sat down to finish his sandwich and his drink. There was no more conversation. She quickly drank about half the glass, excused herself, and left the room, relieved that the mildly irritating episode had ended without further annoyance.

SEVEN

We visited a few more interesting, if archaic, ceremonies or sites of them. We made a trek up to Scotland to a bridge near Edinburgh where one John Howieson was reported to have been granted lands on the strength of his having washed James V's hands – on condition that he continue to wash them when requested. His heirs, the Houison Craufurds, have continued to be handwashers to the monarch right down to the present, though the latest incumbent died not long ago. He had washed Queen Elizabeth's hands on one of her visits to Holyrood House in Edinburgh, and that being sufficient to fulfil his heredity duty, his heir can wait until Charles ascends the throne to do it again. The family still lives on the land old John was given by old James – a fact I found nearly incomprehensible. 'In our restless society, I can't even imagine what it would be like to live in the same place for – how many generations would it be?'

'A good many,' said Alan unhelpfully. 'That's part of the stability you admire so much.'

'Mmm.'

The summer waned slowly. In early autumn, we visited the Lord Lieutenant and Custos Rotulorum of Gloucestershire. To my great surprise, 'he' turned out to be a woman, whose title was nevertheless 'Lord Lieutenant'. I learned that the title dated from Henry VIII's time, and like many of those royal appointments, once carried duties and privileges but was now purely ceremonial – and unpaid. 'I've to show up when the Queen visits,' she told us, 'but as she's scaled back her duties a bit in her declining years, I'm mostly a figurehead for various charities. Rather a pleasant job, actually.'

So there went another of my uninformed ideas about the multitude of unnecessary officials eating up tax money at a great rate.

Then when November rolled around, we girded our loins and

went to London for our last planned outing in the Amuse Dorothy campaign: the biggest and gaudiest extravaganza of them all, the Lord Mayor's Show, held on the second Saturday of November every year, rain or shine.

'It begins at eight thirty,' Alan had warned me back in June. 'In the morning. And lasts most of the day, off and on.'

'So we'll plan to spend a couple of nights, then.'

'I've already booked a room at the Grosvenor. They fill up fast; I got one of the few doubles left. This is a big occasion, you know.'

That was in June. Now, on a chilly November evening as our train pulled out of Sherebury station, I said to Alan, 'I suppose it would be very American of me to ask why anyone would celebrate being elected to an office that doesn't pay anything and doesn't run anything.'

'It's important, though. The Lord Mayor and his staff are ambassadors of the City, and help to keep its immense wealth flowing.'

'So it's all about commerce.'

'Most human endeavours are, love. But the Lord Mayor's job supports thousands of other jobs, in the City and throughout the world of finance. If he did nothing else, the revenue he generates through the tourists who come to the show is significant. Besides that, it's a great deal of very British fun. So relax and enjoy it!'

It would be tedious to detail that long day. It began when a fantastically elaborate boat took the Lord Mayor down the Thames to the Tower for the first leg of the show. After that we had the rest of the morning to kill, so we opted for breakfast at a little café just a few yards from our hotel. It was full of hungry tourists, but the wait wasn't too bad, and our breakfast was delicious. I abandoned worries about cholesterol and ate everything except those ubiquitous baked beans. Years of living in England have not reconciled me to the idea of cold beans, straight from the can, with my breakfast.

We didn't feel comfortable about lingering over our meal, with people waiting for a table, so we finished quickly and stood to go. As we headed out the door, a young man said tentatively, 'Mr Nesbitt?'

'Yes?' A couple trying to get in the door frowned at our

blocking the way. Alan moved the few inches that he could. 'I'm afraid I don't—'

'Edwin Montcalm, sir. You – oh, I'm so sorry.' This to the woman he had just elbowed, who glared at him.

'We can't talk here,' I said, the schoolteacher in me coming out. 'Let's move out of the way. You may lose your place in the queue, though,' I said to the young man. I moved out onto the pavement, which was also crowded with pedestrians, but there was a sheltered spot by the café window. 'Now. You were saying?'

'Yes, this is better. Thank you – you'd be Mrs Nesbitt?'

'Mrs Martin, but yes, I'm Alan's wife. And you are?'

'Sorry! I got off on the wrong foot. Mr Nesbitt, you won't remember me at all, but you were once a good friend of my uncle Andrew. When you were both on the police force in Penzance?'

'By Jove! Andy Montcalm! Yes, of course, we were very close back then. So you're his nephew. Louis's son, that would be?'

'That's right.'

'I'm afraid I've lost touch with him, and Andy as well. He is – that is, he's still living?'

'Oh, I'm sorry you didn't know. Uncle Andrew died some years ago, not long before my father.'

Something crossed Alan's face for an instant, something that told me he was neither entirely sorry to hear that Louis was dead, nor entirely surprised. He made the appropriate noises, however, and went on, 'And you? I believe the last time I had a letter from Andy he mentioned that you had married.'

'Yes, I'm an old married man, with three children. Look, I don't want to keep you, but it was the most marvellous luck running into you. I didn't have your address, and I've been wanting to ask you a favour. Something you'll enjoy, I hope. Would there be a good time to phone you?'

Alan produced his card. 'I'm retired, as you probably guessed, since I'm much the same age as your uncle. My wife and I live in Sherebury, but we're in London for the Lord Mayor's Show. We've seen the flotilla off to a good start, and we're going to watch the procession this afternoon from the Embankment. After that we haven't a thing to do until the fireworks. Would you like to join us for a drink around four? We're staying at the Grosvenor.' He pointed to the hotel, just up the street.

'That would be very kind of you, sir! I'll phone first, shall I?'

Alan gave him his mobile number, and Edwin went back to the scrum around the door of the café.

'I hope you don't mind, love. I haven't seen that chap since he was a baby, but I've always felt a bit sorry for him.'

I waited. The man, well-dressed and healthy, had not looked like an object of pity.

We walked to the front door of the hotel, slowly because the foot traffic made any other speed impossible. The Grosvenor, virtually in Victoria Station and only a short distance from Buckingham Palace, is a favourite with tourists from all countries, so there is almost always a swarm of confused people near the entrances, wondering in several languages which way to turn and risking death by looking the wrong direction when crossing the streets. Alan avoided several of them and pointed the way to the palace to several others. We gained the haven of the hotel lobby before further conversation was possible.

'Whew! I do love London, but sometimes the noise and rush is a bit much.'

'Indeed. Do you want some coffee?'

'No. I want some peace and quiet.' We reached the elevator and started up. 'And you were going to tell me about what's-his-name.'

'Edwin, Edwin Montcalm. Sir Edwin, actually. Some remote ancestor was the French General Montcalm who died fighting the British in the Seven Years' War. In Canada,' he added, seeing no recognition on my face.

'Oh, *that* Montcalm! In the French and Indian War. Something about Quebec and the Plains of Abraham.'

'One of those bits of history you never mastered, I take it. It isn't important, really, except that Montcalm was a nobleman, and had numerous descendants in several lines, some of whom moved to England in the late eighteenth century and gained minor titles here. My friend Andy had ancestors named André, and his brother Louis, Edwin's father, pronounced his name the French way.'

'And you didn't like him.'

Alan just looked at me. 'I never said—'

'Hah! You've accused me of having an expressive face. Your look when that man said his father was dead spoke volumes.'

We arrived at our room.

'Very well. You're right. I hadn't a lot of use for Louis Montcalm.' We sat down at our minuscule table. Alan tented his hands in his lecturing mode. 'Louis was a lot younger than Andrew. He was brilliant, but even when I first knew him he was only in his teens but already something of a rakehell. It was a considerable embarrassment to Andy to have a brother who was continuously getting into trouble.'

'The usual teenage sort of trouble?'

'That, yes. Drinking, shoplifting, general rowdiness, but a lot more, too. Back then hard drugs weren't so prevalent, but Louis was not only using coke and heroin, he was dealing. He stole a car or two, got into trouble with a few girls. Use your excellent imagination. He was always repentant afterward, and he was a charming lad, so his father used to forgive him, and Andy did, too, most of the time.'

'And the parents of the girls?'

Alan heard the edge in my voice.

'The girls themselves pleaded for him. As I said, he was charming.'

'I've always mistrusted charm, at least the ingratiating sort.'

'Me, too. I never liked the boy, and both Andy and I were grateful when he went off to university.'

'He got into university?'

'I said he was brilliant. He got a scholarship and went off to read for a degree in law. I found that highly ironic. He certainly knew a great deal about law on the wrong side; I wondered if he'd ever end up practicing on the right side. Somehow I doubted it.

'And as it turned out, my doubts were justified. He didn't change his ways at all up at Oxford; he merely expanded his horizons and exercised that well-developed charm. Unfortunately he had money enough to go in for gambling in a big way, and also went on drinking and having a jolly time with the ladies. His father began to get tired of rescuing him and dealing with complaints from all and sundry, and it was at that point that Louis found himself wildly in love with a woman, I think a niece or something of one of the dons, a lady who just happened to have a great deal of money. They married.'

'And lived happily ever after, I presume.'

'Sarcasm, as you so frequently remind me, is the tool of the devil. I had moved to London by then, and although Andy and I corresponded regularly for quite some time, he didn't write much about Louis. The one clue I had about how it might have been working out was when Andy wrote me that Louis had had a son. Something about the way he said it made me wonder a bit.'

'About what?'

'I don't quite know. There was just a hint of something in his voice that made me think the baby might not have been the lady's fondest desire.'

I tried not to let my face change, but Alan knows me rather well. It was beyond my comprehension that a woman might have the opportunity of motherhood and not want it. However, I patted Alan's hand to tell him to let it go. 'So go on telling me about old rakehell Louis.'

He spread his hands. 'Very little more to tell. Louis never took his degree. I doubt he could have, in any case. From what Andy let slip, I gathered the boy had done almost no studying and stood no chance, really, of passing his examinations. And he now had no need to work, which was a good thing in a way, because he much preferred the life of a dilettante. I did go up to see his son christened. Andy was godfather, and invited me to come with him. It was the last time I saw him. He seemed to be quite himself. Of course that would be nearly thirty years ago.' Alan shook his head sadly, and I brought him back to the subject at hand.

'Louis' son. That would be the Edwin we just saw.'

'Right. It was rather a curious christening. Did I tell you that Andy was a bart?'

'A *what*?'

'A bart. A baronet.'

'Oh. You did mention that the family was granted some minor titles somewhere along the way.'

'Yes, and that was one of them. It's the lowest noble rank in the kingdom, and as the saying goes, that and a few pounds will buy you a cup of designer coffee. Andy never paid any attention to it, never wanted to be called "Sir" anything, but Louis was forever talking about "my brother the baronet". Used it a few times to get out of trouble. I doubt Edwin uses it much, either.

'The point is, the title is hereditary, through the male line, so Andy's eldest son would have inherited it. But Andy never had a son. Never married, in fact. We used to chaff him about it, say he was married to his job. It was almost true. He was a fine policeman, a fine man.' He paused and cleared his throat. 'Well. So there was an extra little fillip at Edwin's christening. There's a dagger that has been handed down in the family for generations. The story is a bit garbled, but it seems that the dagger, a fine bejewelled specimen, once belonged to a king – not a king of England, but I don't recall where – and some long-ago Montcalm is said to have taken it from the king's bedside to save the life of the king's infant son from an attack by a wolf, or something of that sort. The grateful father gave the dagger to the brave man, and said that it was for him and his heirs forever, and must always be displayed at the christening of the heirs.'

I sighed. 'Another of those essentially meaningless traditions.'

'I agree with you. But over the centuries the king's command came to be interpreted as a legal requirement, so that the dagger had to be in evidence at a Montcalm baby's christening, or the boy was not the legal heir.'

'But . . . I'm still not following. Edwin was the son of a younger son. So how could he be the heir?'

'Remember that Andy had no children. So Edwin was the heir presumptive. When both his father and his uncle died, he would be the baronet. Hence the dagger at his christening. The ceremony was not conducted in the parish church; the vicar took a dim view of a dangerous weapon being brandished in a sacred space. So Andy held the baby over a silver punchbowl in Louis's house, a rather grand place in Suffolk called Something-or-other Manor, and the vicar poured water on his head, while Louis held up the dagger for all to see. Then there was the usual bibulous party to "wet the baby's head" and everyone went home, and that's the last time I saw young Edwin, or any of the rest of them, until today.'

'I wonder what he wants from you.'

'No idea. Now, love, would you like to go shopping, or hit a museum or two, or just idle until our next little foray?'

Idleness won out.

EIGHT

Now, I've seen a lot of parades in my time, but this beat them all. There were more bands than I could count: army bands, navy bands, air force bands – many of each, from various squadrons. Salvation Army bands. Fife and drum bands. We had picked up a programme, and they were all listed, but I lost track after a while. Interspersed with the bands were the floats, representing every organization you could think of: most of the livery companies who had founded the whole shebang. Schools. The Bank of England, for Pete's sake! And then there were the street performers, mimes and dancers and acrobats. And the dogs. And the donkeys. And Boy Scouts and Girl Guides. And, and, and.

At one point I clutched Alan's arm. 'Look, there's Dick Whittington and his cat. How funny to mix in a fairy tale. I suppose because it mentions the Lord Mayor.'

'It isn't a fairy tale, my dear, or not entirely. There's no historic record of a cat, but a man named Richard Whittington did come to London in the fourteenth century. He wasn't poor, but he was a younger son, so he had to make his own way in the world. He did become a wealthy cloth merchant and did, in fact, become Lord Mayor, not three but four times. So throw in the cat, and there you are.'

Even with the nap, I was quite tired after the Lord Mayor passed in his resplendent coach, grander and even more bedizened than the barge in which he'd made his first appearance in the morning. He didn't sit and wave genteelly like the Queen, but leaned head and shoulders out, beaming and calling to the crowds, who loved it. It was all great fun, but just watching absolutely wore me out.

'I've had it, love,' I said when the crowd began to disperse and we could fold up our camp chairs. 'I think I've barely got enough energy to make it to the Tube.'

'I wish we could take a taxi, but the streets are all closed. It will have to be the Tube, I fear.'

Edwin called Alan's mobile shortly after we got to the hotel, and we arranged to meet in the bar in a few minutes. 'And I have to say, even though it's a bit early, I'm more than ready for that drink.'

'Too much noise,' said Alan, 'too much sensory input. The brain can't process it all, and it passes along the overload to the body. Let's totter to the bar, old dear, and refresh mind and spirit.'

The bar was amazingly quiet, and I sank with relief into a lovely leather armchair as a waiter approached. Alan raised his eyebrows in query.

'I don't know,' I replied. 'I can't think. Anything.'

'Jack Daniel's for the lady. Water on the side; no ice.' That, I knew, was in case the waiter had discerned my American accent. Brits expect Americans to want ice with everything – with some justification, I admit. 'I'll have Glenfiddich, neat,' Alan continued. 'And we're expecting – ah, here he is. What'll you have, Edwin?'

He ordered a modestly-priced whisky and sat down full of thanks for our hospitality and apologies for interrupting our holiday. I was hard put not to roll my eyes. I do love the English, but sometimes they overdo the elaborate courtesy bit. And I'm not at my best when I'm tired. Oh, well. Probably he was just being nice. Our drinks came, and I took a long sip of mine.

We made small talk for a while, how great the show was, but London was too full of people. And what have you been doing the past few years? That's always a good one when people have been out of touch for a long time. In Edwin's case, his whole life, so there was a bit to catch up on. I refrained from asking the normal first question, what do you do for a living, first because it's become identified with pushy Americans, and second because I wasn't sure, if there was wealth in the family, that Edwin did anything at all in the way of work. I lost track of the conversation, which had little interest for me, and drifted away into happy relaxation.

I was brought back to my surroundings when Edwin's voice took on a different tone. 'So you see, spending so much time out of England the past few years, and moving from place to place, I've very few close friends. And of course there's no family left. And that's why I need to ask you.'

'Ask me what, Edwin?' Alan was trying hard not to let impatience colour his voice.

'Oh, Lord, haven't I said? It's the christening, you see.'

Alan waited. Edwin reached into a pocket and pulled out his phone. 'This is Joseph. My son.' He proudly handed the phone to Alan, who passed it to me.

I suppose I shouldn't say so, but one baby looks much like another. The one in the picture couldn't have been more than a few hours old. He was red and wrinkly, his face screwed up in what would soon turn into a howl. His eyes were shut, his abundant black hair showing from under the little knitted cap they make newborns wear these days.

One cannot tell a proud father that his child is ugly. 'What a sweetheart,' I said with all the enthusiasm I could muster. It wasn't necessarily a lie. The child might be a little darling, even though he looked like nothing human. 'Your first?'

'My first son. This is his very first picture; he's almost five months old now. We're so excited about him! We'd almost given up hope. The girls are wonderful, of course. Cynthia's in school, and doing very well, and Ruth's starting next year. Clever, both of them, and pretty, and loving. But they can't inherit.'

I kept my mouth shut with difficulty. I had thought that the rigid system of primogeniture had bitten the dust. Even in the royal family, now, a daughter could inherit the throne in preference to a younger brother. At least as I understood it, Charles would inherit the throne from Elizabeth, and William from Charles, but then if something happened to Prince George, the next in line would be Charlotte, even though she now had a baby brother. And yet in Edwin's family, he of the very humble title, the girls were out of the picture. How very unfair!

'You've kept the estate, then?' Alan asked. 'I'd have thought, since you couldn't be there much of the time, you might have sold it.'

'No, we've kept it up. Rented it out now and then, of course, for several years when I was travelling a great deal, before the children were born. For one thing, I couldn't sell it, even if I wanted to; it's entailed. But beyond that, I've wanted to feel that Judith and the girls had a permanent home, even if we've lived in most of the four corners of the globe. That's why Joseph's birth was so important. You see, if I'd been killed somehow – and it wasn't all that unlikely in some of the places I've been – the estate would have passed to the Crown, if no heir could be found. My wife and daughters would have been left homeless.'

I could keep silent no longer. 'Surely that could be changed! Have you never tried to break the entail, or whatever the term is? I'm sorry, I know it's none of my business, but really, in this day and age!'

Alan looked disapproving, but Edwin smiled, somewhat wryly, I thought.

'Believe me, Mrs Martin, I've thought long and hard about that. I have a good income just now, but finance is the sort of field that can come crashing down with very little warning. If the worst should happen, I could realize enough from the estate to keep us financially secure for the rest of our lives. The problem is, although the entail and the primogeniture rulings could probably be overturned, the cost in legal fees would be prohibitive. I've spoken to my solicitor about it; he was not encouraging. If Parliament had passed the recent proposed legislation about primogeniture, known as the Downton Law – you can imagine why – it would all have been very much simpler – but they didn't. So the estate and the title descend only to my male heir, that is, to little Joseph. That is – he isn't my heir yet, which is why I'm here.'

Now I was completely and utterly confused, but I could see the light dawning on Alan.

'The christening,' he said. 'The dagger.'

'Exactly. Joseph is to be christened next month, with the dagger at hand. And since I've no family or close friends, Judith and I very much hope that you and Mrs Martin will stand godparents at the ceremony. Since you were such a good friend to my uncle, my godfather – well, it would mean a great deal to me to have you there for my son.'

'So shall we?'

It was nearly five. Alan and Edwin had talked about details, where and when and so on, and Alan had said we'd let him know very soon. So as we sat in our not-very-comfortable folding chairs on the chilly Embankment, waiting for the fireworks to begin, we tried to make up our minds.

'You'd like the house,' said Alan. 'Not terribly old, late-eighteenth century, but attractive, well-built and well-maintained.

At least it was when I saw it all those years ago. With an absentee landlord for much of the last ten years or so, who knows?'

'Oh, I'd imagine Edwin saw to it that the tenants treated the place with respect. His estate obviously means a great deal to him. I'm not clear exactly what he does, but he's obviously doing it well, so I'm sure he has some sort of staff, people who stayed there, I mean, while he was off chasing money.'

Alan chuckled. 'As good a description as I've ever heard of the world of finance. You're probably right. His father certainly had servants, to look after both the house and the grounds. But the age of the faithful family retainer is long past, you know, even on estates like Edwin's. I'd think there'd be maids and gardeners who come in by the day. No family could keep up a house that size by themselves, not to mention the gardens.'

'So I'll like the house. All right, is that enough reason for us to go gallivanting off to the wilds of Suffolk two weeks before Christmas? I do enjoy sitting in front of my own fire at that time of year. Mulled wine and mince pies, and warm lap cats, and all that.'

'So do I. But we would have to spend only two or three days at most away from our fireside and our housemates. Drive up the day before, spend the day of the occasion, and drive back the next. I'm sure Edwin and his wife would offer us a room, since it sounds as though no family would be coming.'

'Sounds as though there is no family, in fact. Which is really sad. A young couple all alone on the blasted heath, except for three children – what a way to spend Christmas! All right, I'm in. But that big old house had better be warm. Oh, look!'

The spectacular fireworks captured and held our attention, and we spoke no more of Edwin and his family.

NINE

And then it was December, and we waded into the joyous, exhausting tide of Christmas. Advent wreaths at church and on our dining-room table. Presents to buy and wrap. Worry over what Alan's grandchildren would like. They ranged in age from quite small to teenage, and though we saw one set frequently, others lived far away, one batch in New Zealand, even, and it was hard to know what they wanted, fads changing so fast. Money would be welcome to the older ones, but it was so impersonal, and didn't feel at all grandfather- or grandmotherly. Their parents' replies of 'Oh, they don't really need anything' were no help at all. What a child *needs* at Christmastime has nothing to do with it.

Those decisions settled, and the New Zealand gifts dispatched (in the fervent hope that they would arrive in time) we turned our energies to adult friends, and decisions about Christmas dinner, and the tree, and oh, good grief, did I buy enough Christmas cards, and Alan, don't forget the brandy for the Christmas pudding – all the details, with the certainty that something would be forgotten.

'I keep trying to remember that Christmas will arrive, whether I've done everything or not, and that anyway it's about a miraculous baby's birthday, not frantic preparations, but it's so hard not to get caught up in the trivia.' I plopped down in a chair in front of that fire I so loved, but had very little time just now to enjoy.

'Well, then, you should be glad to escape for a bit.'

'Escape? What on earth do you mean?'

'Edwin's baby boy. The christening. It's this Sunday, remember?'

'Oh, *Lord*! I'd completely forgotten. Alan, I can't possibly go. There's far too much to do. I haven't ordered the turkey, or addressed the last of the cards, or made a single mince pie—'

'I ordered the turkey this morning,' he said calmly. 'Alderney's makes mince pies that are almost as good as yours. The cards will wait, or you can address them in the car. You need a break. And we promised.'

I heaved a great sigh. 'And there's no one else, is there? Then I suppose . . . oh, good grief, should we take them presents? I don't have the least idea—'

'Not for the adults. Edwin thinks we're giving them a great gift by standing godparents. If you've time, you might find a little something for the girls. I have the silver cup for the baby, all engraved with name and date.'

'You are the most incredible husband! Most men wouldn't think of all that, much less do it!'

'Ah, well, I take that as a compliment from one who has such a vast experience of husbands. Now, what can I do while you go out and choose something for the little girls?'

I sat him down with a box of cards and my address book, and sallied forth to Marks and Sparks, where the selection of dolls was limited but pleasant, and chose two traditional baby dolls that I would have loved when I was little. M&S wrapped them for me, and I came home actually somewhat refreshed. Alan was right. We both needed a break to restore our priorities.

I was apologetic to Jane. 'We keep going off and leaving you with the brats,' I said.

'Love them. Even the cats. Not to worry.'

'Well, I'm going to have to find an extra-nice Christmas present for you, to make up for all the nuisance.'

Jane, who hates to be thanked, simply waved me off. 'Something to do. Need it.'

Jane needed something to do less than any octogenarian I know. I sometimes wonder how she finds time to look after her own herd of bulldogs. I hope all the busy-ness keeps her sane and healthy, because I cannot imagine life without her.

Saturday was, fortunately, clear and bright, though cold. I had been dreading snow or, even worse, the freezing rain that loved to make December a misery in these parts. I well remembered my first Christmas living in Sherebury, when rain and sleet and all manner of disgusting weather combined to make me utterly desolate. I had been depressed already; it was my first Christmas without Frank, who had died in May, and discovering the body of a clergyman in the Cathedral on Christmas Eve didn't help a bit. But out of all that ugliness and despondency came the sheer joy of Alan, our growing attraction to one another, and finally our marriage and contentment together.

And now we were driving through a crisp winter morning to welcome a new little boy into the Church.

'I'm glad you talked me into this,' I said, patting Alan's knee.

He smiled and mimed a kiss, without taking his eyes from the road or his hands from the wheel. He's an excellent driver.

In the years when Frank and I visited England, long ago, and in the years I've lived here, I've managed to figure out a little geography. Sussex, as one might expect, is in the southern part of the country. Kent is where one finds Canterbury; check. Northumberland: doesn't take too many brains to work out where that might be, and Norfolk, too, is to the north, where it ought to be. But Suffolk?

'Because it's south of Norfolk,' said Alan the first time I asked him, as if that were an answer.

We'd been there earlier in the year, of course, when we visited Otley Hall, but our destination this time was in a different part of the county, farther north and east, almost to Norfolk. We drove along the North Sea for a bit and then turned inland, through a small place called Grantham. Alan consulted the satnav and the directions Edwin had given him, and finally turned into a gravelled drive that led up a hill.

'Behold Dunham Manor,' said Alan, and brought the car to a stop near the front door.

It was, as Alan had remembered, a nice house. I didn't think it quite grand enough to be called a manor, but I suppose a man can call his house anything he wants. 'Why Dunham? Haven't the Montcalms always lived here?'

'I have no idea, but here comes Edwin. We can ask him.'

We got out of the car, ready to greet and be greeted, but Edwin did not look like a man who was eagerly awaiting an important family occasion. He approached with great hesitancy, and indeed opened and closed his mouth several times before he could frame the words.

'I–I'm so sorry,' he said. 'I've brought you here for nothing, I'm afraid. There's been a . . . well, it's a disaster.'

'Edwin!' I cried. 'Not the baby!'

'Oh. No, nothing's wrong with Joseph. Except – oh, I hate to tell you. It's the end of everything.'

'Pull yourself together, man, and tell us,' Alan commanded. 'If the boy's well, and your wife and the other children?' He made it a question.

'Nobody's ill. It's worse than that.'

How, I wondered, could anything be worse than desperate illness? Money trouble? But he said he had a good income. Even if he'd lost his job in the past few weeks, he couldn't be destitute by now.

Alan made no more suggestions, but simply waited.

Edwin drew a shaky breath, swallowed hard, and said, 'It's the dagger. It's gone.'

It was Alan who saw Edwin into the house, rather than the other way round. I trailed behind, wondering if it wouldn't be better just to turn around and go home. If there wasn't going to be a christening, there was no need for godparents.

Alan took a quick glance around the room where he had deposited Edwin. His wife was nowhere in evidence, nor did there seem to be a butler handy, so Alan simply found the drinks cabinet, poured Edwin a stiff whisky, and waited until he took a sip. 'Now,' he said, very much the policeman. 'Tell me.'

'There's nothing to tell. It's gone. We've looked everywhere.'

'When did you miss it? Just today?'

'No, of course not. We had to make sure it was polished and so on, so we . . . that is, Judith and I – Judith is my wife – we went to take it out of the cupboard where it's kept, a big one in the library. That was two days ago. It wasn't there. Now, of course it hadn't been used since my christening, so we thought one of the servants had put it somewhere else.'

He took a healthy swig of his drink. I looked at the beautiful clock on the mantel, which just then chimed eleven. Well, the man had a right to a stiffener, even at that hour of the morning.

'So you asked the servants,' Alan prompted.

'There's no full-time staff anymore, of course, but we asked Mrs Burton – she's the housekeeper, I suppose you'd say, super-vises the other girls on the days they come – we asked her if she'd seen it, and when she hadn't, she talked to everyone else.

Nobody knew a thing about it. Mrs Burton knew it existed, and knew the story, but had never seen the actual dagger. The servants from my father's time have either died or moved far away.'

'Yes. Go on.' Alan saw that Edwin's glass was empty, but made no move to do anything about it. The drink had steadied him. Any more was apt to have the opposite effect. 'The cupboard. Was it kept locked?'

'Good lord, no! The dagger's of no value to anyone except ourselves.'

I frowned. 'But Alan said it had jewels and all.'

'Jewels, yes, but not fabulous ones. Garnets, peridots, aquamarines, that sort of thing. Pretty, but not precious.'

'Hmm.' Alan rubbed his chin in thought. 'So they wouldn't bring much money if removed from their setting—'

'And the dagger, intact, couldn't be sold at all,' I finished. 'It's too unusual not to be recognized by any reputable dealer in antiques, and not famous enough – begging your pardon, Edwin – to be attractive to an unscrupulous collector. A random thief these days goes for something readily convertible to cash, and a specialist wants the truly valuable. So logically it couldn't have been stolen at all.'

'But it's gone!' Edwin wailed. 'And if it can't be found, Joseph can't inherit, and the estate will go to God-knows-who, even the Crown, maybe, and we're all sunk!' He dropped his head to his hands, near tears.

I snapped. 'Edwin, that's enough!'

The tone had always worked with my sixth-graders. I was pleased to see that it worked with Edwin. He looked up, considerably startled.

'Feeling sorry for yourself isn't going to solve your problem, which isn't as dire as you seem to believe. Are you afflicted with some serious illness that will send you to your Maker before your time?'

'No, nothing of that sort. I'm fit and healthy. But—'

'Have you enemies awaiting you in a dark alley somewhere, ready for murder and mayhem?'

'Don't be ridiculous! But you don't seem—'

'Then why are you falling apart at the thought of what might happen to your property upon your demise, far-distant, one

assumes? You're in good health. So are your wife and children.'
From somewhere in the distance a lusty wail proclaimed the
extremely healthy lungs, and the robust appetite, of young Joseph.
It was the unmistakable sound of a baby who wanted to be fed,
and would brook no delay. 'You have, you've told us, a good
income, so the family estate is not required as a source of funds.
I assume you have insurance policies and so on, so your family
is protected if you're hit by a bus tomorrow?'

He drew himself up. 'It isn't the money. You're an American.
You wouldn't understand.'

'I may be American by birth, but that doesn't make me stupid.
Try me. Explain!'

Alan interrupted my little fit of bullying. 'First, Edwin, do you
think we might have some coffee? We've driven rather a long
way this morning.'

'Oh, lord, I've forgotten my duties as host! I'm sorry, I was
so upset . . . but Judith should be around somewhere . . .' He
glanced helplessly around the room as though expecting his wife
to be hiding in a corner.

'I imagine she's feeding the baby,' I said in my normal voice.
The wailing had stopped. 'Maybe we could all go to the kitchen,
unless you have a cook who would be mortally offended.'

'No, Mrs Walker went home. That is, she was busy until
yesterday afternoon with the christening cake, but when we finally
realized there would be no christening, she was very upset. The
cake was to be her masterpiece, you see, and it's nearly finished.'

Well, the party would have been nice, but to me a christening
was a rite of passage, the welcoming of one small soul into the
Church, far more important than a cake – or a dagger. I kept still
about it for the moment, however, and followed Edwin down a
passage to the kitchen. There was, I noted with some shock,
actually a green baize door, studded with brass tacks in an orna-
mental pattern. Shades of Jane Austen!

The kitchen was charming, a pleasant blend of old and new.
The floor of red brick, faded by age to a rose colour, was made
kindlier to the foot by thick braided rugs, the sort one would
expect to find in a farmhouse rather than a 'manor'. The Aga
was new and shining, but in the traditional cream colour. It
warmed the kitchen gently and had, attached to it, one of the

new gas/electric units with surface gas burners. I wished I had one like it. I've gradually grown accustomed to my Aga, but after more than forty years of cooking on an American gas stove, I have a great liking for heat I can regulate easily and quickly.

Cupboards, counter tops, refrigerator – all spoke of good taste allied to plenty of money. The curtains were of red gingham; the windowsills sported the obligatory red geraniums. All was cosy and warm and very, very traditional. It could have been a set for an Agatha Christie movie. *Early* Agatha Christie. Only missing were the plump, rosy-cheeked cook, the over-worked and not-too-bright scullery maid, and the comfortable old dog asleep in his basket near the Aga.

Edwin looked around vaguely, exactly as he had looked for his wife. 'There must be a coffee pot,' he murmured.

I had thought that the stereotypical male, business shark but completely feeble in the domestic arena, was a thing of the past. Plainly I was wrong. Alan gave the smallest of sighs, located the cafetières on a shelf, and turned on the electric kettle, while I found the canister of ground coffee and measured it into the largest cafetière. Cups, sugar, cream, a tray to put it all on – the kitchen was admirably organized and Alan and I made quick work of the small chore. A large fruit cake, already cut, sat in its tin next to a fresh packet of chocolate biscuits in the pantry, and we had just assembled everything when a very lovely woman walked into the kitchen and stopped, looking surprised.

TEN

To say that she was beautiful is understating the case. Her perfect oval face, her shining cap of blue-black hair, her perfect figure – the details make her sound like a soulless runway model, and she was anything but that. The real beauty was in her animation, the lively interest that shone from her face. She left me, literally, speechless.

'You must be Mrs Montcalm,' I said, once I could talk again. Edwin made no move to introduce us, so I ploughed ahead. 'I'm Dorothy Martin and this is my husband Alan Nesbitt. I hope you'll forgive us for making free of your kitchen, but you were plainly busy with your baby, and we were all in need of some coffee.'

'Don't worry,' she said with a smile. 'Joseph was being difficult this morning or I'd have greeted you when you arrived. I'm so happy to meet you, though you may have made the journey for nothing.'

'I expect Joseph reacted to tension in the house. I know our pets sense when something is wrong, and I imagine babies are much the same, though I never had any of my own. But I'm so sorry about your loss.' Then I heard what I'd said, the conventional formula for condolence, and stopped in confusion.

Mrs Montcalm smiled again. 'It's not as bad as all that. I'm sure the dagger will be found, and meanwhile I've been trying to tell Edwin he needn't get in a swivet. We'll ask the vicar to baptize little Joe privately next week, and then we can have the formal naming ceremony later on, when we can do it properly, according to tradition.'

There was something about her accent and her attitude . . . 'Are you American, by any chance?'

'Canadian, but people often make that mistake. I've got used to it. You're American, though, am I right?'

'I've been a British subject for years now, but yes, I was born in the States.'

'Before we get into complete biographies,' said Alan, 'the coffee's ready. Lady Montcalm, may I suggest we sit down and relax a bit?'

At that Edwin came to life. 'Good lord, I'm sorry! I'm letting you do all the work! I don't know where my manners are. Yes, please sit down. At least – would you be more comfortable in the drawing room?'

'Not I,' I said firmly. 'I love kitchens, and this is an especially nice one.'

Edwin pulled out a chair for me and for his wife, passed around the mugs Alan had poured, and I took a revivifying sip. Ah, that was better. Good coffee makes everything better. Judith had refused the coffee with a sigh, and made herself some herbal tea.

A silence fell. Alan cleared his throat. 'There's no point in trying to ignore the elephant in the room. Edwin, you know, and probably your wife knows, that I'm a retired policeman. You may also know that I've been involved in a few unofficial investigations in my retirement. And so has Dorothy, who is an excellent sleuth in her own right. So if you'd like us to look into this matter of the missing dagger, we'd be happy to do what we can.'

The missing dagger, I thought. Sounds like Nancy Drew. Or no, more like the Hardy Boys, maybe. Adolescent melodrama, in any case.

Except it wasn't. I might think the matter trivial, and obviously Mrs Montcalm wasn't terribly disturbed, either, but she and I were both still foreigners. To Edwin, not only was family tradition sacred, but he had a lot to lose if the dagger wasn't found, and quickly. I focussed again on what Alan was saying.

'. . . reported to the police, of course.'

'No.' Edwin gulped. 'No. We were so sure that it was just some stupid mistake. And then when we'd looked everywhere . . . well . . . we thought it better to keep it all in the family for now. It isn't as if the dagger were valuable.'

Except to you. I didn't say it out loud.

'Edwin, I am not a member of your family. Yes, I attended your christening, but as a friend of your uncle's – your godfather's. And I remind you that I am a sworn police officer, retired or not.' Alan was, when I first met him, chief constable for the county of Belleshire, a very senior police officer indeed. 'If,' he went on,

'I find evidence of criminal activity, I have no choice but to report it to the proper authorities.'

'I told Edwin from the first that we should call them in,' said his wife, sounding more than a little exasperated. 'The thing may not be worth a fortune, but it's a family heirloom.'

'I didn't want the matter broadcast,' said Edwin, also testy. 'It's a private matter.'

'It won't be private once you tell the vicar, which you must do immediately,' I pointed out. 'He's made arrangements for the ceremony. And your cook knows. And I presume you've invited some guests – friends, if not family. You'll have to uninvite them. I should imagine most of them know by now, anyway. This isn't a large community; word travels. Your friends will be most upset, and rightly so, if they learn by word of mouth that there isn't going to be a party tomorrow.'

I stopped. Edwin had turned so pale I thought he might be ready to pass out.

'I've already phoned the vicar and our closest friends,' said Mrs Montcalm quietly. 'I told them Joseph wasn't feeling well and we thought it best not to expose him to a crowd just now. I imagine Mrs Walker will soon spread the truth, though.'

'I told her not to say a word!' Edwin protested.

'Yes, dear.'

The universal 'I don't agree but I'm not going to argue about it' response. Mrs Montcalm and I exchanged what was not quite a wink.

'The news will certainly get out,' said Alan patiently. 'The police may well come to you to ask why you didn't make a report. However, for now I'll stay my hand. I want you to give me the names of everyone who might have had access to the dagger since you saw it last. That would have been when?'

'That's one of the problems,' said Mrs Montcalm. 'We don't take it out very often. We did have a look just before Cynthia was born, in case the doctors were wrong and she turned out to be a boy.'

'And she is how old?'

'She'll be seven in February.'

'So the last time you actually saw the dagger was roughly seven years ago?' Alan persisted.

'No, of course not!' said Edwin. 'We dust it from time to time, give it a rub up, that sort of thing. It can't tarnish, of course, being gold, but even gold gets a bit dull if it just sits for years, and of course the steel blade could rust. Anyway, that time just before Cynthia came along is the only date we can pin down with any certainty.'

Alan sighed. 'Then I have to say you're up against a nearly impossible task. In theory anyone who was in this house could have taken the thing at any time during a period which can't be determined.'

'And that's the other reason I haven't been to the police. I knew they'd ask the same questions you're asking, and I'd feel such a fool having no good answers.'

'Yes. Well. I'm not sure I can help you, given the situation. Perhaps we should simply be on our way. Thank you for the coffee.'

He rose, and so did Mrs Montcalm. 'Please don't go,' she said quietly. 'You've come a long way. The least we can do is give you a bed for the night, or longer if you want to stay. Your room is all ready, and you've not met the girls yet.'

I hesitated, thinking about Christmas and all there was to be done still. And then I thought about two little girls in a household in turmoil, and two pretty dolls sitting in our car, and I made up my mind. 'Alan, it's up to you, but I'd like to stay. But only,' I said, turning to Mrs Montcalm, 'if you'll allow me to help out. With three children and this big house to run, and no cook, guests are the last thing you need. I'm a good cook, and this is a lovely kitchen. It would be a privilege to work in it.'

Edwin started to bluster, but his wife laid a hand on his, silencing him. 'It's a generous offer, and we gladly accept. Edwin will show you to your room, and then we can think about lunch.'

When we had gained the privacy of our room, I said to Alan, 'It's abusing hospitality to say so, but he really *is* a bit of a fool, isn't he?'

Alan shook his head. 'More than a bit. That ridiculous dagger may not have any great intrinsic value, but its value to the family is immense. If he had any sense he would have put it in a bank long ago, or at least in a safe here in the house, if he insisted on keeping it here.'

'He should have taken steps to break the entail, if we're talking about sense. He talks about expense, but in the same breath he moans about losing the estate. I think he's interested in maintaining the mouldy old family traditions, no matter what.'

'An English set of values which, as I recall, you used to find charming.'

'Okay, guilty as charged. I do find many of the traditions charming. They preserve England's stability, its identity as a nation. But maybe, sometimes, they preserve it in the sense of bottling up in glass, like . . . like strawberry preserves. Those strawberries are nice, but they're not living anymore. Oh, I don't know. I'm muddled.'

Alan laid a comforting hand on my shoulder. 'You're tired and hungry. I'll unpack; you go put on an apron. I'll try to keep Edwin away from the kitchen, so you and his wife can talk. She seems much the more sensible of the two.'

When I got downstairs, Mrs Montcalm had her head in the fridge, looking for something that could be turned into a reasonable lunch. She pulled her head out and gave me a look of comic despair. 'Eggs and milk, and a bunch of spinach that's looking a little tired. I think Mrs Walker might have intended it for a soufflé, but my culinary skills aren't up to that. Do you have any ideas, Mrs Martin?'

'Look, if we're going to be cooking side by side, I'm Dorothy. And I'm good at soufflés, but not in somebody else's oven. We could always cream the spinach and put it in omelettes and achieve much the same idea.'

'Brilliant! And I'm Judith.'

We solemnly shook hands and then burst into giggles. 'Okay. Where's an apron? And by the way, will the kids eat omelettes?'

'Probably, if we don't let them know they're good for them. Cynthia was very good about eating what was put in front of her until she went to school, where she learned from the others that only pizza and chips are edible, and of course chocolate. Naturally Ruth follows her sister's lead.'

'Ah. Well, we can add a little ham or bacon and say they must eat only a little, since the fat content is so high. I never had kids of my own, but I was a teacher for years, and I do remember how well reverse psychology worked. Where are the girls, by the way? Or is Cynthia in school?' I had washed the spinach and was now chopping it, while Judith beat up eggs.

'No, it's the Christmas holiday; they're upstairs playing. There's a big playroom at the top of the house, what used to be called the "day nursery" way back when children were kept out of the way of parents by an omnipotent nanny. Actually it's not a bad place for them to spend their time. They're old enough to play pretty well together without supervision, and they can make all the noise they want.'

'And Joseph?'

'Napping, thank heaven. It won't last long, but I think I've time to eat my lunch before he starts screaming for his next meal. Did you say something about ham or bacon?'

'If there is any.'

She rummaged in the fridge and then the freezer and found a small chunk of ham, probably left over from some earlier meal. 'Mrs Walker may be saving this for something, but she's not here to ask, so do you think we could use it? It's frozen solid.'

'We can nuke it. Mrs Walker wouldn't approve – it doesn't do the texture any good – but we're just going to chop it up anyway, so it doesn't matter. Do you want to make the cream sauce, or shall I?'

For answer she handed me a saucepan and a bottle of milk. I found the butter and flour and an onion and proceeded with a simple but flavourful white sauce. 'So what,' I asked when it had thickened nicely lump-free, 'do you think about this whole dagger business? Do you have any nutmeg?'

She started to open cupboards and drawers. 'I don't know what to think, except I wish to goodness Edwin had put the thing in a vault years ago. It's a millstone around our necks. Here's some whole nutmegs, but – oh, and here's a little tin of the grated.'

'Thanks.' I stirred a pinch of it into the sauce. 'Brings out the flavour of the spinach. I've been wondering why on earth he hasn't just broken the entail. It seems really outdated in this day and age. I mean, what would have happened if Joseph hadn't been a boy? Would he have expected you to go on having one baby after another until you produced a boy? Shades of Henry the Eighth!'

'His wives didn't have much to say about it, did they?' She put the chopped ham in a frying pan on the Aga and began to stir it, sending out a tantalizing aroma. 'I'm not quite that much of a doormat. I love Edwin dearly, though he sometimes drives me mad, but I told him from the start that three children were the absolute limit. So he was absurdly relieved when the scan showed that Joseph was unmistakably male.'

'He wouldn't have considered adoption, if the scan had shown another girl?'

'Adoption wouldn't have served. I believe the old documents are quite clear about it. No adoptees.'

I sighed. 'That old nonsense about bloodlines. I can sort of understand if the point is to prevent some undesirable genetic trait from entering the family, but the people who came up with these absurd ideas didn't know anything about genetics. Their idea was that simply to be a Tudor, or a Stewart, or a Windsor – or a Montcalm – was to be of a superior race, and God forbid that anyone who was not should inherit the family fortune and power. I'm afraid I have no patience with that idea. My first husband and I would happily have adopted, since we never had any kids of our own, but by the time we looked into it the adoption agencies thought we were too old.'

I dropped the subject, which was growing painful. 'Okay, the sauce is almost ready. Now is when the timing gets tricky. If you'll call everyone and then set the table I'll stir in the spinach and ham. The heat from the sauce will cook the spinach in no time, and then I'll start the omelette pan heating. I don't want to cook the eggs until everybody's on the spot. An over-cooked omelette is fit only to sole shoes, and a cold one is an abomination unto the Lord.'

'I think Mrs Walker sometimes puts finished ones in that oven,' Judith said, pointing. 'It's only warm, not hot, and it'll keep them for a minute or two, anyway.'

'Right.'

I had expected her to do a quick sprint from the kitchen to get the girls. Instead she went to an odd-looking piece of brass hanging on one wall. If I'd thought about it at all, I'd imagined it was an archaic electrical switch of some sort, or a place to plug in something, though I couldn't imagine what. Judith lifted a sort of lid on the thing and blew into it. A shrill whistle resulted, the kind of demanding noise you get from a frantically boiling teakettle. She whistled a pattern, two long blasts and one short, paused, and then did it again.

'Wow! A speaking tube! Was it Poe, or . . . no! Sherlock Holmes!'

'"The Speckled Band",' said Judith with a smile. 'That one summoned a nasty snake. This one will bring my children, and they'll collect the men – the third whistle means "find Daddy". I was no end pleased to find this in the house, and find that it still worked. The girls think it's such fun, they always respond at once. You can talk into it, too, but the whistle code is more fun.

'Here, I'll stack the plates on the warm burner, and they'll be ready by the time you are. Mind you use the hot pads.'

ELEVEN

Sure enough, two little girls appeared in no time, their elders behind them. The children, not in the least abashed by the presence of strangers, helped distribute knives and forks and napkins, while Judith poured orange juice for the girls and herself, and Edwin opened a bottle of white wine for us. I made omelettes and slid them onto plates, Judith filled and folded them and popped them into the warming oven, Alan found bread and butter and set them on the table, and in a very few minutes we sat down to our meal.

Alan can be very diplomatic when he finds it necessary. He kept a gentle flow of small talk going throughout lunch, refusing to come near the subject that was foremost in everyone's thoughts. Well, not everyone. The girls chattered happily about what Santa Claus was going to bring them. 'Father Christmas,' Edwin muttered, as I might have expected. Stick to tradition at all costs, even when the subject under discussion was mythical. The children paid him not the slightest attention. They were, fortunately, so intent upon their hopes and wishes that they forgot to question what they were eating, and beautifully cleaned their plates.

'What's for pudding, Mummy?' asked Cynthia.

'Use your napkin, darling,' said Judith. 'You've a crumb of something on your chin. And I'm afraid we didn't think about dessert. You may have a chocolate biscuit if you like – oh, dear.'

For from somewhere not far away came a lusty roar, announcing that the son and almost-heir was once again in need of attention.

Cynthia made a face, but said, 'It's okay, Mummy. We'll help clear. May I have two biscuits?'

'Yes, but no more. Excuse me, everyone.'

'Lady Montcalm has no help with the baby?' asked Alan when she had left the room.

His tone was neutral, but Edwin interpreted the question as criticism. 'No, she doesn't. She doesn't want or need help. I do my bit when I'm home, but obviously I can't feed him.'

Well, you could, I thought. It seemed likely that Judith was nursing the baby, but there are such things as breast pumps, so bottles of the mother's own milk can be given when the poor woman is exhausted. It wasn't my place to tell Edwin that, but I was beginning to take quite a dislike to Edwin Montcalm.

'I see,' said Alan, still carefully neutral. 'Then I'd like to ask you some questions, while you're not busy.'

A buzzer sounded. Edwin stood. 'Dratted doorbell. I wish I'd never installed it. What was wrong with the old bell that one pulled, I'd like to know. I'll get rid of whoever it is.'

I stood to direct the children in clearing the table and loading the dishwasher. Edwin had broken from tradition to the extent of installing that machine, probably because it would get him out of helping wash up.

Stop that, Dorothy! I scolded myself. *You're feeding your antipathy, which may be quite unjustified. He bought the dishwasher to save his wife work.*

Which led me to musing about servants. One cook, who didn't live in and felt free to leave in a huff when things weren't to her liking. A housekeeper and an unspecified number of 'girls' with no schedule stated for any of those – daily, weekly? No nanny. I looked around the kitchen, which was spotless and gleaming, aside from the slight mess Judith and I had made preparing lunch. With three children to look after, Judith couldn't possibly keep it looking like that by herself, so it looked as though the non-resident cleaners did their work efficiently.

'Mrs Martin, may we go and play now? We've finished the table,' Cynthia asked with grave courtesy. Plainly she took after her mother.

'Yes, of course. You've been the greatest help, both of you. Oh, and don't forget your biscuits.' I got the box from the pantry and turned aside, but out of the corner of my eye observed that Cynthia carefully took out four: two for herself, two for Ruth. But before they scampered upstairs, she said to Edwin, 'Daddy, don't forget to tell Mr Nesbitt about the man who wants to buy the house.'

I tidied up a few loose ends and joined Alan at the table, but before I could sit down, I heard angry voices coming from the front hall, Edwin and another man. Alan shook his head in exasperation and stood, saying, 'I suppose I'll have to see if he needs help.'

'I've told you before,' Edwin said in a near-bellow. 'I am not under any circumstances interested. I've also told you I wasn't prepared to discuss the matter further. If you come again I shall be forced to—'

'Oh, so it's threats you're making now! There'll come a day when you're not so high and mighty, a day when you'll come begging to me—'

'*That's enough!* Leave this house! I have guests, and I'll not—'

They had approached the kitchen door, where Alan loomed. 'Spot of trouble, Edwin?' he asked quietly.

Alan is a large man, and he has kept himself in shape, even after retirement. His voice is deep, and he has, in his years as a policeman, developed a look that can transform his normally genial face into one that makes even criminals think twice about crossing him.

Both the men stopped shouting. The man with Edwin was smallish, with sandy hair and a scruffy beard. His face at the moment was red with anger; his nose, I thought, might be red much of the time from another cause. He glared at Alan and Edwin impartially, gathered the rags of his dignity about him, and turned toward the door. 'I'll be coming back! And don't think you can keep me away!' But he fled, quite promptly. Edwin slammed the front door after him, locked and bolted it, and returned, shaking, to the kitchen table.

'Goodness, what was that about?' I made my voice as calm and normal as possible.

'I'm so sorry you had to hear that,' Edwin said, trying to match my tone. His voice, though, still shook with anger. 'The bast– er, the scoundrel keeps coming round wanting to buy the estate. He can't seem to grasp the basic fact that I couldn't sell even if I wanted to, because of the terms of the entail. And I don't want to, in any case. And certainly not to him! Do you know what he wants to do?'

It was obviously a rhetorical question. 'I'm curious about that, I admit.'

'He doesn't believe in inherited wealth, he says. He's a total rotter! Had the nerve to come here and insult me to my face, and then offer me a pittance for the property. I told him to get out and stay out!'

'Could you be a bit more specific about his behaviour? What exactly did he say to you?'

'A string of insults, I told you. Sounded like an anarchist!'

I had to turn a disbelieving laugh in to a cough. Anarchist! Surely no one had used that term for the past century!

'What led you to that conclusion?' Alan was determined to get some details out of Edwin, no matter how long it took.

'Well, what would you conclude when a man calls you an effete aristocrat, an exploiter of the poor, living on unearned income? I could have told him I earn every penny of my income, every penny, and I've never in my life exploited anyone! But I didn't choose to bandy words with him. I consider I behaved very well indeed not to kick him into next week. Next time I swear I will!'

'Why would a man like that want to buy this property? Surely his principles wouldn't allow him to live in such a conspicuous house?' I was genuinely curious. Even discounting about three-quarters of what Edwin had said, it still seemed odd that someone who sounded like an extreme radical would make such an offer.

'Didn't want to live in it. Had the face to say the house should be torn down and the land used to build cheap little boxes for working families.'

'Ah. And did the man say – by the way, what is the chap's name? Can you remember?'

Edwin barked a humourless laugh. 'I'm not liable to forget. He told me his name was John Smith.'

Alan finally let a sigh escape. 'I see. There is some small chance that is his name. There *are* people named John Smith.'

'Not many Irishmen, though,' I put in.

'Dorothy, we don't know that he's Irish. The appearance I'll grant you, but the diction and accent sounded forced to me. However, as I started to ask, Edwin, did "Mr Smith" tell you who was to build these homes?'

For the first time Edwin appeared to actually think about his answer. 'No,' he said finally, 'I don't think he did. I got the impression the enterprise was his, some company of his own, but I don't think he actually said so. I was a good deal upset, you understand.'

'I do understand.'

And Alan really did, I thought. Edwin, ineffectual and annoying as he might be, was facing a disturbance of his whole way of life, all his assumptions being called into question. It was a crisis of belief as profound in its way as a loss of faith. It *was* a loss of faith, in fact, secular faith, to be sure, but just as seismic in its consequences.

'There's an interesting point, you know,' Alan added. 'I know this house isn't particularly old, but surely anyone wanting to tear it down and build something else on the estate would have a good deal of trouble getting planning permission.'

'I told him that, too! We're a Grade II listed building, and we have to jump through hoops to do any alterations.'

His temper was improving, and I tried to help keep it that way. 'You know, Edwin, I've wondered about the name, Dunham Manor. Why not Montcalm?'

'Ah, well, you see, the Montcalms didn't build the house. My branch of the family didn't move to England until the early nineteenth century. This house was built in 1785 by the Dunhams, who were landed gentry, but untitled. Sadly, their family fortunes diminished rapidly after that, so that when my many-times-great-grandfather came over from France in 1805, the Dunhams were desperately in need of capital. As it happened, the Montcalm fortunes were in the ascendant at the time, owing to my ancestor's financial aid to Lord Nelson and the British fleet. By that time the family's loyalty to France had all but disappeared, you see – none of them cared much for Napoleon. At any rate, Great-great-et-cetera-Grandfather Louis was rewarded with the baronetcy and decided he needed a house appropriate to his position. He liked this part of the country, the Dunhams needed money – *et voilà!*'

'I'm surprised he didn't change the name.'

'Oh, that would never have done. Even though the house was relatively new, the Dunhams had lived hereabouts and had been the local squires since the Ark. They were well-respected. Old Louis was canny enough to keep up the noblesse oblige traditions, and leave the name of the house so as to minimize the offence to the tenants and villagers.'

I stood. 'I don't know about anyone else, but I could use some coffee.' As I assembled what I needed, I continued to listen. Having tactfully dealt with the subject of the irritating 'Mr Smith', Alan got onto the subject of servants. 'Right,' he was saying. 'Mrs Walker, every weekday. A housekeeper/cleaner, Mrs Burton, three times a week, with two assistants when needed. Gardener three times a week in season. What about general maintenance, small repairs and so on? A house of this age must require attention almost constantly. I know mine does, but of course it's a good deal older, early seventeenth century.'

Oh, well done, Alan. Casually suggesting that we're not the Johnnies-come-lately that he may suppose. Of course we bought our house a few years ago; it didn't come down through anyone's family. Alan's father was a fisherman in Cornwall; mine was a teacher in Indiana.

'Yes,' said Edwin, 'there's always something. And with people coming in to see the house from time to time, we've had to keep it up properly.'

I could almost hear the groan Alan didn't utter. People in and out. Casual servants, tourists who probably didn't even leave their names. We'd been handed an impossible task.

I brought in the coffee.

Alan said, 'Just what I needed,' in the tone of a man holding on desperately to his sanity. He took a sip, scalding though it was, took a deep breath, and continued asking questions, which Edwin answered incompletely if at all.

How on earth could a man so apparently unobservant or downright incompetent be holding down a big-deal job in finance? Not that I had any idea what 'in finance' meant. Maybe he was a sort of international banker who was very good with numbers but bad with people? Or maybe, just maybe, he was faking the stupidity because he was involved in some sort of fraud. But what? Was this some kind of insurance scam?

Or maybe, Dorothy, he's so upset by the threat to all his hopes and dreams that he can't think straight. I was becoming ashamed of my judgmental attitude and trying to think more charitably when Judith came back into the room. This time she was carrying in her arms a small, blanket-wrapped bundle.

'Dorothy, Alan, I'd like you to meet the newest member of the family. He's had his lunch and gone back to sleep, so I thought I'd show him off when he's at his best. Meet Joseph Montcalm.'

All that could be seen of him was his face, round and rosy-cheeked. A little black hair poked out from beneath his knitted cap; a sweet little round mouth was still now; eyelashes that would be the envy of any Hollywood star lay peacefully against silken cheeks. It seemed impossible that such a tremendous volume of sound could have come from such a small bundle of humanity only a few minutes ago.

'He's a love,' I said, honestly this time. The red-faced newborn of the picture Edwin had shown us had metamorphosed into this adorable baby, so angelic-looking that my throat tightened up. I once thought I'd eventually come to terms with my grief over my own childlessness, but it never happened. A baby brings it all to the fore, fresh and painful as it ever was. I swallowed and blinked, and Alan, perceptive as always, picked up the cue.

'He's a delightful boy, Judith, but Dorothy has been nursing a slight cold. Nothing serious, but we wouldn't want her to pass it along to the baby, so perhaps . . .'

Judith looked at me. I tried hard to smile, since I couldn't have said a word. Somehow she understood. 'He's pretty hardy, but no, we don't want to risk it. I'll put him back to bed and hope he stays quiet for a while.'

She whisked him away. I found a tissue and blew my nose, and Alan went doggedly back to his extraction of information from Edwin.

Or at least he tried, but Edwin was oddly unresponsive. He didn't seem to be paying attention to Alan's questions, and finally held out his hands in the classic fending-off gesture. 'Look, I'm being an ass, and I apologize. It's no excuse, but I simply didn't want to face the loss of the dagger – which would mean the loss of everything I possess.'

'Not everything,' I said in a voice I tried hard to keep steady.

'No. I saw that just now. My children – my wife – they're what really matter. I want them to have what they should, a stable home, the things that are theirs by right. But it doesn't have to be here. I guess.'

'No,' said Alan. 'Ancestral acres are important, but not essential. Of course, I speak as one who never had any, and I may say I've never felt the lack of them. Edwin, does this shift in your attitude mean you're no longer interested in finding the dagger?'

'Yes. No. I don't know!' He buried his head in his hands. I exchanged glances with Alan. I had changed from aversion to sympathy for this volatile young man, but I was sorrier for his wife, who had to deal with him all the time. I wondered if his moods were always this variable, or if it was only the current crisis that had brought them out.

I also wondered what we should do. When one's host is in a state of near-collapse, it creates an interesting social situation. I was pretty sure a motherly 'there, there' wouldn't help. Should we just quietly leave? Oh, but our bags were upstairs.

Alan squared his shoulders. 'Edwin, listen to me. This thing has shaken you badly. I understand. But you must face it and deal with it, for the sake of your family. Now pull yourself together and tell me what you want me to do.'

The young man took a deep breath that sounded almost like a sob, but when he spoke his voice was steady. 'I want you to find the bloody thing. Sorry, Mrs Martin. Once it's found, Judith and I can make some decisions, but I'm damned if I'm going to be forced into an unwise move by some bl– ruddy thief.'

'Good man. Ah, Judith. All quiet in the nursery?'

'For a bit.' She sank down into a chair. 'I must say, I'll be grateful when he starts sleeping all night. Oh, I know, I could prepare bottles, so Edwin could take over some of the time. I did do for a day or two when I was really exhausted, not long after he was born, but I do usually enjoy my time with him. If only I weren't so tired! And of course the girls need me, too.'

That gave me an idea. 'Judith, I never had any children, but I have lots of nieces and nephews, and I taught children of various ages for many years, so I'm pretty good with them. I'd enjoy spending some time with your girls, if it would give you a little respite. I think you badly need a nap. And if you'd prepare a bottle for Joseph, I could give it to him when he's hungry again. I promise I'll wake you if there's any problem at all.'

'Well, if you're sure you wouldn't mind—'

'I'd enjoy it very much. Trust me.'

She was too tired to protest much. I followed her to her

bedroom where she extracted enough milk for two small bottles and handed them to me.

'I'm woefully ignorant about all this. Do the bottles have to go in the fridge?'

'It'll be safe for about four hours, and I'm sure Joseph will want one bottle before then. The other can go in the fridge, yes.' She hesitated. 'Are you sure . . . I mean, will it be too hard for you to give him a bottle? I saw how you looked back then, and . . . you don't really have a cold, do you?'

'No, or I would never have volunteered to feed Joseph. That was just my husband trying to rescue me from an uncomfortable situation, and explain my sniffles at the same time. And yes, it will be hard,' I said honestly. 'I wanted babies of my own very badly. When I agreed with Alan to come to Joseph's christening, I had forgotten that it's still hard for me to watch a baptism. And it will be harder still to hold a baby, and feed him. But I will truly enjoy being with the girls, and if feeding Joseph helps you get some badly-needed rest, I'll do it, even if I cry all over his head.'

Judith yawned uncontrollably. 'Oh, sorry!'

'Don't be silly. Look, you lie down and let me pull this over you. I'll close the door, and you sleep as long as you can.'

She yawned again and said something about dinner. I ignored her and left the room carrying two baby bottles for the first time in well over forty years.

TWELVE

I detoured down to the kitchen with them, hoping Alan and Edwin had adjourned to the drawing room, or whatever he'd called the room where we'd first sat. They weren't in the kitchen, at any rate. Good. I thought Edwin would talk more freely without me around. He could at least let himself go with respect to language. His embarrassment about profanity in front of me was a rather endearing quality, and goodness knows he needed a few. I still hadn't quite made up my mind about him.

One bottle went in the fridge; the other I tucked away in a cupboard. I wasn't sure how much the girls knew about breast-feeding, and I didn't want to be the one to explain about the bottle of rather odd-looking milk. I was good at playing with kids, and reading to them, but I felt explaining some of the facts of life was above my pay grade.

No one had told me where to find the girls, but if the house followed the traditional pattern, it would be on the third floor. I trudged up two flights of stairs, the upper one covered in rather less imposing carpet. Tradition, again! With the children using those stairs a lot, I would have thought a good thick covering would wear better, as well as abating noise, but there! It wasn't my house. My opinion was irrelevant.

I was half expecting a chilly room with linoleum on the floor and shabby, cast-off furniture, but here the Montcalms – or probably Judith – had parted with tradition. The room was bright, with yellow wallpaper and white woodwork, and lots of windows. The floor was covered with rugs that looked hard-wearing, but were of a cheerful light blue. There was a soft squishy couch covered in virtually childproof fabric, and best of all, the room was warm. The windows were modern, double-paned ones, and besides the gentle warmth coming from the electric radiators, there was a gas fireplace putting out plenty of heat.

Cynthia was lying on her stomach on a furry rug in front of the fire, looking at a big picture book. Ruth was busily arranging furniture in a dollhouse, the plastic kind made for children to really play with, not the accurately detailed sort collectors love. She was humming something unrecognizable as she worked.

Both girls looked up as I came in.

'Mummy's downstairs, I think, Mrs Martin,' said Cynthia politely. 'Or are you looking for your room? You're staying all night, aren't you? Even though there isn't going to be a party.'

'Yes, my husband and I are staying for at least one night, but I wasn't looking for my room or for your mother. I was looking for you, both of you, and I've found you! I think I've done pretty well, as big a house as this is.'

'You talk funny,' said Ruth with a giggle.

'Ruth!' said big sister. 'That's very rude! Mummy told us we weren't to say anything about that.'

I laughed. 'It's all right. That is, your mother was right when she said it isn't polite to talk about the ways that people are different – but you're absolutely correct, Ruth, I do have an odd way of speaking. I was born in America, you see, and lived there for many years before I moved to England. So I still speak a little like an American. When I go back to America for a visit, though, the people there think I sound English.'

'Why did you leave America?' This was Ruth, eager to find out more about this somewhat exotic person who had invaded her world.

Well, that was a little complicated, and involved some sadness I wasn't sure the girls should hear. 'It's a long story,' I said, 'but I had retired from my job at home in Indiana – that's the place in America where I lived – and my husband had died, and I'd always loved England, so I moved here and found Mr Nesbitt and married him, and I've lived here ever since.'

'Oh.' Ruth, losing interest, returned to her play, but now Cynthia's curiosity was aroused. 'What was your job back in America?'

'I was a teacher, and I enjoyed it very much. Our schools are a little different from yours, but children are alike, I think, all over the world.'

Cynthia nodded. 'That's what I think, too. Daddy goes all over the world for his job, and sometimes we go with him, or he sends us back pictures, and Mummy says the people may look different, but inside they're just like us.'

'Do you have children from other parts of the world at your school?'

'Well . . . they all live near us. But some of them have different sorts of names, and they don't look like us. My best friend, Deva, says her father and mother are from India. Is that where you said you used to live?'

'No, it's a different country.' I looked around the room and spotted a globe. 'Look, this is like a picture of the world, right?'

Cynthia looked condescending. 'I know *that*. Daddy showed me. This is where we live.' She put a finger on the tiny blob that represented the United Kingdom.

'That's right. Very good! Well, if we turn the globe quite a long way, here is America, and here is where I used to live.' There were no states indicated, but the Great Lakes were shown, which allowed me to approximate. 'And when we turn the globe the other way, here's the big country where your friend Deva's parents came from.'

'Ooh! She says there are elephants there, and tigers, but I don't believe her. She tells lies sometimes.'

'Almost everybody does, sometimes, but she isn't lying about the elephants and tigers. They really do live in India, though there aren't as many of them as there used to be.' I looked around again, this time toward the bookshelves. 'There's a book here written by a man who spent much of his life in India, even though he was English. Shall I read it to you?'

'Is it about India?'

'Not really, but it's about some of the animals that live in both India and Africa. It's funny; I think you'll like it.'

'Yes, please,' both girls chorused, so I took down the tattered copy of *Just So Stories*. The stories about the Elephant's Child and the Leopard and the others had been my favourites for years. I wasn't lucky enough to come across them as a child, but I'd read them to generations of school children. They were written to be read aloud, and I loved to do it. We sat on the couch, one child on each side of me, and I opened the old, well-loved book.

'"How the Whale got his Throat",' I began. '"In the sea, once upon a time, O my Best Beloved . . ."'

They were giggling before I'd finished the first paragraph, and I laughed along with them. Kipling knew how to write for children, knew how they loved silliness, and rhymes, and repetition. We were all enjoying ourselves, and had nearly got to the end of the whale story, when I heard a wail, not yet a full-throated demand for food, but working up to it. I put the book down.

'Don't stop! Mummy will look after Joseph.'

'Mummy's taking a nap. She's very tired. I told her I'd mind the baby for a little while.'

'But . . . but you can't! I mean . . .?' She looked acutely embarrassed.

'Yes, usually your mother feeds Joseph. That's what mothers do. But this time she put some of her milk in a bottle, so I could feed him. Shall I bring him in here, after I've changed his diaper – I mean his nappy? Then you could watch him being fed, and maybe even help.'

By now the wail had become a roar, and I was afraid he'd wake Judith. I didn't wait for the children to answer, but hotfooted it down the stairs, following the sound. So I thought I'd avoid the facts of life and female anatomy, did I? Well, come to think of it, of course the girls themselves had been breast-fed, and probably they'd seen kittens born and nursing; even if this was no longer a huge estate, there must be barn cats. Anyway, kids nowadays were so much more savvy than I had been at their age. I was being old-fashioned and foolish. I opened the door to Joseph's pretty little nursery and spoke to him, and my strange voice startled him so much he stopped howling for a moment.

Only for a moment, however. I picked him up, laid him on the changing table, and performed that messy little chore rapidly. It would have been easier had he not been screaming and flailing little arms and legs, frantic with hunger, but I wasn't going to hold him on my lap in his present state. I was an experienced aunt, after all, so I managed fairly well. Then, cooing and rocking him in my arms, I hit the kitchen, put the bottle in my pocket to warm a bit, and trudged back up the stairs to the playroom.

The children were waiting to watch this phenomenon. Sitting down on the squishy couch, I wasn't sure how Joseph would take to the bottle, being used to the breast, but he was very hungry. After a little nosing around, he figured it out and began to suck noisily.

I was glad the girls were there. I could easily have turned into a weepy mess, holding in my arms a baby that wasn't mine, giving him milk that I had never been able to produce, feeling his warmth, smelling the indefinable baby smell – but with the children watching intently, I had to maintain my composure.

'He eats like a little pig,' said Ruth the forthright. '*We've* been taught to eat quietly and not get food all over the place.'

'But you're so much more grown-up, not babies anymore. I'll bet you were just as messy when you were tiny.'

'She was,' said Cynthia in her Big Sister voice. 'When she started to eat porridge and baby food and that, she sprayed it all over herself and the kitchen and everywhere.'

'Did not!'

'Did too!'

'Now, ladies, don't quarrel or you'll upset your brother. And if a baby gets upset when he's eating, he can get pains in his little tummy, and when that happens, he can easily scream the house down!'

The girls glared at each other, but subsided. I looked for a change of subject, but Ruth forestalled me.

'You came for the christening, but it isn't going to happen, so why—'

'Well, you see, we didn't know until we got here that the christening had been postponed.'

'What does "postpone" mean?'

'Put off until later.' Joseph's assault on the bottle had slowed down. I picked him up and put him over my shoulder. 'Cynthia, run and get me a towel, will you? A face towel will do.' Some things are never forgotten, and I had no desire to get baby spit-up on one of my favourite sweaters.

Cynthia obeyed swiftly, but commented, 'Mummy uses one of his bibs.'

'A good idea, but a towel is quicker. Just in case.' I began to pat the baby gently on his back, hoping I hadn't forgotten the technique.

Ruth persisted. 'But Daddy says we can't do it without that stupid dagger. I don't see why. It's just pouring water on the baby's head and saying some prayers. I've seen it in church.'

I didn't think now was the time to go into an explanation of the spiritual significance of baptism, and Cynthia didn't give me a chance, anyway. 'It's because it's tradition!' she said scornfully. 'Every baby – anyway, every *boy* baby – in our family has been christened with the dagger for hundreds and hundreds of years.'

'You don't christen with a dagger,' said Ruth scornfully.

'With the dagger *there*, silly. So without it we can't do it.'

'Maybe we couldn't have done it anyway. Because of what that woman said.'

Joseph obliged me with a resounding burp (a nice clean one), so I took him in my lap again and presented the bottle. There wasn't much milk left, and he wasn't interested. He wasn't sleepy, either. He looked around the room with interest and suddenly smiled, instantly captivating his sisters – and me. And when he started waving his fists and babbling, I completely forgot Ruth's remark.

Cynthia, sitting next to me, was the first one to break the spell. 'Mummy should see this,' she said with a little sigh. 'She loves it when he tries to talk.'

'So she should. Look, sweet, do you think you could hold him for just a second? I can't get out of this couch without using both hands.' I handed him over, and one of his flailing fists caught her on the nose. She just laughed and held him securely until I was safely on my feet. 'Now, we'll go to Mummy's room and see if she's awake.'

She certainly was by the time we reached her. Between Joseph's cooing and his sisters' responses, she had little chance to stay asleep. She did look somewhat rested, though, and she greeted us with a broad smile and held out her hands for her adorable son.

'I think he needs another clean nappy,' I warned.

'He usually does, don't you, lamb? Is that what you're trying to tell me?'

He loudly cooed what might have been an affirmative, and we all laughed. Mother and children were wrapped up in each other; I thought my presence could be dispensed with. I slipped out of the room and went to find Alan.

He and Edwin were sitting in front of the drawing room fire. Like the one in the playroom upstairs, it was gas-fuelled. Rather a pity, I thought, but with Edwin away a lot and no live-in servants, Judith would hardly have been able to keep a coal- or wood-burning one stoked and clean. This was much more practical, and actually warmer. I was a bit surprised, though, that the tradition-loving Edwin had allowed it.

They stood as I entered the room. 'I didn't mean to interrupt,' I said. 'Please do sit down and go ahead with whatever you were doing.' I dropped into one of the comfortable chairs, so as not to keep these courteous gentlemen on their feet.

'We'd just about finished,' said Alan. 'I think I've garnered all the information Edwin can give me about the mysterious disappearance. How did you get on with the children?' He gave me rather a searching look.

'Swimmingly. I read to the girls for a while, and then when Joseph began to demand attention, I took him into the playroom and fed him. We all quite enjoyed that.' That was in response to Alan's unspoken question. *No, my love, looking after a baby didn't leave me unhinged.* 'I coped rather well, I think, considering how many years it's been since my nieces and nephews were that age. I left them all with Judith just now; she was awake and feeling much friskier, and Joseph was chattering away.'

A smile broke out on Edwin's face, the first I'd seen since we arrived. 'He's only a bit over five months old, you know, and already babbling like a politician! We think he's going to begin talking very young.'

'He's obviously an intelligent child,' I said, stretching only a little, 'and so are the girls. Delightful children, all of them. And that reminds me,' I rudely continued over the reply Edwin was about to make, 'Ruth said something I didn't quite follow. We were talking about the delayed christening, and she said she thought it might not happen at all, and mentioned something some woman said. I didn't get a chance to ask her about it, but I did wonder . . .'

I wasn't prepared to see Edwin's face lose all its colour.

THIRTEEN

'Here! Steady, man!' Alan clapped Edwin on the shoulder. 'Dorothy, some water!'

I tried to get out of my chair, but Edwin spoke up. 'No, no, don't trouble. I'm fine.'

'You don't look fine,' I said frankly. 'I thought you were going to pass out. Are you sure you don't want water, or tea, or something stronger?'

'No, truly, I . . .' His voice was raspy. 'Well, perhaps some water. My throat seems a bit dry.'

Alan, by this time, had gone to the kitchen and was now handing a glass to Edwin, who took it with a shaking hand and sipped a little. The poor man cleared his throat and started to speak, but Alan held up a hand. 'I'd like the truth, please,' he said, gently but firmly. 'I remind you that Dorothy and I are here at *your* invitation, and that we have stayed at *your* request, to look into *your* problem. You are, of course, not obliged to answer any of our questions – but neither are we obliged to stay. We both have a good many things to do at home before Christmas.'

Edwin bit his lip, put his glass down, and took a deep breath. 'You're quite right. I've been a fool, and in more ways than one. It's just that I'd hoped you wouldn't have to know about the woman Ruth mentioned. I had no idea she knew anything about her!'

'Children see and hear a good deal more of what goes on in a family than their parents always realize,' said Alan, and I nodded. The school children always knew what was going on in the classroom, too, long before I did. Little pitchers, as the saying goes.

Edwin groaned. 'I just hope she hasn't said anything to her mother. I don't care so much about you knowing, but Judith . . .'

'Is this something that would distress your wife, then?' asked Alan. 'Some youthful infidelity, perhaps? Or not so youthful?'

'No! Or rather, yes, I suppose, but not my own.' He swallowed hard and took a deep breath.

Judith chose that moment to walk into the room. There was a spring in her step and colour in her cheeks. 'Joseph got tired of playing and dropped off, so I put him to bed. Dorothy, you may have saved my life. The girls asked if you could come back and read some more to them. I gathered you stopped just in the middle of a good part?'

I laughed. 'I started them on *Just So Stories*. I expect they want to hear the end of the whale story. I had to leave them hanging when Joseph began to fuss. I'd love to read more to them. They're sweet kids, and it's one of my favourite books.'

'Oh, Kipling! They'll love that. I was just going to start on it when my little tyrant came along, and I've not had a lot of time since. Yes, by all means read as much as you can bear, but not right now. Edwin tells me you two have been doing a tour of sorts, exploring England's oddities. I've not seen many of them myself, so I'd love to hear about them.'

'When did you move to England, then?' I asked. 'You said you were Canadian. How did you and Edwin meet?'

'I lived in Toronto, and he was there on business.'

'Business with the firm her father managed,' Edwin put in with a grin. 'She walked into the office one day, and I was lost forever. She's lovelier now than she was then, but she was the most beautiful woman I'd ever seen, even back then.' He gave her a look of adoration that racked up another few points for him in my estimation.

Judith laughed, a warm, musical sound. 'The man's mad. I'm ten years and three children older. The bloom is fading fast, but he pretends not to see it.'

'I don't agree,' said Alan, 'and I consider myself something of an expert on feminine pulchritude. A truly beautiful woman, one whose beauty is in the bone, and in her character as well, does in fact grow lovelier as the years pass.'

He gave me a meaningful look, and I spoke hastily. 'And before he goes all polite and sweet and starts saying things about me that are obviously not true, I'll say I agree with him in principle. Judith, I didn't know you when you were younger, of course, but there is a calm serenity about you now that does better work than any cosmetics could. You *are* lovely, my dear, so don't bother to deny it. And I have a very good friend whose years have treated her in the same benevolent way.' I smiled, thinking of Greta Endicott at the Rose and Crown. 'She's in her sixties now, and even more striking than when I first met her many years ago. There are grey hairs among the blond, and laugh lines around her eyes, but they only enhance her appearance. So, Edwin, it was love at first sight?'

'And second, and third, and hundredth. I stayed in Toronto quite a lot longer than business required, and before I left I made arrangements to see her again.'

'And that time he asked me to marry him. I hesitated for at least thirty seconds before I said yes.'

'A girl mustn't seem too eager,' I said gravely. 'So where were you married, over there or over here?'

'In Toronto. Of course I wanted my family and friends around me, and since Edwin had no close family, we decided to have the wedding from my home. Then after a honeymoon that wasn't nearly long enough, we came here to the manor just to get me settled, and then Edwin was off again to – I forget where.'

'Brazil. I didn't think Judith would like the climate, so I made my stay there as short as I could, and managed to get posted off to Iceland, where we could be together again.'

I shivered at the very thought, and both Judith and Edwin laughed. 'The story is that the first Europeans to visit Iceland named it that to keep others away,' said Judith. 'It actually has a delightful climate, and amazing scenery.'

'And a very high standard of living,' put in Edwin the financier. 'We very much enjoyed our time there. But of course it didn't last as long as we liked, and we came back here for a bit.'

'And after a few more jaunts Cynthia was born, so of course I wasn't quite as free to go gadding about the globe with Edwin, nor was I free to gad about England. So I'm sadly ignorant about the more peculiar rituals that prevail here.'

One of the most peculiar, I thought, was the one that should have taken place right here in a day or two. Of course I didn't say so, but talked about swan-upping and the Lord Mayor's procession and the moving ceremony at the Tower in memory of Henry VI.

I was just considering how to get rid of Judith so we could ask Edwin about the woman Ruth had mentioned, and his reaction to hearing about her, when the phone rang in a nearby room. Edwin excused himself, quite glad to leave us, I thought. When he had left the room, Judith spoke to us in a low tone.

'Edwin is nervous about something. Has he been talking to you about this dagger nonsense? Because it is nonsense, you know. I'm quite sure the entail could be broken, and what does it matter where we live? The estate actually costs quite a lot to keep running, you know.'

'I'm sure it does,' said Alan. 'I believe I mentioned that our house needs constant attention, and it's much smaller than this one, with no acreage to worry about. Of course it's nearly two hundred years older.'

Edwin came back into the room, looking like death warmed over.

Judith sprang to her feet. 'Dear heaven, what is it, Edwin?'

He held onto the back of a chair to keep from swaying. 'The dagger has been found.'

'But that's wonderful news!'

'No. It was found in the body of a woman. She was burned to death in a fire at the Swan, with our dagger in her back. The police are on their way.'

Alan poured a stiff whisky for Edwin and made him sit down and drink it. I made a quick cup of herbal tea for Judith and then sent her upstairs to keep the children occupied and away from discussions of calamity. Alan went to the door to wait for the police, and I was left to try to get some sense out of Edwin.

'Edwin, quickly, before Judith comes back. Who was the woman?'

'The police don't know. She had no identification, or at least they couldn't find any. They only phoned me because of the dagger. I suppose—'

'Not that woman! The woman Ruth was talking about – the one who said something that made her think there would be no christening.'

'Oh. Her.'

I waited. Most people can't endure a silence and will talk just to fill it.

'She has nothing to do with the theft of the dagger.'

'Maybe not, but you're upset about her. Who was she?'

'I don't really know. She gave me her name, but I've forgotten.'

Right. Forgotten the name of someone whose very memory made him turn white. I waited some more.

'Really, she's irrelevant to all this. She couldn't possibly have taken the cursed thing; she was only in the house a few minutes and never left the room.'

'Did you leave the room? I take it Judith was not at home.'

'No, she wasn't, and no, I did not leave the blasted woman alone, not for a moment. Back in the days when this family had proper servants, no butler would have admitted her at all, no matter what fantastic story she made up.'

I didn't remind him that those days of 'proper servants' were gone with the dodo, and responded instead to what he had let slip. 'Fantastic story? So she had a story?'

'No! She told a pack of lies! She was a beggar, that's all. I – I gave her a few pounds, just because I felt sorry for her, and sent her away.'

'Then what was it that Ruth heard her say? She's young, but she's a very intelligent little girl. I'm sure she must have heard something she thought was important.'

'I didn't know – I mean she couldn't have been close enough to hear anything that mattered. In fact there wasn't anything that mattered. A tissue of lies, as I said.'

'But lies you didn't want Judith to know about,' I persisted.

'No! Look, I don't know why you're going on about this. As I've said, repeatedly, it has no bearing on the loss of the dagger, which is what – yes?'

Alan had come back into the room. Two men followed him. They wore no uniforms but everything about them proclaimed their mission. 'Gentlemen,' said Alan, 'Sir Edwin Montcalm. Edwin, these gentlemen are from the Grantham police. They'd like to ask you a few questions about the poor woman who was found at the pub.'

Edwin stood to greet them. He had not regained his poise, but he had been raised as a gentleman, and early training held. 'I believe we've met,' he said stiffly, 'at church fêtes and the like, but I'm afraid I don't recall your names.'

'Detective Chief Inspector Billings,' said the taller of the two.

He was an imposing man, though running a little to fat. His eyebrows were the bushy sort that always reminded me of woolly bear caterpillars. 'And this is Sergeant Lewis.' A small man, diffident and looking very young, he was the kind you wouldn't remember if you met him every day for a month. I imagined that appearance was very useful to a policeman.

'Ah, yes.' Edwin shook hands with both of them; I noticed that his hand shook just a little, and I was sure that the policemen noticed it, too. 'Won't you sit down? Will you have something to drink?'

'Not just now, sir, thank you,' said Billings, and I could hear, loudly, the unspoken: *Not on duty, sir.*

'Well, now, I understand that Sergeant Lewis told you in his phone call of the circumstances that bring us here.'

'He said something incredible about a dead woman and my – our – the family's dagger. I could hardly believe any of it. Who is – was this woman?'

'That's one of the things we hope you can help us with, sir. The fire – Sergeant Lewis told you about the fire?'

'Only that there was one.'

'It seems to have begun in the room where the woman's body was found. Although it was quickly extinguished, her personal belongings, handbag, and so on were destroyed. We could find no identification in the room, and Mr Bell, the proprietor, had no one registered there. As we had heard of your missing dagger, we thought you might be able to identify her for us. I believe this is yours?'

He gestured to the sergeant, who produced a plastic bag from a breast pocket. I leaned closer. The object inside was certainly a dagger, though its details were considerably obscured by soot and other material I didn't care to speculate about.

'You may take it out and look at it, sir. It has been inspected and searched for fingerprints.'

Well, they didn't say so, but it was obvious to me that the ornate surfaces would be unlikely to yield any fingerprints worth mentioning. Other traces, though, might be enough for a DNA check.

'I don't need to take it out,' said Edwin, his voice raspy and poorly controlled. 'I can see well enough. That is not our dagger.'

FOURTEEN

The chief inspector's eyebrows rose, looking more like caterpillars than ever. 'You're certain of that, sir?'

'Quite certain. This – object – is covered with small gems, probably paste, though I'm no judge of that. They're faceted, as well. Ours, the real one, has fewer, larger stones, which are simply polished, not elaborately cut. Cabochon gems, I believe they're called. This dagger bears very little resemblance to ours, in fact, beyond the general shape and size.'

'Ah. Perhaps you wouldn't mind showing me yours, so I can make the comparison.'

Dead silence.

Edwin sighed. 'I'm afraid I can't do that, Chief Inspector. As you seem to know, our dagger has gone missing. We're rather upset about it, as it was to be displayed tomorrow at Joseph's christening.'

Rather upset. If there were a World Cup for understatement, the English would win it every year. But of course Billings was English, too, and saw through Edwin's words to the desperate anxiety that lay behind them.

'You've had a good look, then?' he said mildly.

Edwin abandoned his pose of slight dismay. 'We've turned the house upside down. It simply isn't here. We've had to postpone the christening.'

'If you'll agree, I'd be happy to ask Lewis, here, to have a look. The police, you know, sir, are trained in search procedures and sometimes see things others might miss. You know, of course, that you are entitled to insist on a search warrant.'

'Lord, bring in a troupe of searchers! No one could be more eager to find the bl– the blasted thing than Judith and I.'

He had missed the implications of the chief inspector's desire to search. Alan, of course, had not, as I could tell from his expression of deeper and deeper concern. There was, first, his obvious, stated desire to prove that the murder weapon was not the Montcalm dagger. But that being the case, then whose was this disgusting thing, now back in Lewis's pocket? How did it end up in the back of some poor woman? And where was the 'real' one, and why had it been taken? And of course by whom?

The questions about that dagger were endless, and all of them centred on one Edwin Montcalm, who was going to be the subject of a lot of official scrutiny. A search of the house might turn up the dagger. It might also turn up other things of interest to the police. It would be better for everyone concerned if that miserable artefact could be found somewhere in this house.

Alan cleared his throat. 'I could perhaps assist in the search, Chief Inspector. It has been many years since I've exercised those skills, but I trust it's like swimming or riding a bicycle. They say one never forgets.'

Plainly Alan had introduced himself when he opened the door to the policemen. Billings looked him up and down, smiled, and made a decision. 'I'm sure you've forgotten none of the bag of tricks, sir. But in this case, if you will, I believe you might be a comfort to your friend while I join Lewis in hunting for our needle in the haystack.'

Or, in other words, I interpreted, keep an eye on chummy while we ransack the house.

'I'll do what I can, of course. Edwin's uncle and I used to be great friends, back when we were both in the uniformed branch in Penzance. In fact, I was present when his uncle stood godfather to the boy at *his* christening, something like thirty years ago.'

And that was code for: full disclosure – I'm not entirely impartial in this matter.

The two men nodded to each other in perfect understanding. Billings asked Edwin where the dagger was supposed to be and then escorted Lewis out of the room.

Alan made sure they were out of earshot before he sat down next to Edwin, who had collapsed on the couch.

'All right, young man, it's time to stop playing games.' This was Alan in full policeman-mode, all business and quite formidable. 'If you know anything at all about the whereabouts of the wretched dagger, or about the dead woman at the pub, tell me now. I can't help you if you lie to the police, and withholding information counts as a lie – and is a felony. And although lying to *me* would not be a felony, as I am not officially involved in this investigation, it would be an extremely stupid thing to do. As well as futile. After all these years I can spot a liar from forty yards.'

Edwin heaved a huge sigh and then sat up straighter. 'Yes. Now you must know everything, though I still hope Judith needn't.'

'That will depend on what "everything" is, won't it?'

'I suppose. I know nothing about the whereabouts of the dagger, I swear by all that's holy. The last time I saw it, years ago, it was where it belonged. Then a few days ago it wasn't. And I know nothing about the woman at the pub. But the woman Ruth talked about – yes, I'll tell you about her.' Another deep breath. 'She said she was my mother, and she wanted money.'

I couldn't quite suppress a gasp, but I tried to turn it into a cough.

Edwin wasn't deceived. 'Yes,' he said to both of us. 'I suppose you know, Alan, that my father was not always quite an angel. No one told me, of course, when I was a child, but when I was older I caught some of the rumours. A word overheard here, a word there. I pieced together a picture of a man who – er – enjoyed his time at Oxford all too well.'

'I know some of the stories,' said Alan. 'You needn't repeat them if it's painful.'

Edwin shook his head. 'It doesn't matter, not now. When I was younger I was distressed, mostly on Mum's account, but my father and I were never close, so I wasn't devastated. In any case all his – er – indiscretions seem to have ended with his marriage, so I suppose in the end I shrugged it off.'

'Then this woman arrived on my doorstep.'

'Describe her, please.'

'Just an ordinary woman, in her fifties, I suppose. She had sort of mousey hair, grey and brown mixed. I don't remember very much more. She was the kind of woman you see on the street and never notice.'

'Height, weight?'

'Shorter than me by an inch or two, I guess. Neither fat nor thin. When she came to the door, I thought she was applying for a job as housemaid. She looked like that.'

'I believe you said your wife was not at home?'

'No, thank God, she was in London for a few days, doing some early Christmas shopping and visiting a friend. She'd taken Joseph with her, of course, so it was just me and the girls here in the house. And Mrs Burton and Mrs Walker – no, it was late afternoon, so they'd both gone home. Later I wondered if the woman knew that and chose that time on purpose.'

'Right. She came to the door.'

'I answered when she knocked, but I wasn't going to let her in. We didn't need any more help in the house. But she looked at me and said, "I'd of knowed you anywhere, Eddie. You're exactly like Louis." Well, that took me aback, her calling me Eddie and mentioning my father. No one's called me Eddie since I was a baby. And she pronounced my father's name the right way, too. So I asked her what she wanted.'

It was chilly in the room, despite the gas fire blazing away, but Edwin took out his handkerchief and mopped his brow. Alan waited patiently.

'She asked if she could come in, said she'd walked from the village. I didn't see a car, so I assumed she was telling the truth. It's a good four miles and she wasn't warmly dressed; I couldn't in decency refuse her a bit of rest and warmth.'

Alan interrupted. 'This was how long ago, Edwin?'

'About two weeks. I'm not very good about dates, but about then.'

'Was it before or after your encounter with the man who wanted to buy the property?'

'After. I'm quite sure about that, because Judith was at home when that chap came around the first time. She heard me shouting and came to see what the fuss was about, and to tell me not to be so loud. She worried that I would wake Joseph. Wake the baby! Hah! If that were all I had to worry about!'

'All right, we'll come back to that later. Let's hear more about the woman. You asked the woman what she wanted. Did she give a name, by the way?'

'Angela something – Wilson, that was it. Angela Wilson. I sat her down in here, by the fire, because she really did look cold. She looked around and said – I'll never forget her exact words – she said, "You've done well for yourself, Eddie, much better than if you'd stayed with me. I guess Louis was telling the truth when he said he was rich." Well, that brought me up short, I can tell you. "What do you mean, stayed with you? Were you my nurse when I was a baby? Who are you?" And that's when she said . . . she said—'

'She said she was your mother.' Alan said it with a trace of sympathy, understanding how difficult this must be.

'I didn't believe her, of course. I remember my mother very well, though she died when I was just a kid. But then this . . . this person started giving me details, about how my father had . . . had had an affair with her at Oxford, and then dropped her to marry an heiress. He'd been living with her, with Angela, I mean, right up to the wedding, and never told her a word about it until the day before. Then he gave her a present, some jewellery, I think, and told her it was goodbye – and just left.'

I made some small sound of disgust. Both Alan and Edwin heard it.

'Believe me, Dorothy, I absolutely agree,' said Edwin. 'If my father behaved that way, he was an utter blackguard! Not that I believed it, but it was a shock to hear her talk about him that way.'

I couldn't keep still any longer. 'And where do you come in?'

'She said that she didn't know she was pregnant until after my father was married and gone, and she didn't know where to find him. She went on working – she was a waitress – until she couldn't do it any longer and then went to stay with a cousin to have her baby. After the baby was born she went back to work, trying to make as much money as she could, because she had a child to support now. She sold the jewellery my father had given her and it helped to make ends meet, but it didn't last very long, and she was about ready to go on the dole when she heard from my father.'

'She hadn't tried to reach him?'

'She tried, but without the money to hire a solicitor or detective, she didn't get very far. He, of course, had those resources and found her without much trouble.'

'Why?' I demanded. 'He doesn't sound like the sort to try to atone for his sins.'

Alan shook his head at me, but I shook mine right back. It was a reasonable question.

Edwin stood, went to the table where the decanter stood,

poured a little whisky into a glass, and drank it straight down. 'Forgive me. This is the hardest part. According to this woman, Angela, my father said his wife was unable to have children. She'd known that before they married, but hadn't told him. He wasn't happy about it, and insisted she go to doctors, but they all said the same thing. Well, he knew about Angela's baby, I don't know how, and said he wanted to adopt him. Since, he said, the boy was his own son.'

'We're talking about you.' Alan left just a hint of question in his voice.

'According to Angela. I don't believe it.'

'It would be easy enough to prove, either way. There would be adoption papers, or failing that, DNA testing.'

Edwin sank back into his chair and shook his head. 'According to Angela, the adoption was private. No papers, nothing official. The isolation of this house made it all possible. She simply brought the baby here and handed him over. He was only a few months old. If anyone asked about my sudden appearance, it was easy to pretend that – that my mother had been ill before I was born, and afterward, and had not left the house.'

He listened to what he had just said, shuddered, and looked at his empty glass.

I had noted the change of pronoun. 'You do believe it, don't you?' I asked it gently.

'Oh, God! I don't want to. But it's all so plausible! She had all the details right. And I never had brothers or sisters.'

'What about a birth certificate?' Alan asked. 'You'd need one to get a passport, if nothing else, and you've had to have a passport, as you've travelled extensively.'

'I don't know. My father got my first passport when we went as a family to New Zealand for a holiday. I was about ten, I suppose. He must have used my birth certificate, but I've never seen it, nor needed to.'

I took a deep breath. 'So once your mother had told her story, what did you do?'

'Don't call her that! My mother was the one who put me to bed at night, read to me, soothed me when I had nightmares. She was never very strong, and was often ill, but she was very dear to me. I was only fifteen when she died. I was away at school at the time. They rushed me home, but I was too late. I never said goodbye.'

Most men would rather suffer torture than be seen weeping. An Englishman would rather die. So Alan and I both made sure we didn't see Edwin's tears, but simply waited for him to regain control.

He blew his nose and cleared his throat. 'So you can understand that, no matter what the truth of that woman's story may be, she is not and never will be my mother. It seems probable, however, given my father's reputation, that he might have treated her shabbily, and though I had no strong bond with my father, I didn't want his memory dishonoured. As I said, I have quite enough income for my family's needs. So I gave the woman some cash and said I would see about setting up some sort of annuity for her – without, however, acknowledging her claim, simply as an act of Christian charity.'

'And did you in fact do that?'

'Not yet. I do keep my promises, you know!' he snapped, in answer to the criticism we hadn't voiced. 'The money I gave her was quite sufficient to carry her over for several weeks. After the christening – oh, Lord, if there is any christening – I'll see to it.'

'So Ms Wilson gave you her address and so on?'

'Well, obviously, I was going to need it!'

'Edwin, calm down,' I said in my best schoolteacher voice. 'We're trying our best to help you, but you're making it very difficult. Have you really not seen that if Ms Wilson's story is true, and you were adopted, there is no need to worry about the christening, no need to find the blasted dagger? Judith told me that an adopted child could not inherit. So . . .'

He had not thought of it. We could see his world collapse as he took it in.

'So,' he said at last, 'so I might not be the legal owner of this property. All this worry about passing it on to my son and heir, and it might not even be mine!' His laughter held a note of hysteria.

It was at that inauspicious moment that the two policemen walked back into the room.

FIFTEEN

Edwin stood. The two men were empty-handed, but I thought the expression on the chief inspector's face was a bit too grim to be explained only by the failure to find what they were looking for.

'We did quite a thorough search, sir, and found nothing,' he said. 'We have, however, had a call giving us some news about the victim of the fire. The medical examiner has some preliminary findings. The woman was not stabbed to death.'

'Not? Then all this fuss about the dagger—'

'Let me finish, sir. She was stabbed, but not fatally. She died in the fire, almost certainly of smoke inhalation. We'll know more after the full autopsy. It's possible that the fire was started deliberately, perhaps to cover up the stabbing.'

'But . . . I don't understand. You say the dagger was left in . . . was left behind. There could have been no hope at all of covering anything up. It makes no sense at all.'

'No, sir, but we know very little as yet. We have, however, learned the woman's identity. She was in fact booked into that room, where she had stayed before. She simply neglected to sign the register. Her name was Angela Wilson.'

This time Edwin did faint. Alan managed to catch him before he hit the floor.

'I'd better find Judith,' I murmured, and when no one disagreed, I left the room. She was bound to be upstairs in the playroom, and as I climbed stairs, I tried to work out what to tell her. Did the whole story about Edwin's adoption have to come out? Eventually, I thought, but perhaps not now.

She was reading to the girls when I poked my head in the door. Cynthia was the first to spot me. 'Hi, Mrs Martin. Mummy's reading to us from that book you started, only she doesn't make the animals sound all different, the way you do. Can you read to us after supper?'

'If Mummy agrees, until your bedtime. Right now I need to

help Mummy start to cook that supper, so you two will have to fend for yourselves for a few minutes.'

Judith gave them each a hug and a kiss and followed me downstairs. 'There's actually a cottage pie in the freezer that just needs to be popped in the oven. But you didn't come up about that, did you?'

'No. I'm afraid Edwin has had some news that upset him badly, and he needs you with him. I'll let him tell you about it,' I added, forestalling her questions. 'He's a little wobbly just now, but it's nothing serious – he'll be fine.'

In the brief interval since I'd left the drawing room, Edwin had been given a restorative and was sitting, or half-lying, in a comfortable chair. He still looked pale, but at least he was compos mentis. He gave Judith a weak smile. 'Sorry, love, but they've told me not to try standing up for a few minutes. Did Dorothy tell you I was ass enough to throw a fainting fit?'

'No, only that you were very upset. What is it? What's happened?'

'I think I can explain,' said the chief inspector. 'We have learned the identity of the person who perished at the pub. She was apparently someone whom Sir Edwin knew slightly, and he was distressed to learn she had died, and in such a wretched way.'

'You knew her?' She turned to her husband, puzzled but not, I thought, in the least suspicious.

'Hardly that.' Edwin was now in full possession of his faculties and ready to pick his way through this minefield. 'I had met her. Once. She came to the door, begging, one day when you were out. She seemed utterly indigent, and said she had once known my father and hoped I could help her. I believed her story and gave her a bit of money, promising to try to help from time to time in the future. She did give me her name, which is why I recognized it just now. I do feel a bit guilty for not giving her more assistance; perhaps she might then have left the area and this wouldn't have happened.'

'Oh, you poor dear! But surely you owed her nothing, even if she did know your father years ago. You were acting out of kindness, so you oughtn't to feel any guilt.'

Billings cleared his throat. 'I wonder, sir, if you'd be good enough to come with us to the village to identify the body.'

Judith frowned. 'I am just about to put a meal on the table. If Edwin must accompany you, it will have to wait until after he's had his dinner. This has been a trying day for him, for all of us, and he needs to relax and regain his strength. Your dead woman isn't going anywhere, so there's not all that hurry.'

Alan said, 'My wife and I are staying here for a day or two. I'd be happy to run Sir Edwin down to the village after dinner, or tomorrow morning if that would suit. It will be Sunday, of course, but . . .'

'As you would know, sir, there are no holidays in the midst of a murder investigation. Tomorrow will do. It's possible that we might have more information by then.' They discussed details, and I beat a hasty retreat to the kitchen to help Judith with the meal. She wanted to ask questions. I wanted to talk about anything else. With a good deal of effort I managed to steer her onto Christmas, her preparations, what the girls wanted from Father Christmas, what still needed to be done.

'Actually, I've done most of the shopping, though I still want to pick up a few small things in the village for the girls. Perhaps tomorrow—'

'Oh, that reminds me,' I interrupted rudely. 'Alan and I brought a gift for each of the girls, just dolls, but they're young enough to play with dolls still, aren't they?'

'They adore them, but they have so many – really, you shouldn't have gone to the trouble!'

'When would be a good time to give them to the girls? Are they too excited tonight, with all that's been going on? Or would tomorrow be better? We were going to do it at the christening, so they'd have gifts themselves, not just little Joseph – who is too little to know or care anyway. But now, perhaps you think it would be better to save them for Christmas. We won't be here then, of course.'

I put a plaintive note into the last remark, and Judith, bless her heart, picked up on it.

'Oh, no, you'll want to see their reactions! Perhaps not tonight. They are a bit tired, and Ruth's apt to get fractious when she's tired.'

'So am I, for that matter. I can sympathize. So I'll read to them tonight, as promised, and we can do gifts in the morning.

We had our cottage pie, after which I went up and saw the girls into bed in the room they shared, faces washed, teeth brushed, and prayers said. Then I finished the whale story and began 'How the Camel got his Hump', but the girls fell asleep before I could finish. I straightened the blankets, turned off the lights except for one small night-light to keep nightmares at bay, and tiptoed from the quiet, peaceful room. Truth to tell, I was reluctant to re-join the adult world downstairs. I very much doubted that I'd find much peace and quiet there.

The room was in fact very quiet when I entered. It wasn't, however, the quiet of peace but of tension. Edwin sat alone; Alan was on the couch. I sat down next to him and took his hand, not wanting to speak for fear of saying the wrong thing. The atmosphere felt full of something explosive that a single word could touch off.

Finally Edwin spoke. 'Alan's explained to me,' he said dully. 'I must be the world's prize ass not to have guessed.'

'We've told Judith everything,' Alan said quietly. 'She's gone to feed Joseph and put him to bed for the night.'

I studied Edwin's face, and he nodded. 'She took it well. I didn't want her upset; the least little thing can affect the baby, too. She didn't seem to care a lot about . . . about maybe losing the house and estate and all.'

'I think,' I said cautiously, 'that perhaps things like that aren't quite as important to women. And of course she's not English by birth.'

'No.' Edwin tossed it away. 'I do understand the reasoning of the police. I didn't kill her. I didn't even know she was staying at the Swan. I never saw her, except that once. But they won't believe me, will they?'

Alan said, with the patient air of having said the same thing several times before, 'Once they learn of the possible relationship, they're bound to suspect you, Edwin. You can see why. But motive is the least important leg of an investigation. Means and opportunity rank much higher. The police are also capable of employing common sense. There seems little reason for you to plant that dagger on the scene. It isn't the murder weapon. It isn't even yours.'

'But that will be hard to prove unless mine can be found.'

'Photographs?' I ventured.

Edwin shrugged. 'There might be one someplace, I suppose. I believe my father had the thing insured. You have to understand, it's simply not important to us, not in our everyday life. It was brought out once a generation, for the christening of the new heir, and then returned to obscurity. It has little intrinsic value, even for its history, which is legendary at best. It was just . . . always there. I couldn't describe it in any detail; I've seen it perhaps two or three times as an adult. Alan, you saw it at my christening. Could you describe it? Would you even recognize it if you saw it?'

Alan shook his head. 'I remember it only vaguely as colourful and ornate and rather unsuited to its purpose as a weapon. That jewelled hilt must be terribly uncomfortable to grasp. I would urge you, Edwin, to try to find that photo you mention.'

He shrugged. All the life seemed to have gone out of him. 'I hope you'll forgive me if I go up to bed. I'm . . . it's been a difficult day. Good night.'

'He's given up, Alan,' I said when he had left the room. 'He looks like a scarecrow that's lost its stuffing.'

'Too many blows, one after another. He's like a punch-drunk boxer. Emotional blows can be as damaging as physical ones. I'm a bit off-balance myself. I don't think Edwin would mind if I helped myself to a drink. You?'

Well, it was Scotch whisky, and I much prefer bourbon, but I was tired and disturbed, too. 'A small one. With water.'

'What's going to happen?' I asked when I'd taken a sip or two.

'Edwin will be asked to identify the body, first of all.'

'Will it be identifiable? Do you know how badly she was burned?' That thought sent a deep shudder down my spine; I drank a little more of my nightcap.

'Steady, old girl. I don't think that will be a problem. Remember that Billings said she probably died of smoke inhalation. So I gather she was not in fact badly burned.'

'And he saw her not long ago, so he should be able to make a positive identification. Then what?'

'Then they'll question Edwin more closely about his relationship with this woman. I've told him that, and advised him in the strongest possible terms to tell them the whole truth.'

'Will he?'

'I intend to go with him and make sure he does. Only candour will do.'

'Because, if he doesn't tell the whole story, and they find out later, he'll be in much worse trouble.'

'Exactly.'

I finished my drink and decided, after a small struggle with myself, not to have any more. 'Alan, can they do DNA testing on someone who's dead?'

'You know the answer to that, love. You followed the Richard III saga with the rapt attention of the true believer. He'd been dead and buried for 500 years, but it was DNA that eventually proved it was his body under that car park.'

'So they can test this woman. And if it proves she isn't Edwin's mother, that takes care of that.'

Alan shook his head sadly. 'It solves one possible problem for Edwin, the question of his right to this estate. But it doesn't help him find the dagger that will establish little Joseph's right to inherit. Nor does it make the slightest difference to his presumed motive to wish Ms Wilson dead.'

'But if . . . oh.' I looked again at my empty glass. 'He didn't know, one way or the other, at the time she died. So the motive is still there. So they'll start to grill him, won't they?'

'They'll question him, certainly. I'll be there to ensure fair play. I still have a certain amount of influence, even in these parts. And of course there's his title – a minor one, to be sure, but still a factor.'

'Are you telling me,' I said indignantly, 'that a baronet gets treated with kid gloves just because he has some silly title?'

'Simmer down, love. Your beloved traditions, remember? This is England, and still a hierarchical society. America is just the same, you know, except your aristocracy is one of wealth rather than ancestry. If Bill Gates fell into the hands of the Law, would he be treated in quite the same way as Joe Schmoe?'

I muttered something.

'Quite. To continue. If the police have been able to narrow down an approximate time of death, they'll ask Edwin to tell them his whereabouts at that time.'

'And he lives way out here in the country with no close

neighbours, so if he says he was at home, there'll be no one to verify his statement – no one except Judith and the kids, who won't count.'

'I'm afraid that's true.'

'Phone calls?'

'If he still has a landline. Many people don't, and of course a mobile—'

'Can be used from anywhere on the planet. Well, almost.'

'Actually, that's a point, Dorothy. They might not be able to use their mobiles from here, unless there's a tower nearby. So they might still have a landline, at that.'

I shook my head and sighed. 'The police were able to take a call here. Someone called to tell them about what killed Ms Wilson, and who she was. If they can get reception, the Montcalms can. Wait, though. When the police called to say they were coming, wasn't that on the phone in the library or wherever? I'm sure I heard it ring, and it sounded like a real phone.'

'I do believe you're right, love! So that makes a phone call proof of location at least possible.'

'It's an awfully thin possibility. There's email, I suppose.'

'But there again, if he has a laptop or a tablet . . .'

I hit the arm of my chair. 'Drat it, modern communications have made things way too convenient! How on earth does anybody ever prove where they were on the night of the umpteenth inst?'

'Witnesses,' said Alan wearily. 'If Edwin was at his office in a meeting with several other people, or on a transatlantic phone call, or having lunch at a place where they know him, or almost any place except here, he should be able to prove it. If not . . .' He lifted a hand and let it fall, heavily.

'If not, I hope he has a good lawyer. Solicitor.'

'He mentioned speaking to his solicitor about the entail question.'

'Well, I hope the man's office is nearby and not off in London. And I hope Judith has a good friend to help her through this.'

'We'll do all we can, love. And right now what we're going to do is make sure the house is locked up, and turn off the lights, and go to bed. Things may look brighter in the morning.'

SIXTEEN

Things looked very bright indeed in the morning. At least, the light coming into our room was almost bright, though it wasn't casting shadows. Good grief, we must have overslept. I found my glasses on the end table and looked at the clock. Barely eight o'clock. It must have stopped. I managed to focus, and saw the second hand going busily on its round.

I'm not at my best before I've had my coffee. It was several minutes before I had the sense to go to the window and see why the sky was so light so early on a December day.

It wasn't the sky. The sun wasn't up yet, and from the looks of the clouds, we wouldn't see it for a while. It was the earth that was light. Everything I could see from the window was covered in snow. A lot of snow.

The first thing any woman my age has to do upon awakening is find the loo. Fortunately it was just across the hall. I tried to be as quiet as I could, in case the family was still in bed, but the toilet was an old-fashioned one with a pull chain. The resultant rush of water made a racket, and when I opened the door the two little girls were waiting for me.

'Goodness! You look frozen!' They were clad in flannel nightgowns, with no bathrobes or sweaters, and their little feet were bare on the oak floor. The hall was draughty, and I was freezing myself, even in a warm robe. 'Your mum will fry me for breakfast if I let you stay here and catch cold. Back to bed with you, this minute!'

'We thought you might read to us some more,' said Cynthia, politely but firmly.

'I want to know how that silly camel got his hump,' said Ruth. She was equally firm and didn't bother much about manners.

'I promise I'll finish that story, but we all need some breakfast first. Shall I help you get dressed?'

'We can dress ourselves!' said Cynthia indignantly. 'At least, Ruth sometimes needs help with buttons, but when it's only shirts and jeans she can do everything. We're not babies!'

'I do know that. It's just that it's been years since I've spent time with girls your age, and I'd forgotten how grown-up you are. All right, off you go, and while you get into some good warm clothes I'll do the same, and we can rustle up something to eat.'

'What does that mean?' Ruth cried over her shoulder as Cynthia tugged her away.

Our conversation had waked Alan, and he was getting dressed when I got into the room. 'I refuse to shower in this icebox,' he said, pulling on his socks. 'A nice hot tub would be a boon, but I don't want to take time for that. I need to shepherd Edwin to the police as soon as possible.' He got up to find his pants.

'You're spoiled by our central heating at home in a much smaller house. I'll bet as a boy you didn't have such luxuries. And talking of going to the police, have you looked outside?'

Our windows faced the back of the house. We couldn't see the road or the drive, but everything we could see was white. It looked to me like the kind of heavy, wet snow we used to get in Indiana, sticking to every branch and twig, really beautiful, and really hard to deal with. Even with proper equipment, it used to take the city quite some time to get the roads clear.

'Does it snow like this often in this part of the country?'

'Almost never.' He had sat back down on the bed.

'Then they won't have snowploughs and all, will they?'

'Depends on who you mean by "they". The Montcalms will almost certainly have nothing more sophisticated than a shovel or two. The county may have some ploughing capability, but streets in town will certainly take first priority. And no one is going to deal with private drives except the property owners.'

'Then I think you might just as well have that lovely bath. I'm going to dress and go down to see if Judith needs help with breakfast. Or perhaps Mrs Walker has returned.'

'Have you looked outside?' Alan said.

I decided not to throw my hostess's pillow at him.

I hadn't brought comfy, warm clothes. I had a lovely dress to wear for the christening. It was a lightweight wool jersey in my favourite ice blue; it even looked cold. The slacks and pullover I'd worn yesterday would have to do. Maybe Edwin could lend me a cardigan; I'd never fit into anything of Judith's.

The house had central heating, but it didn't cope well with the more remote areas. The Aga would be keeping the kitchen toasty, though. I wouldn't be cold, really. It was just the thought of all that snow outside that made me shiver.

The little girls had got to the kitchen before me. Of course. Children are quicker than old ladies, and far more single-minded. Breakfast, and then story time. That was what I'd said, and they did not intend to let me forget.

They knew where to find various breakfast necessities. Bread, butter, and a pot of marmalade sat on the counter, along with two glasses half full of milk. 'Mummy doesn't let us make toast,' said Cynthia, 'or boil eggs.' It wasn't quite a command. Not quite.

I was just debating about the etiquette involved in rummaging for a saucepan in someone else's kitchen when Judith walked in. Her face had a grey tinge and her eyelids were at half-mast. 'I'm sorry to be down so late,' she said. 'No way to treat a guest!'

'You look as though you needed the sleep, and I'm perfectly happy to deal with breakfast. Do you know where Mrs Walker keeps the egg pan? I'm guessing she won't be able to get here, what with the snow and all.'

She laughed a little at that. 'She never comes in on a Sunday, unless we're having a party, so I do know how to cope without her. No, I doubt she'll be here tomorrow, even. She usually phones if she can't make it on one of her regular days, but she doesn't have a mobile, and I imagine the landlines are out. The least little storm puts paid to them. Do you prefer your eggs boiled or fried?'

'Scrambled, actually, but if you and the girls are having them boiled, that will be fine. At home we don't usually have eggs at all. Cholesterol, you know. So I'll make the toast if you'll do the eggs, and maybe the girls can set the table?' I wanted a word with Judith, and the task would keep the little pitchers occupied for a bit. Not that they wouldn't still be listening.

'Judith,' I said under cover of a clatter of silverware, 'there'll be no driving into town today, and the police won't be able to get here, either, until the roads and your drive have been ploughed. So we're on our own with this thing for a day. We need to do some serious thinking.'

'I've thought of nothing else, all night.' She tried to keep her voice even, for the sake of the girls, who weren't making much noise with the table-setting. 'It isn't so much the dagger and the inheritance. I wouldn't say so to Edwin, but I think the whole dagger charade is a load of . . . codswallop.'

I nodded my agreement and put four pieces of bread into the toaster. That wouldn't be anything like enough, but since the English eat their toast cold, it didn't matter how long it might take to produce an adequate supply. 'Have you remembered napkins, ladies?' I called out to the girls at the other end of the kitchen. 'And don't forget coffee cups for the grown-ups.' I hoped some of those things were kept in a far corner.

Judith broke some eggs into a bowl and began to beat them. 'We all like them scrambled.' She beat vigorously, and noisily. 'Tell me the truth: do you think Edwin is in any danger?'

'Not if *he's* telling the truth. I don't know him well enough to be able to tell. He's certainly in for suspicion and a fair amount of annoyance, though. Frankly, none of this makes any sense. If he had wanted to—'

Judith warned me with a look. The girls had returned. 'Can we have some more milk, Mummy?'

'*May* we. Yes, you may, but be careful pouring it, love.'

'We never have to worry too much about spills in our kitchen,' I commented. 'With two cats and a dog, nothing edible stays on the floor for long.'

'Ooh, Mummy,' Cynthia pleaded, 'can we – may we have a cat? Then we wouldn't have to cry over spilt milk!'

For some reason that struck both the children as hilariously funny. I took the bottle of milk out of Cynthia's giggle-impaired hands and poured it myself.

The men came down just as the eggs and toast were done – perfect timing – and we tried to find innocuous topics of conversation for the meal. It wasn't easy. It would have been impossible without the children's chatter. Of course, without them, we could have talked about what was on our minds.

The moment Cynthia had eaten as much of her breakfast as she considered necessary, she pushed her plate aside. 'Mummy, may we be excused?'

Judith looked at the half-eaten food and was about to protest when I gave her one of my best schoolteacherly looks, the one that said *stop that this minute*. Judith bit her lip and said, 'If you'll promise to clean your plate at lunch time. Put your dishes in the sink before you go.'

They did that and then came back to the table. 'We'll see you upstairs, Mrs Martin.'

It was a royal command, and of course I obeyed. 'Fifteen minutes. Enough time for you to brush your teeth and make your beds, and for me to finish my coffee. Off you go.'

The adults all looked a little surprised. 'I promised them I'd finish the story about the camel and his hump. And if I go on to the rhinoceros and his skin, it'll give you all time to work out what you're going to do about this mess. I'd much rather be in on the discussion, but I think I can be more useful keeping the girls happy. If you want, Judith, I can give Joseph that other bottle when he starts fussing.'

'I just fed him, before I came down. He should be good now for a while. No, don't worry about clearing the table, or washing up. We can let that go, for once.'

'Yes,' said Edwin firmly. It was the first note of authority I'd heard from him. 'We can all pitch in later. Right now we need to talk. You're very good to offer to keep the girls out of our hair for a bit, Dorothy.'

I finished my coffee and went up to the playroom.

The girls were ready for me, the couch pulled close to the fireplace, an afghan ready to throw over my elderly knees if necessary, the book at hand. 'Daddy won't let us turn on the fire, even though it's dead easy. The switch is right there.'

I was beginning to think that, if something were to happen to the entire Windsor family, Cynthia could take over as monarch with very little training. She had the art of the indirect command down pat. I obediently dealt with the fire and picked up the book. 'Now, do you remember where we stopped last night?'

'We fell asleep,' said Ruth with a frown. Obviously it was my fault that they didn't stay awake.

'Oh, yes, so you did. Shall I start again from the beginning?'

'No,' Cynthia pronounced. 'We know about how the camel was lazy and wouldn't do anything and kept on saying Humph. And I think the other animals were trying to find someone to make him work, but I can't remember what happened then.'

'Ah, then we'll go back to the Djinn and see what he did.'

'Gin?' Ruth giggled. 'Our gardener says it sometimes makes him see things.'

Cynthia nodded. 'Pink elephants, he says.'

'That's a different kind of gin, something grown-ups drink,' I said, trying hard to keep a straight face. 'This kind is a sort of magic person, like a genie. You've heard of genies in fairy tales, haven't you?'

'They come from lamps. And grant wishes.' That was both girls together.

'Yes, well, a Djinn is very much the same kind of thing. This one is very magic, and very good, as you'll find out.'

I spun the story out, getting the girls involved, talking about the pictures, reading the poem at the end and talking about that, and I really did enjoy myself, but all the time I was thinking about what was happening downstairs. Were the three of them able to come up with any scenarios for recent events that were even possible, let alone probable? Had they had any ideas about what might have happened to the real dagger? Did that really matter anymore, if Edwin was illegitimate?

'You stopped,' said Ruth.

'Oh, so I did. I must have been thinking of something else.'

'You're thinking about what Mummy and Daddy are thinking about that they won't tell us. Why won't they?'

Oh, dear. Think fast, Dorothy. 'I think they're worried about something, but they don't want to trouble you about it.'

'You know what it is, don't you?'

'Yes, but it doesn't worry me very much, because I'm not involved.' One shouldn't lie to children, as a rule, but there are times when a fib is advisable. 'And it doesn't really involve you, either, so just you stop bothering about it. Shall we have the story about the rhinoceros?'

'I want to know what's happening,' said Cynthia. 'If my Mummy and Daddy are sad, I want to know how I can make it better.'

'*I* think it's something about that woman,' said Ruth, pummelling a stuffed dog, as one might pound a pillow into shape. 'Daddy didn't like her.'

'How could you tell?' Cynthia sounded scornful. 'You told me you couldn't hear what they said.'

'They sounded angry. Well, Daddy did. The woman just sounded sad. And Daddy was making faces.' The little girl twisted her own face into a fearsome scowl.

'You're just making it up! I don't believe you know anything at all.'

'Do too! Stop being so . . . so consenting!'

Condescending, perhaps? Cynthia wasn't sure, either, but she took exception anyway. 'Stop using big words when you don't even know what they mean!'

'Speaking of big words,' I said, raising my voice over what threatened to turn into a first-class row, 'there are some wonderful ones in another story, the one about how the elephant got its trunk. Settle down, now, and I'll read you about the Elephant's Child and his "'satiable curtiosity".'

Ruth sat back, but her lower lip protruded. 'I did too see Daddy making faces,' she muttered. 'And I saw something else, too, but I'm not going to tell.'

'"In the High and Far-Off Times the Elephant, O Best Beloved",' I began, rather loudly, ignoring Ruth and trying to immerse myself in the story. My own 'curiosity' about what was going on downstairs was becoming more and more insatiable, but I firmly told myself that I was being useful here, and concentrated firmly on Kipling's delightful tale.

The girls enjoyed it, but they grew restless at the end. 'Thank you,' said Cynthia, taking the book away from me, 'but now we want to go out and play in the snow.'

'Do you have snow boots?'

'We have wellies.'

'Hmm. Well, if Mummy says you may go out, you'll have to put on extra socks to help keep your feet warm. Have you ever played in the snow before?'

'Not this much. Just a little. This is much nicer!'

Ah, well, I was once a child who loved snow. Sledding, and snow angels, and snowmen. I think perhaps one is irretrievably grown up when snow is seen primarily as a nuisance. 'All right, get into your warmest clothes, and I'll go downstairs and see if Mummy and Daddy say yes.'

SEVENTEEN

I arrived at the bottom of the stairs just as the doorbell rang. It startled me considerably. There were no close neighbours, as far as I knew, and surely no one could have arrived by car. Who would even try? I kept thinking about snowstorms back home, and even there, with five or six inches of the messy stuff, it would have taken an emergency to tempt someone up an uncleared drive, even if the roads had been ploughed. So who on earth . . .?

'Who in the world?' Judith echoed my thoughts as she came hurrying into the hall. The windows on this side of the house were so obscured by frost and wind-blown snow that we could see only the faint outline of a human form at the door. 'You don't think,' she said in a low tone, 'the police again?'

'I don't see how they could have gotten here, failing a sleigh and eight tiny reindeer.'

She giggled, a little nervously, and opened the door an inch or two, ready to slam it shut again in the face of an unwelcome caller. Then she pulled it open fully.

'Why, Sam! Come in and get warm! You must be frozen. Is there trouble at your house?'

'No, ma'am,' he said, not moving from his place on the doormat. 'I come to dig you out, me and Silver. Wanted to tell you, case we scrape up a bit o' grass. I'll look to it come spring. Thank you, ma'am.'

He touched his cap and turned away. I saw now, in the drive, an old white horse hitched to a remarkable object, part tractor, part snowplough. As I watched, Sam stood on the tractor, clucked to the horse, and off they went slowly down the drive, clearing away the snow and turning it up in curls on either side.

'Goodness,' I said weakly. 'I never saw such a contraption. And . . . um . . . Silver?'

Judith giggled. 'Sam's our gardener, as you've guessed. He loves cowboy movies.'

'And his favourite hero is the Lone Ranger. I see. Well, Sam's certainly a hero. Where in the world did he find that thing?'

'Made it out of bits and pieces, I imagine. He's something of a blacksmith, too. Jack of all trades, in fact, and takes a proprietary interest in the place. He lives not far away; his family have lived around here forever, I believe. He keeps the garden spick and span in summer, and provides us with such a bountiful supply of fruit and vegetables that Mrs Walker can freeze and can enough to see us through most of the winter. He even does odd jobs around the house when the need arises. He's a treasure.'

'I can see that. It amazes me, though, that he'd be prepared with a snowplough, however makeshift, when the area seldom gets snow like this.'

'It used to, though, back in the day. Mrs Walker's regaled me with stories about walking to school through snowdrifts when she was a girl.'

'Remembering with advantages?'

Judith laughed. 'Possibly. At any rate, that rig-up might have been sitting around in Sam's barn for years.'

'Anyway, he's going to make it much easier for you to get out.'

'True.' Her smile was gone. 'And for the police to get in.'

The sound of children's laughter reminded me of the reason I'd wanted to talk to Judith. 'Oh, I almost forgot. The girls want to go out and play in the snow. I told them I'd see if you were okay with that.'

'Oh, goodness, yes. This snow is nothing to what I grew up with in Canada, and I never caught pneumonia. They'll have a glorious time getting cold and wet. Might as well enjoy it while . . . yes. I'll hunt out their warmest coats, and those wellies.'

I watched out the library window for a little while, watched Sam making sweep after sweep up and down the drive, his elderly horse pulling the heavy load with stoic patience. Watched Cynthia and Ruth rolling snowballs for a snowman, with their mother's help. Watched them learning from their mother to make snow angels, with giggles all round. And my heart ached for them. It was all very well to say that they could live anywhere, that this house and this estate weren't necessary to the family, and it was true. But for the children, who had never lived anywhere else, and for Edwin, who had lived here since he was tiny, if perhaps not from birth, leaving would be a terrible wrench.

I shook myself. Wallowing in sentiment wasn't useful. I left the window and went to the drawing room.

Alan and Edwin were sitting, trying to pretend they were absorbed in day-old newspapers. I wasn't sure if they were annoyed with each other, or just talked out, or both. When they saw me, they made half-hearted attempts to stand, but I gestured them back to their seats and took a chair myself. 'So,' I said brightly. 'Have you reached any decisions?'

Edwin shrugged, looking defeated. Alan didn't look much happier. 'Only what we already knew, that the police must be told the whole story.'

'And do you think they're competent?' I asked. 'Will they draw the same conclusions we have?'

'Probably, for what they're worth. The trouble is that what few facts we have are contradictory. Edwin had a very good motive for killing the woman. She died in a fire Friday night, at a time, presumably, when Edwin could have been there. He says he was here with his family, continuing the despairing search for the dagger and preparing for our visit. I believe him, but there's no proof. Judith will vouch for him, but a spouse's word is worth little. No one phoned, no one visited. The cook, Mrs Walker, was here until about five, but then she left.'

'Nearly in tears,' Edwin said. 'This christening meant almost as much to her as to us.'

'So no witnesses,' Alan continued. 'Then there's the dagger itself. If it had been the real one, the historic, symbolic one, then it would have pointed straight to Edwin, and his guilt would have been very hard to disprove. But it was a cheap replica, not even a very close replica, and furthermore it wasn't used to kill. So what was the point of it?'

I refrained from saying that the point of it was the sharp part, and forced myself back to a proper focus. 'I think we're concentrating too much on what has happened. I'd like to think about who might want Edwin to suffer. Because if you think about it, the theft of the dagger, which is where this all began, was intended to do just that.'

'As it certainly did!' Edwin groaned.

'Dorothy, we don't know for a fact that the dagger was stolen.'

That was Alan being the policeman again. I suppose he couldn't help it, poor dear.

'Well, we can't *prove* that it was stolen, no. But it's gone and can't be found, even by those trained in search procedures, and neither Judith nor Edwin hid it away somewhere. Theft is, I think, a reasonable assumption.'

I probably sounded a bit tart. Alan held up a placating hand. 'Peace, woman. I agree, but the police prefer to deal in verifiable fact. We need to remember that.'

'All right, but for now, I intend to call it a theft. So, there were two results of that theft. One was the utterly predictable one that the christening had to be postponed. The other totally unpredictable one is that a woman has died, a woman in some way connected with this family. Possibly Edwin's mother.'

Edwin groaned again. 'Not my mother,' he muttered, and I couldn't tell if he was denying the fact or reiterating his definition of the word.

'Right. Both ways, damaging to Edwin. So, back to the question. Who wants you hurt, Edwin? Who are your enemies?'

That actually brought a laugh. 'Enemies! What a melodramatic word. No one except politicians has "enemies" these days. Business rivals, yes. There are two or three people I can think of in London who wouldn't be sorry to hear I'd moved to Outer Mongolia. Or no, to Mars. There are fairly lucrative business opportunities in Mongolia.'

'Right. Scratch professional enemies. For now.' I reached in my purse and got the notebook I'm never without. 'Neighbours. Any boundary disputes, complaints about noise, animals – whatever?'

Alan rolled his eyes, but let me continue.

'I have no close neighbours. Sam is probably the nearest, and he's about three miles away at the very boundary of the estate. We've never had any difficulties about it. He's not only my gardener, he's a friend, in his rather crusty way.'

'Yes, I've met him.' I turned to Alan. 'Just this morning, while you two were talking. He came with the most astonishing horse-drawn snowplough to clear the drive. He's at it still, I think. Remarkable devotion to duty, I'd say.'

'Yes, he takes good care of us. And as I say, he's the only

near neighbour. I barely know any of the others. Judith may know more about them; she's here far more than I am.'

'So check off neighbours, unless Judith has had a run-in with the local witch.' They both looked startled. 'Joke. Though you're remote enough here that there probably is a local witch. So that leaves family. What's the possibility of a long-lost heir, third cousin twice removed, or something? Someone who's just panting to do Joseph out of his inheritance so he, or she, can take over?'

Both Alan and Edwin were shaking their heads. 'We've gone into all that, Dorothy,' said Alan. 'When Edwin's Uncle Andrew died, his father delved into the family history very thoroughly. The family had run to daughters for generations, with just one son here and there to carry on the line. Andrew and Louis were the very last, with no cousins of whatever degree anywhere in the genealogy. There are quite literally no surviving heirs except young Joseph.'

I sat back, defeated. 'In that case, who will inherit if Joseph has no sons?'

'The Crown,' said Edwin in a dead sort of voice. 'Her dear old majesty, who obviously has need of one more house to live in.'

'And who, I imagine, has better things to do than go around stealing daggers. So scratch family.' I looked down at the spanking-clean notebook page. 'Well, then, it really does come down to our fiery Irishman, doesn't it?'

Both Alan and Edwin frowned.

'Come, come, gentlemen,' I remonstrated. 'You're not thinking! If the dagger is gone, Joseph cannot be named the official heir. In that case, since the child can't inherit, Edwin might be pressured into breaking the entail and selling the property. To the anarchist who wants to tear everything down and build council houses or something of the sort.'

'So you think he stole the dagger.'

'I don't think anything, except that the possibility is worth looking into.'

'But in that case—'

'But then why would he—'

The two men spoke together. 'I have no idea! All I'm saying is, that man whose name is certainly not John Smith has good reason to try to do Edwin out of his estate. He, that is, or whoever is backing him, whoever wants to build the shabby little houses.'

'Dorothy, that theory leaves at least twenty questions unanswered,' Alan put in, unhelpfully.

'And you think I don't know that? I don't have any answers to anything at all! But that man has been here to the house, several times in fact.' I looked at Edwin, who sighed and nodded. 'He's no friend to Edwin, and he could have had access to the dagger. Edwin, do you keep your doors locked?'

'Not until we knew the dagger was missing. I know, I know, the stable door, et cetera. But so far out in the country, it never seemed necessary. And anyway how would the wretch have known where the dagger was kept?'

'I don't know! Stop expecting me to have all the answers!' I realized I was shouting. 'I'm sorry. I'm as frustrated as you are, Edwin. I can come up with only that one idea, and it's nothing we can do anything about, it's for the police to deal with, and I don't know where to go from here!' My voice had risen again.

'I think,' said a quiet voice, 'we are all in need of some attitude adjustment.' Judith had come into the room, a sleepy Joseph in her arms. 'It's early for Sunday lunch, but I think some pre-prandial libations are in order. I'm going to make myself some herbal tea, since I can't have the real stuff right now, or anything stronger, but Edwin, dear, why don't you ask our guests what they'd prefer?'

'Of course! I'm sorry, I should have offered sooner. Alan, I believe whisky is your tipple. I've some rather nice single malt I picked up on a trip to the Orkneys.'

Alan's expression improved markedly. 'Ah, yes, Highland Park. I know it from our recent visit. Certainly I'll have a nip.'

'And you, Dorothy? There's wine, or . . .?'

'My preference, actually, is for bourbon, but if you don't happen to have any—'

'But we do!' Judith sounded delighted to be able to offer me something besides doom and gloom and frustration. 'I like it, too, so we picked up some on our last trip to London. I'd love to have some with you if I could, but I'll just have to enjoy you enjoying it.'

Joseph, waking up, waved his fists and made a loud sound

that could have been interpreted as approval, and we all laughed – a break we badly needed.

'No caffeine, either?' I asked when we were all settled with our various beverages.

'I have a little coffee after I've fed him in the morning. The doctor doesn't absolutely prohibit it, but certainly I want him to sleep as much as he can, for all our sakes, so I don't take chances.'

'Speaking of chances,' said Alan, raising his glass, 'I'd like to propose a toast to our chances of solving these many mysteries. May they increase and blossom!'

'The chances, not the mysteries,' I put in. 'Here, here!'

And when Judith toasted with her teacup, it reminded me of the time I'd heard about years ago, when a meeting of the Dorothy L. Sayers Society was held in America at a tee-total college. I told them how, at dinner in the college dining room, the various toasts were drunk in iced tea or water, to the amusement of the English and the horror of a naval wife, who said that to drink a toast in water meant sure disaster of one kind or another.

I should have kept my mouth shut. The word disaster brought back to mind just the things we'd been trying to forget, and our moment of congenial respite collapsed into a morose silence.

'Me and my big mouth,' I muttered, and stood up. 'Judith, I don't know what you have planned, but may I help?'

'You can come and talk to me while I add the final touches,' she said, 'and bring your drink. There's almost nothing to do. You forget that today was to have been party time. Mrs Walker prepared enough food for an army. It's mostly cold, of course – cold ham, cold beef, cold salmon – but I've heated up soup from the freezer and there are jacket potatoes, so we'll feast. You can help me organize it all, and keep this little nuisance occupied.' She gave Joseph a kiss on his nose; he chortled. 'And Edwin, would you make sure the girls have dealt properly with their clothes? They're all sopping wet, and I wouldn't be surprised if they left them in sodden heaps in the bathroom.'

He trudged out, Alan following – I suppose to try to cheer him up.

EIGHTEEN

'Judith, you amaze me,' I said as I followed her into the kitchen. 'You're the perfect example of the Kipling ideal.'

'Keeping my head when all about me are losing theirs? Well, they're not blaming it on me, at least. And someone has to stay sane and focussed. Edwin is a lovely man, but he's always had a tendency to fall apart. I have to think of the children, you see. I don't want them drawn down into the pit with their father.'

'They know something's up, you know.'

'Of course they do. They're quite bright, though I says it as shouldn't, and they've always been observant. Have they talked to you about it?'

'A bit. They know you and Edwin are upset and hiding something from them, and they think it has to do with the dagger and the christening. I tried to fend them off by saying it wasn't anything that they need worry about, but of course they didn't buy that. Cynthia, especially.'

'Do you think we should tell them? Here, can you hold him for a moment?'

'Give them a bowdlerized version, perhaps. Maybe say that Daddy's sad because . . . I know, because today's party had to be postponed. I just taught them that word; they'll like hearing it again. And maybe point out that it will happen at some later time, after Christmas, and that it'll be almost like Christmas again. And then if you can manage to get Edwin to climb out of his slough of despond and put on a decent show for the girls, that'll help a lot. And after you've given them the pep talk, I'll present them with the dolls. What do you think?' I tickled Joseph under his chin and sent him into peals of laughter. What a happy baby!

Judith, meanwhile, had been setting food out on platters, stirring soup, taking potatoes out of the oven and a salad out of the fridge.

'There, now! I'll just retire to the drawing room to feed him.

He doesn't act hungry, but if he has a little now, he'll let me eat my lunch in peace. And here are the girls to set the table, and the men to pour the wine!'

I wish I'd ever been that well organized. If I'd had to juggle housekeeping duties and three children, I don't know how I'd have coped. Perhaps, I thought with a secret sigh, it was actually just as well I'd never been put to the test.

When we sat down to eat, the girls saved us from gloom. They wanted to tell us all about playing in the snow, about the wonderful snowman they had made. 'Only it's a snow woman, with one of Mummy's old hats—'

'And my scarf, the pink one, so everybody will know it's not a man—'

'And we found two flowers on the jasmine by the shed, and used them for earrings!'

'They'll just die,' said down-to-earth Cynthia. I surmised that she had not approved of the 'earrings'.

'But there wasn't anything else. The snowdrops won't come for ages, and anyway they're white and wouldn't show up.'

'We could have used buttons from Mummy's button box.'

'Not the same! And anyway we put buttons down her front.' Ruth gave her mother a sidelong glance. 'We couldn't find five all alike, so we just used the prettiest ones.'

Judith gave a mock-groan. 'Probably just the ones I was keeping for replacements when one falls off a coat or dress. Mind you find them and bring them back to the house when the snowman . . . er, woman melts.'

They ignored that. 'And Daddy, Mummy showed us how to make angels in the snow. That's how we got so wet. It's fun! You have to fall backwards and then wave your arms and legs, and then the hardest part is getting up without spoiling it. I had to help Ruth.'

'But I know how to do it now. Can we go back out this afternoon, Mummy?'

'"May we". We'll see. Perhaps, after your outdoor things dry.'

'You could put them in the tumble dryer,' said Cynthia. Again the command veiled as a suggestion.

'Already done,' said Edwin, sounding just a trifle smug. 'I remember what I was like in snow, when I was a child. I wanted to be out all day. It was a rare event, you understand, so I had to make the most of it. Though it was a bit trickier then. My winter things were wool, and took forever to dry.'

Cynthia thought about this, perhaps trying to picture her father as a child. 'Did you have snowball fights? I mean, if you were a boy . . .?'

'I lived here, sweetheart. There weren't any boys living nearby, and I didn't have any brothers. I did shy a few snowballs at the squirrels and rabbits, as I recall, but they escaped easily.'

I was pleased that Edwin seemed to have climbed out of his slough. I hoped that childhood memories wouldn't make him slide back in again.

'So anyway, Mummy, can we – may we – go back out now?' That, of course, was persistent, on-track Ruth.

'No, darling. You promised to clean your plate, remember? There's quite a lot of potato left. *And* there's treacle tart to follow. Mrs Walker made it before she left, specially for you.'

'Oh. Well. But after we've finished?'

'As soon as you've had a bit of a nap. No argument, now. Finish up that potato, and Mrs Martin and I will fetch the tart.'

Treacle tart happens to be one of my favourite desserts, too, so I was happy to help clear away and make coffee. 'If there's decaf available, I'll make some for you, too. Something that sweet absolutely has to have coffee to set it off.'

She nodded agreement and pointed to a cupboard.

The children were getting restless and a bit snappish. They did indeed need a nap, little as they wanted to take the time for one. I could have used one, too, as a matter of fact, but I doubted I was going to get one. I only hoped *I* could keep from getting snappish.

The girls polished off their treacle tart in record time, and I shooed Judith off to tuck them in while I loaded the dishwasher and drank another cup of very strong coffee. I was about to see if we could decide on a plan of action, and I needed to be firing on all cylinders.

'Judith will be back as soon as she can,' said Edwin when I re-joined the men, who were in the drawing room. 'Joseph woke up and wanted his food.'

'And, I suspect, some attention.'

'Oh, yes, he's very good at making demands. We're soon going to have to start making him wait for a bit, or he'll turn into a right tyrant.'

'All babies are tyrants,' I said with the authority of one who'd never had any. 'Or so I'm told. Certainly my small nephews and nieces were, as well as their progeny.'

'And so are four-footed children,' Alan put in. 'Though they don't stop their tyrannical ways when they grow up. At least not the cats.'

'Yes. Well.' In effect, I called the meeting to order. 'We'll need to have Judith in on this, but meanwhile, have you two decided what we're going to do next?'

'There's only one thing to do,' said Edwin. He sounded weary, but determined. 'As soon as I can get through to Grantham, I'm going to the police, and I'll tell them the whole story about the woman. Ms Wilson. I'll identify the body, if necessary, and answer any questions they ask. I know they may well decide I'm their prime suspect. I can't help that. I didn't kill anyone, and eventually the truth will come out.'

'I would strongly advise you to have your solicitor present if they question you,' said Alan.

'You think I'm guilty too, don't you?'

Alan didn't even blink. 'No, I don't. That's why you need legal advice. My first impression yesterday of the police was favourable. The chief inspector seemed to be both intelligent and competent. But he can't afford to ignore your tie to the victim, once he knows it in full. You need to watch your step and say nothing that will reinforce his, shall we say, his possible inclination to find an easy answer. You need, in short, a good lawyer. Do you have one? Near here, I mean, not just a company man in London?'

'I do have a personal solicitor, yes. But in London. I don't believe he deals with – er – criminal matters.'

'Then ring him up and tell him to find someone for you and get him here as soon as possible.'

'It's Sunday. I don't know if—'

'Oh, for – look, man! This is a serious charge you could be facing! It's no time to be playing etiquette games. Your mobile is still working, yes? Even if your landline is not. Call the solicitor's office now. If you get voice mail it will almost certainly include an emergency number. If it does not, keep calling anyone you can reach in your firm until someone can recommend a good criminal lawyer.'

'I don't know that I want my employer to know—'

Alan stood up and began to pace. 'God give me patience! If you're arrested on a murder charge, they'll know soon enough. Get cracking!'

'Oh. I suppose I hadn't – yes, very well.' He pulled his mobile out of his pocket and began to search his contacts.

The doorbell rang.

We all looked out the window. The drive was clear, and a police car stood before the door. Oh, not a marked car, but there was something about its very deliberate discretion that identified it beyond doubt.

Edwin put down his phone.

'No,' said Alan. 'Carry on. I'll answer the door. They've come here instead of waiting for you to come to them. The situation has changed. I don't know how, but it doesn't bode well. Get a solicitor here the very minute you can.'

The bell rang again, sounding impatient.

'Keep at it, Edwin,' I said quietly. 'Whatever the police have, it can't be evidence of your guilt, because you're not guilty. Find that lawyer and try not to panic.'

The sound of male voices approached. 'Quick!' I urged Edwin. 'Kitchen. Make your calls from there.'

He scooted away just in time. The baize door closed behind him as Alan and the chief inspector walked in from the hall, accompanied by the almost-invisible sergeant.

All three men stopped, the inspector with a frown on his face. 'Mrs Martin.' He nodded an acknowledgment. 'I understood Sir Edwin was with you.'

'He was.' I smiled blandly. 'He stepped out to make a few phone calls.'

'I believe the landline is down, madam.'

'Yes, I think it is. But the mobiles seem to be working. And the roads must have been cleared in record time! We were of course planning to go into the village first thing this morning, but the drive was impassable, and we could only imagine what the secondary roads must be like. We wouldn't be dug out still, but for the fact that the Montcalms' gardener came with the most amazing contraption and set to work. Mrs Montcalm and I – oh, dear, is that right? Or should it be "Lady Montcalm"? Or "Lady Judith"? I'm hopeless about titles, coming from a country where we have very few more interesting than Mr and Mrs.' I was chattering as idiotically as I could, to give Edwin time for his calls, but I had to pause for breath, and the inspector stepped in.

'"Lady Montcalm" is correct, madam. Perhaps you could tell me where to find Sir Edwin. I have some rather pressing questions to ask him.'

Alan cleared his throat. 'I believe he is calling his solicitors, Chief Inspector. At my suggestion, in fact.'

The inspector's frown deepened. 'You believe he has reason to avoid questioning?'

'On the contrary, sir. I believe him to be innocent of any charges you might think of bringing against him. However, he is innocent in another sense as well. Strange as it may sound, he is naïve to a degree one would scarcely expect in an international financier. I know as well as you, sir, that police interrogation can cause many an innocent man such anxiety as to make him appear guilty as hell, if you'll forgive the expression, Dorothy. Hence the innocent may often need a lawyer quite as much as, if not more than, the guilty.'

Alan was nattering on, too. He could have said all that in a very few words. Somehow his prattle sounded more impressive than mine, though. It must, I thought, be that deep voice. Or perhaps it was the badge of exalted office which he now wore invisibly, but which was still apparent.

The inspector was still trying to frame an appropriate response to Alan when Edwin came back into the room. He looked weary, but somewhat relieved. He gave me and Alan the slightest of nods and then turned to the inspector. 'I'm very sorry that I was not able to speak to you just now. As Mr Nesbitt and Mrs Martin may have told you, I was phoning for a solicitor, not the easiest task on a Sunday. However, my man is coming down from London. He'll arrive at Lowestoft on the 4.52, if all goes according to schedule, and will hire a car there. Given the state of some of the roads, it seemed the quickest way. Now, how can I help you, Chief Inspector?'

The man coughed. 'I have a good many questions for you, Sir Edwin. As I expect you've worked out for yourself. There's no question yet of charging you with anything, so I'm not obliged to caution you. However, as you've indicated that your solicitor is on his way, I gather that you'd rather wait and answer those questions when he is present. So may I ask you to come to the station in Grantham at – shall we say six, sir?'

He nodded impartially to everyone and left the room with his sergeant, who had not uttered one word.

NINETEEN

Edwin dropped into a chair. 'They have some new information.'

'That's my assumption. If it were still just a question of identifying the body and checking on your whereabouts, the inspector wouldn't have been quite so intimidating.'

'He didn't say anything to you?'

'He wouldn't. You must remember, Edwin, that I'm walking a tightrope here. I'm a retired police officer of high rank, but I'm here as your friend and the proposed godfather of young Joseph. So while Chief Inspector Billings is respectful of my position and my expertise, such as it is, he is also obliged to keep some matters private. I wouldn't ask him to reveal anything confidential, and he wouldn't if I did.'

'No. No, of course not. But . . . do you have any idea what's made him change his mind about me? Because he has changed his mind. Yesterday he thought I was a blithering idiot, but probably not a murderer. Today he thinks I'm very likely guilty.'

I was a little surprised. I hadn't thought Edwin was that observant, perhaps because I'd gone rather far toward the 'blithering idiot' assessment myself. The inspector wasn't the only one having to change his mind.

'I doubt Billings has got quite that far. I imagine he's been looking into Ms Wilson's background and come up with some information about her tie to this family, back in Oxford. He's a good, competent policeman, Edwin. I've dealt with enough coppers in my time to recognize the bullying ones and the corrupt ones and the stupid ones. This man is none of those. He's intelligent and courteous, but he's of the bulldog breed. It's his job to find out what's going on here, and he'll do it, avoiding sensitive toes if he can, but stepping on them if necessary.

'So there's only one sensible thing for you to do at this point. I want you to tell me everything you can remember that might have any bearing on our two problems, the loss of the dagger and the death of Ms Wilson. I'll ask you some leading questions if you like, but I'd far rather you simply stir your mind and see what floats to the top.'

Edwin held up his hands in the classic gesture of bewilderment. 'I wouldn't know where to start.'

'Ah, yes, always the difficulty. This is a free association exercise, Edwin. Start with the first time you ever saw the dagger.'

He laughed a little. 'I suppose the first time would have been the only time you ever saw it, at my christening. Of course I don't remember a thing. I was – how old – six months?'

'Eight or nine, I think. Too young to remember much, at any rate. Did your parents ever talk to you about the event?'

'I think Mum told me I howled when I felt the water on my head, and the parson said that was always a good sign, the devil was being knocked out of me.'

'You did indeed howl, as I recall. Babies often do. Go on, you're doing fine.'

'Do I remember . . . was there a party? With cake? I have some vague memory of something very sweet, the first really sweet thing I'd ever tasted. I know I didn't like it. Howled again, most likely. Maybe that was some other time, though.'

Alan smiled and made no comment.

'I wonder if they cut the cake with the dagger, rather like the sword at a military wedding. Gosh, I am beginning to get bits and pieces! I've had a dream all my life about something bright and sparkling that shone in my eyes and bothered me. I wonder if that could have been the jewels on the dagger catching the sun. Was it a sunny day?'

Alan shrugged and shook his head. He didn't remember.

'I do remember, quite clearly, that Mum gave me a piece of cake for a birthday, my fifth, I think, and told me she'd saved it from the christening. I know I picked off the icing and just ate a little of the cake. And I remember feeling that I was being very good to eat it at all, because I never have much liked sweet stuff. I ate it to make her happy.'

I saw his eyes glisten for a moment as the memory of his mother touched a nerve. But then the memory changed. 'And the dagger was there! This time I remember for certain. They had saved a whole tier of the cake, frozen, I suppose, and it was there on a big plate, and my father cut the piece for me with that damned dagger! I remember because it didn't cut very well and my father was extremely annoyed. And Mum said it was never meant to be used that way, that it was just a symbol and not sharp, and besides the cake was old and hard. At least I think she must have said something like that, because then my father got really angry and jammed the dagger down into the cake and left the room. I remember I was scared, and Mum cried because the plate was broken.'

A picture was emerging, a picture of a surly and ill-tempered father and a loving, and dearly loved, mother. A mother long gone but still called 'Mum' by her thirty-something son, and a father simply 'my father' – not even 'Father'. Edwin's mother must have been a wonderful example, even if she hadn't been all that keen on motherhood at the start. Edwin had to have learned his parenting skills somewhere, and he was good with his own kids, if a little distant. The girls were stable and loving, and plainly fond of both their parents. No wonder Edwin remembered 'Mum' with great fondness and refused to accept the idea of Ms Wilson as his mother.

Alan nodded and murmured something encouraging, not wanting to interrupt the flow.

'After that there isn't much. I went away to school when I was twelve, and was only home on holidays. Mum tried to come to school events, sports day and all that, but she was pretty much an invalid by that time and often couldn't make the journey. My father never bothered. I wasn't good at games, and didn't like them, so he thought I was a disgrace to the family. Then after Mum died I came home for good. I told you I was too late to say goodbye, but I had to go through the horrible funeral. Oh, they dragged out the cursed dagger for that, too. I'd forgotten that, on purpose, I suppose. They had laid it on her coffin, God knows why, and I saw it as a desecration and pushed it off. My father was furious, although I did it here at home before they took her to the church, and there were people around. That was probably what kept him from saying, and doing, what he wanted.'

Edwin stopped, gazing into space, and Alan had to venture a question. 'Was the dagger damaged at all?'

'I don't know. I didn't care. I think not; it fell on the carpet, if I remember. I'm sure there wasn't a loud clang or anything. Although I was so angry I might not have heard it. Have you ever been in such a state that you could hear your blood pounding and blocking out everything else?'

We both nodded. Oh my, I certainly remembered a couple of occasions – but we were losing the thread. 'Gold is soft,' I said. 'If the dagger hit something hard, it would probably have been dented, or marred somehow. Do you remember seeing any damage later?'

'No, but it was years before I saw it again. My father allowed me to stay home – hired a tutor to prepare me for university – but I spent as little time as possible in the house. It was better that way. We . . . didn't get on, my father and I. I was useful to him as an heir, but he never cared about me, personally. I used to walk a lot. There are splendid walks in this area. We kept a couple of horses, but I didn't ride much. My father hunted.'

Oh, and you wanted nothing even remotely associated with your father, I thought. What a sad little boy! Your father used the horses for hunting, so you missed the pleasures of riding.

'So the next time you saw the dagger . . .' Alan prompted.

'Was when Cynthia was to be born. I told you. We had been told Judith was going to have a girl, but just in case, we hunted the thing out and polished it, and all that. I'm quite sure it was in good repair then. Old, of course, and looking a bit shop-worn, but all intact. Then again before Ruth I checked, and of course before Joseph, since we knew he was a boy.'

'You didn't tell me that when I asked before,' said Alan, his voice sharpening. 'Nor about the time before that, when Judith was expecting Ruth. Now you're telling me that you last saw the thing only a few months ago, before Joseph's birth.'

'Yes, well, you see,' he said, looking at his feet, 'Judith was there when we talked before, and I didn't want her to know. She had some idea that getting the dagger out before the birth was unlucky somehow, that we should wait until the baby was actually born.'

'Not really!' I burst out. Alan frowned at me, but I couldn't help it. It was such an extraordinary remark. 'I would not have believed that Judith was superstitious. Judith, of all the sane, sensible people!'

Alan sighed. 'Dorothy, I truly hate to say this, but you've never given birth. You have no idea what peculiar ideas women can have during pregnancy, even the most sane and sensible ones. Even Helen, who was certainly a sensible woman. Helen was my first wife, Edwin. I had to watch my step for at least six months before every one of my children. The doctor said it was hormonal, and perfectly normal, and I was not to worry. That did not, of course, stop me worrying.'

He had talked long enough for me to swallow the lump in my throat. I even managed a smile. 'Okay, score one for you. That makes, I believe, the second time in my life I've been wrong about something. I'm spoiling my record. So . . . let's see. Joseph was born when, exactly?'

'Seventeen July.'

'Right. And you knew some time before that, from the scan, that he was a boy. So about seven or eight months ago the dagger was where it was supposed to be, and in good condition. And then last week it wasn't.'

'That,' said Alan, 'helps a bit. Not a lot, but a bit. I've no doubt dozens of people have been in and out of this house in that time, but you might be able to remember a good many of them.'

'Especially,' I added, 'anyone who might have been in any way unusual.'

Judith returning, we left it at that for the moment. We weren't getting anywhere, anyway, just going over the same ground again and again. I sighed and stood up, a bit creakily. 'I've been sitting too long. Are the girls awake?'

I was answered by the sound of their feet running down the stairs. They slowed a bit as they neared the drawing room; I heard Cynthia whisper something to her sister that sounded like an admonishment. They came in, doing their best to look like a pair of little angels. I nodded to their mother and slipped out of the room.

Ruth was her usual direct self when I came back. 'Mummy said you had a surprise for us, before we go out to play,' she said, eyeing the carrier bag in my hand.

That explained why they weren't already in their outdoor things.

'And I do. You see, Mr Nesbitt and I thought it wasn't fair

that Joseph was going to get lots of presents, with none for you two, so we brought you a little something. This one is for you, Ruth,' as I pulled the smaller package out of the bag, 'and this for Cynthia.'

I watched anxiously as the girls opened them and inspected them. Ruth was the first to decide that the gift was acceptable. She plopped down on the floor, cradled her doll in her arms, smoothed its hair and its dress, and began gently crooning to it. Cynthia turned her face to me with a smile that lit up the room and said, 'She's beautiful. I'm going to name her Josephine.'

'Because of Joseph?'

She nodded emphatically. 'Because he's the reason you gave her to me. And because it's the name of a queen, once long ago. And I love her very, very much.'

Judith opened her mouth to utter the usual motherly reminder. I shook my head. 'It's all right,' I murmured. 'They've thanked me in their own way. The formality can come later, when they remember. I'm just so happy that they like them. One is never sure about presents.'

Children have short attention spans. It wasn't long before Ruth looked out the window, saw the snow, and stood up. 'Now I want to go out, Mummy. Sarah will need a warm coat and hat. She can wear Paddington's wellies,' she added, looking critically at the doll's patent leather shoes.

'I'm not sure it will be good for Sarah to play in the snow,' said Judith. 'She might catch cold.'

'That's why she has to have a coat and hat and wellies. I'll look after her, Mummy.'

'Very well. I'll hunt out some of your old things to fit her. Paddington's boots will be far too big for her, though. Better let Cynthia have those for Josephine, and I'll give you your old trainers for Sarah.'

Ruth's lower lip began to protrude ominously. Cynthia said, 'Josephine isn't going out. She doesn't like to play in the snow. It would spoil her clothes, and her hair would get wet.'

'It's no fun by myself! I want you to come, too!' Ruth wasn't used to being thwarted; her temper was rising.

'Look, I have an idea,' I interposed. 'It's getting close to teatime. Why don't you leave your dolls inside for now while you and Cynthia build a snow table and chairs for tea? Then Josephine and Sarah can have tea with you outside, and not get wet playing in the snow. They're a bit young for that sort of game, don't you think?'

Ruth considered the matter gravely and then nodded. She sat Sarah carefully on a chair and told her to behave until she, Ruth, came back. 'Come *on*, Cynthia,' she commanded, and Cynthia, recognizing determination, put Josephine beside Sarah with a similar admonition and followed her sister to the hallway where their coats were hung.

'She wants what she wants when she wants it,' I sang as the front door closed behind them. 'It's a good thing Cynthia usually goes along with her wishes, or there'd be trouble.'

'I suppose she's badly spoiled,' sighed Judith. 'She got used to being the baby, and when Joseph came along she wasn't best pleased. She loves him now, but he's too little to impinge on her world much. When he starts toddling and wanting to play with the girls, then things could get dicey.'

'She'll adapt,' I said comfortably. 'Above all she's a realist. I think she should go in for politics. I can see her as Prime Minister one day, following in Mrs Thatcher's footsteps.'

'Heaven help us all. Well, I'd best go and find some old baby sweaters and hats for the dolls to wear to their tea party, and get out the dolls' tea set.'

'Will the girls be happy with pretend food and tea, or will they require something real?'

'Oh, pretend, I think. Then it can be anything they like, strawberry tarts in December, even.'

'Yes, a definite advantage over boring reality. Can I help with tea for the grown-ups? It's early, but we lunched early.'

'There are some scones in the freezer you could pop in the oven if you like.'

'Right. And shall I cut the remains of the cake, and round up the men? They were both here just a little while ago. I don't know where they've taken themselves.'

Judith made a face. 'They've probably gone off to worry away at our problem. Men can be so . . . I don't know what to call it. So dogged about pursuing a solution, whether it's a minor repair to the plumbing or where to send the children to school.'

'Yes. Whereas women are multitaskers by nature, and happily juggle several projects, or several ideas, at the same time. I do think it's healthier, though I sometimes drive Alan mad by what he considers my irrelevant asides. They may well be wallowing in gloom, but I'll bet I can distract them with the prospect of tea.'

I found them in the library, still gnawing at the problem like a dog at a bone. They were happy enough to drop it for the moment and indulge in some refreshment. We had set the table and put out scones and cake, and Judith had just put the kettle on, when cries from outside stopped us in our tracks.

Even I can tell the difference between childish shrieks of joy and screams of pain and fear. Judith was the first to the door, with Edwin close behind. Cynthia ran up to her mother, crying so hard she couldn't speak coherently, but her intent was unmistakable. She frantically towed Judith down the drive to where snow lay in ragged piles on either side, the result of Sam's efforts. And there by one pile lay Ruth, her face nearly as white as the snow, a small pool of blood growing slowly under her right hand.

TWENTY

Alan took over. He unceremoniously pushed everyone aside and knelt by Ruth, feeling for a pulse, pulling one eyelid open, checking for the source of the blood.

'She's all right,' he said brusquely, 'but she needs medical attention. She's cut her hand rather badly, and the pain probably made her faint.' As he spoke he pulled off the little girl's muffler and wrapped it around her hand. 'She'll need stitches. It will probably be quicker for us to drive her to the nearest trauma centre than to wait for a doctor.' He picked up the limp little body and stood up. 'Judith, she needs warmth. Hot-water bottle, anything. And blankets. Edwin, my car is snow-covered; yours is garaged and warmer than mine. Bring it round, as quickly as you can.'

Judith picked up Cynthia, who was still sobbing and clinging to her mother, and ran to the house. I followed her, feeling useless and somewhat in awe of my husband. I had never before seen his police first-aid training in action. Plainly years of retirement hadn't made him forget the essentials.

At least I could help Judith fetch and carry. When I got into the house, at my age-diminished pace, I saw that the poor woman was frantic. Cynthia was calming down a little, but she still wouldn't let her mother leave her, and somewhere upstairs Joseph had begun to howl. 'Okay,' I said. 'I can find blankets. Where are the hot-water bottles?'

'There's one in each bathroom upstairs, in the cupboard with the towels. And the kettle has just boiled. Cynthia, darling, do stop crying. It's going to be all right, truly.'

Cynthia was trying, but she'd been nearly hysterical, and it's not so easy for a child to regain control. Her breath was coming in heart-breaking sobs. I decided to try a distraction.

'Cynthia,' I said in a brisk schoolteacher voice, 'it will be a big help if you'll go and get the eiderdown from your bed and bring it downstairs. On your way, stop in the nearest bathroom and get the hot-water bottle, while Mummy sees to poor little Joseph. This is a family emergency, and we all need to work together. Scoot, now!'

She was an obedient child. Still sobbing, she headed for the stairs, and Judith followed her, first shooting me a look of gratitude.

I went to the kitchen and filled the big kettle with water from the hot-water reservoir, placing it on what I hoped was the hottest burner of the Aga, in case the electric kettle didn't hold enough water.

Cynthia was back almost before I had finished. Her sobs had turned to hiccups. Her face was red and tear-streaked, and her coat was dripping water all over the kitchen.

'Goodness, child, you'll catch your death of cold if you don't get out of those wet things. You do that while I fill this bottle, and then I'll take the bottle and the blankets out to the car, and you can hop into a hot bath.'

'I want to go with Ruth!' The tears started again.

'I know you do, but honestly, my husband and your parents can cope better without one more person. I'm not going; I'm going to stay here and look after Joseph. And here he comes, with Mummy.'

And then Alan was in the house looking for bottle and blankets, and I handed them over and took Joseph from Judith, and somehow we all got ourselves sorted out, the door closed, and there was peace, except for Joseph's discontented grunts. I found the leftover bottle of Judith's milk, heated it for a few seconds in the microwave, and carried it and the baby upstairs to Cynthia's bedroom.

The sound of running water came from the bathroom across the hall. I knocked on the door and found Cynthia testing the water with a small hand.

'Not too hot? Sorry I can't help, but I've got my hands full, as you see. I thought I'd sit with you and feed this little rascal while you get nice and warm. Can you make it into the tub by yourself?'

'Of course.' The take-charge attitude was beginning to surface. Good. She was on the mend.

'Well, you needn't sound so smug about it! I have a really

terrible time getting into a tub, and an even worse time getting out.'

'But you're grown up!'

'I've grown old, my dear. My joints don't work the way they used to. I do love to soak in a tub, but I always have to ask my husband to help me get out.' I had settled by that time on the neat white chair by the window, and Joseph was steadily working his way through his meal. Cynthia got herself into the tub and began, half-heartedly, to wash her arms. For a few minutes the only sounds were splashing and the rhythmic pop-pop of Joseph's little mouth at the nipple.

Then Cynthia spoke in a small voice. 'I thought she was dead.'

'I don't blame you! She was awfully white, wasn't she? And then there was the blood. No wonder you were so scared.'

'I'm not a baby.'

'No, you're not, and you didn't act like one, if that's what you're worrying about. You acted like a loving big sister who knew exactly where to get help. I'm proud of you.'

Silence. Splashes.

'Is she really going to get well?'

'Really and truly. My husband said so, and he doesn't lie.'

'Yes, but does he *know*?'

'He does. I'm not just trying to make you feel better. My husband was once a policeman, and he's trained to know what to do for people who are hurt. He can tell when someone is badly hurt, and when it's just painful, but not serious. So you can trust what he said. Cross my heart.' With Joseph occupying both my hands I couldn't make the gesture, but I gave Cynthia a reassuring look, and she heaved a deep, shaky sigh.

Joseph was nearly asleep. I put him over my shoulder and burped him, and then laid him gently on the fluffy rug while I struggled out of the low chair. 'Now, my dear, before I take him back to bed, do you need some help with your face? That's the tricky part; you don't want to get soap in your eyes.'

'I'm okay. Are you going to stay here?'

'I'll just put Joseph to bed and then come to your room. I thought we might have a bit of tea, just the two of us, when you're all dry and warm. The scones are cold by now, but we can heat them up again, and there's cake.'

'And chocolate biscuits?'

'*And* chocolate biscuits. I'll be back in a tick.'

Joseph didn't stir when I put him in his crib, and I hurried back to Cynthia's room. She'd been in too much distress to put away her wet things, so I helped her with that little chore once she was dressed in jeans and a warm pullover.

'Now, shall we have our tea downstairs or up in the playroom? We could light the fire, if you like?'

'Oh, yes, please!'

'Good. Then I'll go down and get the tea. It's nearly ready.'

'No!' The note of panic was back in her voice. 'I mean, I'll come and help you.'

Of course. That was stupid, Dorothy. She doesn't want to be alone. 'That's a good idea. You can help carry things up.'

'And if Joseph cries, we can bring him in there with us.'

'Only there's no more milk for him, so we'd better hope he stays asleep. Come on, then.'

When we got up to the playroom with the tea tray and had turned on the fire, the world was twilit. A December evening falls early in northern climes, and we were nearing the shortest day of the year. The room was cosy with firelight and lamplight, and I made the decision to allow Cynthia a cup of weak tea with lots of milk and sugar, as a special treat. But she was still unable to relax, and didn't even want a chocolate biscuit. 'Ruth really is going to be fine, you know,' I said soothingly.

'Yes, but . . . it's all my fault.' She was trying hard not to cry.

'What do you mean? She fell, didn't she?'

'No.' Cynthia took a deep breath. 'We needed more snow for the table and I told her to go get some from the pile and she said it was packed hard and she couldn't get any out and I called her a baby and she pulled off her mitten and tried harder and dug in deeper and that's when she screamed and pulled her hand out all bleeding and it's all m-my f-fault!'

'But . . . I don't understand. Was there an animal in there that bit her?'

'I d-don't know! But she's only little and I shouldn't have made her dig there and it's all—'

'Now stop that this minute! It is *not* your fault! It was an accident. And we're going to finish our tea, because it's far too

good to waste, and then we're going to go out and I'm going to
get a shovel and find out what on earth injured Ruth's hand. Lord
knows what you're going to wear in the way of a coat, with
yours still sopping, but we'll find something. This is a mystery,
and if there's something like broken glass there, we need to get
rid of it before it does more damage.'

I managed to get her to nibble a little bread and butter and
drink some of her milky tea, but she refused everything else. I'm
no child psychiatrist, but I worked with children for so many
years that I thought I could diagnose her problem. Not only was
she torn by irrational guilt and worried about her sister, but she
was quite terribly afraid of the unknown horror that might be
found in that pile of snow. I'd done what little I could to deal
with the guilt and the worry; now it was time to destroy the fear
by unmasking the monster.

'All right, then, off we go.'

She shrank back.

'Cynthia Montcalm, you're to come with me, right now!'

Her lip trembled, and I felt awful, but I was sure a straight-
forward approach was the only way. She stood and headed for
the stairs, but she wouldn't let me take her hand. I felt a little
like crying myself.

A short jacket of her mother's covered her adequately. It was
miles too big around, of course, and the sleeves were far too
long, but I rolled them up and tied a scarf around her waist. She
was hating the whole procedure, but she made no protest, just
stood like a doll and let me do what I would. I pulled my flashlight out of my purse, and we headed out.

I had to ask her where I might find a shovel; she pointed silently
to one of the outbuildings, a garden shed apparently, and stood
unmoving while I went to fetch the necessary tool.

I didn't need to ask where the accident had taken place. The sun
had set, but there was enough light, with my flash on the snow, to
see the blood marking the spot with cruel certainty. Cynthia followed
me with great reluctance, still not speaking a word, tears streaming
down her face.

Am I doing the right thing? I prayed silently. *Or am I
traumatizing this child for life?*

I could only trust my instinct and press ahead.

The child stood there, trembling, as I thrust my spade into the stained and disturbed snow. The pile had softened under the brilliant sun of the afternoon. All would thaw soon.

I dumped a shovelful of snow to the side, and another. Cynthia, poor child, had turned her back. A less obedient child would have run away. I didn't force her to turn around; I couldn't be that heartless.

Another thrust of the shovel and I hit something that gave a muted metallic clink. Ah! A piece had fallen off that ridiculous jerry-rigged snowplough. I dropped the shovel and went in with gloved hands.

'Don't,' cried Cynthia. 'Please, *please* don't. You'll hurt yourself.'

'I'll be very careful. I think it's a scrap of metal.'

My hands felt the shape. Something long and somewhat lumpy.

'Oh, good heavens! Surely not!'

It was somewhat dirty and crusted with snow. A sodden, bloodstained cloth was half-wrapped around it. I pulled it all free and let the cloth fall to the drive and held, unmistakably, the missing dagger.

TWENTY-ONE

My exclamation had at last broken through Cynthia's terror. She moved closer to look and said, 'Is that really the dagger? Why was it buried in the snow?'

'I have no more idea than you do, my dear. And of course I can't be sure it's "the" dagger. But it certainly fits the description, and the handle, hilt, whatever, is certainly gold. Any lesser metal would have rusted.'

'Maybe it hasn't been there very long. Doesn't it take a long time for something to get rusty?'

'I think it depends on temperature and how much air is available, and all sorts of other things. I don't know enough about it to say, really. But when the dirt and the snow have been wiped away, this will be bright and shiny, even the blade.' I turned it over and over, cautiously. The edge didn't look very sharp, but the point certainly was.

'Look, one of the jewels is gone!' Cynthia exclaimed.

'Goodness! So it is. You have sharp eyes, child.'

I hadn't noticed that there was an empty setting near the place where the hilt met whatever-it's-called, the wide bit before the handle meets the blade. There was a row of small bluish-green stones encircling the hilt there, and I could see the gap, where bent prongs had held the missing stone.

Cynthia had gone over to the snow pile and was digging carefully. 'It might still be here. I'm going to try to find it.'

'Whoa! You don't have gloves or mittens, and if I let you get frostbitten fingers your mother will have something to say to both of us. And it will be really dark soon. If you're determined to find it, we'll need a garden trowel and a sieve of some sort. I'm going to forage in the shed.'

'I know where Mummy keeps a sieve in the kitchen. I'll go fetch it.'

She ran off toward the house, and I breathed a prayer of thanks. By some miracle, my solution to her panic attack had been the right one. She seemed even to have forgotten her hatred of my domineering attitude. I hoped I could continue to walk the tight-rope with this intelligent and sensitive child.

She came back in no time with a spotless sieve, probably used by Mrs Walker to strain custard. Well, if we ruined it Alan and I could replace it. Right now I cared more about Cynthia's feelings than Mrs Walker's.

'Splendid! That's just what we want. I found a couple of trowels, so we can each have a look. Now, what we want to do is—'

'I know! I saw a programme about archaeology once. You dig very, very carefully, sometimes with your hands . . .' She paused and gave me an imploring look.

'On no account! I'm sorry, I really am, but with your mittens still wet you truly mustn't. The small trowel will serve you well, and I'll use the big one.'

'Oh, well. Then every bit of snow has to go in the sieve, every single one, and then –' she produced from a pocket, rabbit-in-the-hat fashion, a kitchen brush of the kind used for scrubbing vegetables – 'we scrub at the snow until it's all gone through the sieve, and see what's left behind.'

'Bravo! That's exactly right. I'll tell you what. I'm not so good at getting down on my hands and knees, so suppose you dig and I'll do the sifting, and hold the flashlight – the torch. But quickly, mind. It'll be completely dark soon.'

As a distraction for a small child, or for many adults, for that matter, it's hard to beat a treasure hunt, though its charm fades after a while. Fortunately it didn't take us too long to find the missing gem. There in the sieve it lay, next to bits of grass and mud and an elderly, cracked marble. Cynthia picked it up with awe. 'A jewel! I've never held a real one before.'

'Not a very valuable one, though. The diamond in Mummy's ring probably cost a lot more.'

She dismissed Mummy's ring with a wave of her hand. 'But it's just plain. This one is a pretty colour. I wish I could keep it, but it belongs in the dagger. We'd better see if we can put it back.'

She reached for the dagger, but I caught her hand. 'I think we'd better leave it the way it is until Daddy sees it.'

'We have to clean it up.'

'Not right away. Cynthia, you watch television. Have you ever seen any of the detective programmes?'

'Mummy won't let me.' She looked away. 'Sometimes I watch a little when she doesn't know.'

'Then you may know about what is called evidence.'

'Fingerprints and things,' she responded promptly. 'Of course. Everybody knows about that.'

'Well, you know this dagger, if this is the right one, was missing. It's possible that someone stole it, and if that's true we need to keep from wiping it clean until your father and my husband have had the chance to take a look at it.'

'Oh.' She was disappointed but then brightened up. 'Anyway, now Joseph can be christened, and Daddy and Mummy can stop being sad.'

I wished it were that simple. I ignored her remark, asked for her scarf/sash and carefully wrapped the dagger in it. The cloth that had surrounded it was disgusting, and I nearly threw it away, but one never knows what might be significant, so I laid it carefully on the snow, and we both trooped back to the house.

My mobile rang just as we got inside. It was Alan.

'They've patched Ruth up nicely. It was a rather nasty cut, fairly deep, and she had to have a few stitches, of which she's quite proud. She won't have much use of her right hand until it has healed, but fortunately children heal quickly.'

'Wait a minute, Alan.' I turned to Cynthia. 'They've fixed Ruth up. She's fine and is going to want to tell you all about her stitches.' Back to the phone. 'All right, love, go ahead.'

'Well, they took a lot of anti-bacterial precautions since we don't know what caused the wound, and gave her a tetanus jab on general principles. Judith is going to bring her home in a few minutes, but I'm afraid Edwin and I have to stay here in town. It's nearly six, and we mustn't miss our date with the police.'

'Have you heard from the lawyer?'

'Yes, he called from Lowestoft. Apparently the roads from there aren't too bad, so he plans to meet us at the police station.'

'Well, then, there's something you should know. We found out how Ruth got that cut. She was digging in the snow and her hand met something sharp.'

'Dorothy, we *had* worked that out for ourselves. Edwin and I really must leave now.'

'Wait for it. The sharp thing buried in the snow was the dagger.'

'The . . . are you sure?'

'I'm sure it's *a* dagger. It's gold, or gilded at least, and fits the description.'

'What have you done with it?' His voice was sharp.

'Nothing, other than digging it out. The snow was so disturbed anyway there was little point in leaving it where it is. We've not cleaned it at all.'

'You're sure it caused the cut? Is it bloodstained at all?'

'Yes, Cynthia's right here.'

'Ah. And you don't want to talk about blood in front of her. Right. Keep it safe, and don't touch it, and I'll send that young sergeant to fetch it as soon as I can. Judith says love to Cynthia, and they'll both be home soon.'

'Did you talk to Daddy?' asked Cynthia, the moment I'd ended the call. 'What did he say about the dagger? Is he excited?'

'There was only time to talk to my husband; he's the one who called. But yes, he was excited. He and your father are going to have to talk to the police about all this for a little while, so Mummy is bringing Ruth home. They'll be here in just a few minutes, so we'd better fix them something to eat, don't you think? They'll be hungry, both of them. What's Ruth's favourite thing, besides chocolate biscuits?'

'Macaroni cheese. Mummy and I like it too. Could we make that?'

'Let's get out of our wet things and go to the kitchen and see what we can find.'

I would be the first to admit that I'm a decent cook, but not at the gourmet level. Years ago when I lived in Indiana I was perfectly content to make mac and cheese out of a box, with a few extra flourishes. However, given the ingredients, I was confident I could make a reasonable facsimile from scratch. So I was busy scavenging in Judith's kitchen when she and Ruth came home.

Cynthia instantly abandoned her efforts to help and took Ruth under her wing. The bandages had to be admired and Cynthia had to hear the whole saga of the stitches and the rest of the procedure, and then Ruth had to hear about finding the dagger. I carefully unwrapped it to show Judith, who identified it without question.

'But what was it doing out in the snow? It can't have been there long; the snow only fell last night.'

'Exactly. I can only think that it was buried somewhere under the drive and Sam's plough dredged it out.'

'It couldn't have been very deep,' she said dubiously. 'And why would it have been there at all?'

'I imagine Alan and the police will have to try to figure that out. And speaking of whom –' I looked out the window – 'I think that's Sergeant What's-his-name just pulling up.'

The young man, admitted to the kitchen, took the scarf-wrapped dagger, nodded and smiled, and left, all without a word.

'I suppose he *can* talk?' I said doubtfully.

Judith shrugged. 'I suppose. Now I'm going to go up and feed Joseph while you tell me all about it.'

'There's not a lot more to tell.' As we went up the stairs I related what Cynthia had told me about how Ruth had come by her injury. 'She was determined to blame herself, because she encouraged Ruth to dig in the snow there. I thought it would be a good idea to find the broken glass or whatever it was, because it would keep Cynthia busy and might take her mind off her worries. She didn't want to. She really was in a bit of a state, but I pushed a bit. I did the actual digging, because I didn't want her to hurt herself. And then when we found the dagger, astonishment took over. I think she's all right now, but you may have to keep a watch out for nightmares for a while.'

'I think you did exactly the right thing. You might not think so, because they do quarrel, but the two of them really are very close.'

'I could see how upset she was, but when she saw the dagger she forgot most of her anxiety. She was the one, in fact, who noticed that one of the stones was missing. Oh! I forgot to give that to the sergeant, or even tell him about it.'

'A missing stone? I didn't notice it.'

'It's a really little one, a greenish one down at the end of the hilt. An aquamarine, I thought maybe. I didn't see the gap either, but Cynthia's eyes are a lot sharper than mine. Then nothing would do but that we hunt for it, and Cynthia gravely instructed me about the proper excavation method, gleaned from television. I'm afraid we borrowed a sieve from the kitchen, and I suppose we must have left it down on the drive. And I think I put the gem in my coat pocket, or maybe my pants pocket. Don't let me forget to give it to you.'

By this time Judith was laughing. 'She's been mad keen to do some archaeology ever since we saw that programme. I tried to tell her that it was mostly boring digging and finding nothing but bits of dirty pots, but now she'll think there's treasure everywhere. She's going to be a frightful bore about it at school, I fear. There, I think my greedy son has had enough for now.' She laid him gently in his crib, and we went back downstairs.

'I promised Cynthia I'd try to put together some macaroni cheese for our tea. I'll be glad to do that, if you'll show me what kind of cheese you use.'

'Well, actually, when Mrs Walker isn't here, I cheat.' She went to a cupboard and pulled out the familiar blue and yellow box.

We'd both been under a good deal of strain. I started to giggle, and Judith caught the contagion, and we had both fallen into chairs, tears streaming down our faces when the girls came back.

'Mummy!' said Cynthia severely. 'What *are* you doing? We haven't had our tea and we're *starving*.'

Supper – 'tea' – was made and eaten in short order. 'All right, ladies,' said Judith when they had cleaned their plates and polished off the treacle tart by way of dessert, 'you've had a day to remember. Now it's bedtime for you both.'

'But Mummy! It's much too early! And we want to wait until Daddy gets home.'

That, of course, was Cynthia. Ruth's eyelids were already beginning to droop.

'No argument, now. If you're very good and in bed in fifteen minutes, I'll let you leave the light on for a little while for you to play with your new dolls. Scoot, now.'

'Can Mrs Martin read to us?'

'Not tonight. She's tired. We're all tired. Tomorrow, perhaps.' Cynthia opened her mouth for another protest, but Judith said firmly, 'That's enough, Cynthia. Off you go. I'll be up in a moment to tuck you in.'

'They'll be asleep before I get there,' she said softly as they left the room. 'I have a pill to give Ruth if she's in pain, but I think she'll sleep right through. What a day!'

'Indeed. I'll make you some herbal tea – no, you sit still – but I wish you could have something stronger!'

'Me, too. Ah, well. He'll soon start on solid food, and then it won't be too long before I can wean him.'

I hesitated, and then said, 'Is that difficult? I would think you'd miss the intimacy. If that isn't too personal a question.'

She laughed. 'A very sensible question! Of course I'll miss it. I missed it with the girls, but then I gained so much freedom, and we began to bond in other ways.'

'I had hoped to nurse my own children, and back in those days it wasn't a popular option. But then the babies never happened.'

'Well, you missed out on a great deal, there's no denying. But considering the way children can turn out, you missed some heart-aches as well. And your teaching gave you the experience of hundreds of children, not just the two or three you might have had. Obviously you learned how to deal with them; look at the way you handled Cynthia today. I'm not sure I could have settled her down so easily.'

'You were caught up in worry about Ruth. I was a bystander. Easier to be calm at a slight remove. And good grief, I need to make that tea. When do you suppose the men will be home?' I got up and busied myself at the Aga, and blinked away the foolish tears.

TWENTY-TWO

I poured myself a cup of the tea, as well, and sat down with Judith. 'Will the men be home soon?' I asked again.

Judith's face clouded. 'Edwin didn't sound happy when he called me. I gathered he was about to tell the police about the woman claiming to be his mother. Alan said he must, but—'

'Alan's right, you know. It's a really, really bad idea to lie to the police, even by omission. When they find out, they're apt to draw conclusions, usually not favourable ones. I wish Alan would call and tell me what their reaction was to finding the dagger. I hope they won't decide Edwin put it there himself.'

'But he couldn't have! The snow didn't fall until yesterday, and the dagger certainly wasn't just lying there in the drive waiting to be covered.'

'We know that. But the police don't know that Edwin didn't have it stashed away somewhere, and put it in the snow yesterday or today.'

'Why would he do that?'

Judith was becoming combative. She was sitting bolt upright in her chair, and her voice had become almost shrill. I poured her some more tea. 'Again, we know he wouldn't. And we know that his distress and yours were genuine when the dagger went missing. But the police have to be suspicious of everyone. Here, drink up. It has some camomile in it, well known for its calming properties. Don't forget that when you get upset, you may disturb Joseph, and what you don't need to deal with right now is a colicky baby.'

Judith took several deep breaths and a few sips of tea, and sat back. 'All right, I'm trying. But I don't understand why the police might refuse to believe us about the dagger.'

'Look at it from their point of view, Judith. A woman is found dead with a dagger in her back. It resembles the Montcalm dagger. Edwin says it isn't, but can't produce the real one for comparison. The police learn that Edwin has an excellent reason for wanting the woman out of the way. Then the real dagger turns up, but by that time its value as evidence on Edwin's side is greatly diminished, especially if, as the police may believe, he put it there himself thinking it might exonerate him.'

Judith sighed. 'It's awfully convoluted, but I see. I guess. What's going to happen now?'

'That depends in part on how good Edwin's lawyer is. He'll certainly keep Edwin from saying anything that might sound incriminating. Probably he won't let him talk much at all.'

'But won't that seem suspicious?'

'Not necessarily. The police are used to dealing with lawyers and know they keep their clients as silent as possible. And of course he – the lawyer, I mean – will keep reminding the police that Edwin has a sick daughter at home, and will make it sound much worse than it is, for the sympathy value. I imagine your poor husband will be sent home soon, with the understanding that he's not to go very far afield for the time being. And don't forget Alan is there, as well as the lawyer, to assure fair play. Edwin's in good hands.'

'You have a lot of faith in your husband.'

'I do. And it's justified. He sometimes makes me furious, especially when he goes all English and overprotective, but even when I'm annoyed with him I love and trust him. He has a good mind and a good heart, and there's nobody I'd rather have on my side when the chips are down.'

I had probably embarrassed Judith, I thought, with such a very un-English display of sentiment. But then she wasn't English, either. Maybe Canadians were given, occasionally, to speaking what was really in their heart. At any rate, I meant every word of it and wasn't sorry I'd said it.

Judith just looked at me for a moment and then said, 'I'm glad to hear it. I'm trusting him with a lot just now.' She stood. 'I'd better go and see if the girls are in bed, and check on Joseph.'

'They're probably fathoms deep by now. It's been an eventful day. I could drop off myself without any trouble. Don't bother about clearing the table. I can do that.'

I stood, not without difficulty. That brief spell of digging in the snow had delivered more stress to my knees than they liked. I had just managed to get moving when I heard the car door slam.

I hadn't thought I could run, but I managed a fair turn of speed and got to the front door just as it opened. Judith, carrying Joseph, was just behind me.

Edwin, who looked exhausted, brightened a little at the sight of his wife and son. 'Here I am, darling, back safe and sound. Though for how long I don't know. Murbles says I've nothing to worry about, but then he has very little experience with criminal matters.'

'Then he ought to be the perfect man for this, since you are not a criminal.' Judith kissed his cheek and handed Joseph to him. 'Here, have your boy while I deal with a meal for you. I don't suppose they gave you anything to eat.'

'They offered,' said Alan with a dry chuckle. 'Canteen sand-wiches. The cuisine has not improved since my time. Nor has the coffee.'

'Right.' Judith was back on form, setting her worries aside to deal with first things first. 'Alan, since Edwin's got the baby, would you mind pouring drinks while I cope in the kitchen? It's just macaroni cheese and it's all ready, but it needs hotting up, so come in and sit while I work. And I think you all need a stiffener.'

I certainly did. I settled back gratefully with bourbon to listen to what the men had to say about their experience with the police.

Edwin had a good swig before he began. 'Where are the girls?'

'In bed and asleep,' said Judith. 'We all ate as soon as Ruth and I got home, and the girls were so tired, even Cynthia made only a token protest. So we can talk freely, but be careful not to sound upset. Joseph picks up on that, and it worries him.'

'We'll be careful,' said Alan. 'Edwin, suppose you let me fill in the outline. Jump in when I miss something.'

'I'll try, but half the time I didn't understand what was happening.'

'First, of course,' Alan began, 'Edwin identified the body. That was just a matter of form, since they were reasonably sure of her identity anyway. Then we went back to the station just about the time you called, Dorothy, with the news about the dagger. Then Edwin had to identify that, which of course he did.'

'I cannot *imagine* how the thing ended up in a snow bank,' said Edwin. 'Oops, sorry, old chap. Didn't mean to shout. It's all right; go back to sleep. The inspector seemed inclined to think I put it there,' he went on. 'Which is totally absurd.'

'None of us can work that out,' I said. 'It's as big a mystery as how and why it disappeared in the first place. But go on.'

'Actually, I'm reasonably certain the inspector was just trying that on to see your reaction. Which was, I may say, exactly right. Any policeman can tell the difference between genuine surprise and bafflement and the imitation variety. Unless, that is, we're dealing with a superb actor.'

'Which you certainly are not, darling,' said Judith. 'Your thoughts are always written clearly on your face.'

'Oh, my, Edwin, I'd shake your hand if both yours weren't otherwise occupied.' I smiled at him. 'I'm the same way. I've always been told I should never, ever play poker.'

Alan smiled at me. 'I've always been grateful you never attempted a life of crime. You'd have been wildly unsuccessful.'

Judith brought plates to the table and put them down in front of the men. 'There's nothing much for afters unless you'd like some ice cream, so make the most of this. And don't stop talking.'

'There isn't a lot to tell. DCI Billings took Edwin over the story he'd already told.'

'And damned boring it was, too.' This time he spoke in a quiet tone belied by his words, the better to keep Joseph happy. The baby had awakened and was cooing softly. The tranquil sound made an odd background to talk of violence and sudden death. 'I just said the same things over and over again, that I didn't know where the woman went when she left me, didn't know she was in the area, had seen her only that once and she'd never got back in touch with me.

'I have to say Murbles wasn't a great deal of help with that part of it. He kept trying to stop me saying anything at all, which I thought made the story sound terribly fishy. I saw no reason why I shouldn't just keep on telling the truth.'

'Billings also wanted to know about the Irishman, or whatever he is,' said Alan. 'The man who keeps on trying to buy the estate. And of course Murbles didn't want Edwin to talk about him, either.'

'Why not?' asked Judith. 'Smith, so-called, sounds to me like one of the most suspicious characters in the whole scenario.'

'I don't think I agree,' I said slowly. 'At first glance, yes. He's not a pleasant man, certainly. And assuredly he wants Edwin out of the picture. But what would he gain by murdering Angela Wilson? If the woman really was your mother, Edwin – your biological mother, I mean – then you'd be out of the estate, true. But that would be the case whether she was alive or dead. And if her claim was false, she was irrelevant to Smith's aims. All her death has accomplished, as far as Smith is concerned, is to make the truth of her story somewhat harder to prove or disprove.'

'You're forgetting about the dagger, Dorothy,' said Alan. 'It appears the weapon was used to try to implicate Edwin. An inept attempt, true. Not only was the dagger a poor imitation of the Montcalm artefact, it was not used effectively. The autopsy hasn't been completed, but I had a word with the police doctor. It's his opinion that the wound was little more than a bad scratch, and the woman would certainly have lived to tell who attacked her had it not been for the fire.'

'Then we're dealing with someone who's stupid as well as evil,' I pronounced. My voice was rising, and Joseph looked over at me, his face beginning to pucker. 'Oh, dear. I didn't mean it, sweetheart. Or I did, but I wasn't talking about you. You're a fine boy, and brilliant as well!'

Joseph calmed down, but still eyed me with some suspicion.

'And as soon as the police give the dagger back – the real one – we can have my son christened, and establish his claim to his inheritance. If in fact there's anything to be inherited.'

The bitter tone in Edwin's voice started Joseph off again, and this time he refused to be placated. His whimpers turned to full-fledged howls.

'Now he's hungry and tired,' said Judith with a little sigh, 'and probably needs a clean nappy. I'd best see to him. And then, if you all don't mind, I'm off to bed. It's early, I know, but it's been quite a day.'

She stood and took her flailing and screaming baby from Edwin's arms. We all stood, not quite certain what to do next. I was tired, but not sleepy. Edwin looked nervy as well as weary; Alan was at his blandest, which usually meant his mind was working at full speed.

That was when the doorbell rang.

'Damn!' Edwin's oath was subdued, but vehement. 'Sorry, Dorothy, but I've had all I can take today. If that's the police again I may slam the door in their faces!'

'I wouldn't advise it,' said Alan quietly. 'I'll answer the door for you, if you like, but stay nearby.'

He opened the door, Edwin standing behind him. The light from the hall shone on the man in the doorway, a bulky, somewhat stooped figure, dressed in warm but well-worn clothes.

'Sorry I've come so late, Mr Edwin,' said Sam. 'I've only just heard. I've come to confess.'

TWENTY-THREE

'No! I don't believe it! Not you, Sam!' Edwin strode to the door, too astounded to invite his guest inside. 'There's some mistake. You'd kill a fox that was after the chickens, or a mad dog, but not a woman! Never!'

'No, I'd not kill anyone. I've not made myself understood. Maybe I could come in and tell you?'

Edwin, shaking his head in bewilderment, stood aside, and Sam came in, his manner subdued and deferential, but not obsequious. He refused an offer to come into the drawing room and stood in the hall instead, his feet in their worn boots planted foursquare.

'It's a bad thing I did, sir, and I'll not try to make less of it. It began as an accident, but I made it worse with every step I took after that. And now it's hurt your girl that I love like my own, and I must tell you all of it.'

I began to see a glimmer of light in this murkiness. 'This is about the dagger, then?'

'Yes, ma'am. When I was doing some work in the house a while back, I saw that a drawer in the big cupboard in the library needed repair. It wouldn't close quite right; I thought one of the joints had got dry and come away. So I opened it to see, and tipped out what was in it onto the desk. I was careful, mind you. I didn't want to scratch the leather, nor yet damage anything in the drawer. There wasn't much, only some papers and a bundle wrapped in velvet. The drawer didn't need repairing, it was only that a bit of paper had got jammed at the back. So I pulled that out and put everything back, only when I picked up the velvet bundle, it came unwrapped and I saw it was the dagger, and I dropped it, right to the floor.

'The carpet there is good and thick, so I thought the knife would come to no harm, but when I picked it up I saw that one of the jewels, a little greenish one, had fallen off. And that's when I did wrong. I was ashamed that it had come to harm through me, because I know you set great store by it, so I thought I'd just take it home and put the stone back and no one the wiser. Gold is soft; I was sure I could put it right in no time.

'Then I got sick. You won't remember, Mr Edwin. You were away at the time. But I came down with a cold or the flu and it hit me hard. For two, three weeks I could hardly get out of bed. As soon as I was able, I went to work on that dagger. But everything went wrong. First I couldn't find the stone, little bitty thing that it was. It had rolled into a corner of the box I'd put it in, and my eyes aren't so good as they were. Then I moved one of the prongs of the setting that bit too far, and it broke off. That was when I began to think I'd have to take it to a jeweller, but I managed to weld the prong back on. Made a nice neat job of it, too.

'But I'd lost track of time through being sick and out of things, and just when I was ready to slip the dagger back where it belonged, it was almost time for the christening and you'd gone looking for it and putting about that it had been stolen, and then there was the to-do about the woman being killed, and I was afraid, sir, and that's the truth of it. I'm ashamed of it. I'm ashamed of all I did, sir.'

'Then . . . then it was never stolen, after all.' Edwin was slow to understand, as I think we all were.

'Not stolen by intent, but stolen by deed, as I see now. And then I went and made it even worse.'

He cleared his throat. 'I couldn't see my way to returning the dagger without putting myself under the eyes of the law. And then the snow came and I thought I saw my way clear. I'd bury it in a snow bank and then find it and pretend not to know how it got there. I see now it was a fool idea, but I'd got myself tangled in a web of deception by then and wasn't thinking straight. And then it was your girl who cut herself, and I'd rather have cut off my own hand, I swear to it. So I knew I'd have to tell you the whole story and take what's coming to me.'

There was a long pause while we assimilated what he had said. Then Edwin shook his head, rather like a dog shaking off water, and put his hand out to Sam's.

'Come in to the kitchen, man, and sit down and have a drink. You have to be dry after that long tale, and I'll not take no for an answer.'

This was plainly a men's conclave. I slipped away and went up to see if Judith was asleep yet. She needed to hear this story.

She was just settling Joseph for the night. I said nothing until we left the room and closed the door. 'Will he sleep all night now?'

'Most of the night. He'll probably want to be fed around five, since he's going to sleep so early. But that's all right. I'm going to sleep early, too!' She yawned mightily. 'I heard someone at the door. Tell me it wasn't the police again!'

'No, it was Sam. Go ahead and get ready for bed, and I'll tell you the story he told us.'

She heard me out and was as astounded as the rest of us. 'Sam, of all people! The most reliable person I know. It's hard to believe. Why on earth didn't he just tell us? He'd have saved us all kinds of worry.'

'I think he was embarrassed, first of all, that he'd been clumsy, and hoped no one would have to know. And then he got sick. But I can't make out why he didn't say anything as soon as you and Edwin missed the dagger. He said something about getting involved with the law.'

'But surely he knew we would never accuse him of theft! I don't understand.'

'Neither do I. But anyway, now one mystery is solved. And Joseph can be christened.'

'I'm glad of that. Not that I care about the inheritance question, though Edwin does. But . . . oh, call me superstitious, but I'm uneasy until a baby has been baptized. I don't believe all that nonsense about unbaptized babies going to hell, or whatever it is. I'm not sure I even believe in hell. In fact, my beliefs are a little vague. But I like the idea of my children being blessed, and welcomed into the church, and all that.'

She sounded a little embarrassed, as many people are when they talk about religion. I smiled. 'Tradition and ritual are comforting, aren't they? Myself, I believe there's more to it than that, but I'm glad you find it important. We'll have a good argument about it one day, but we're both far too tired now. Go to bed, and don't think about anything at all until your tyrant wakes you. Good night.'

I very much wanted to go to my own bed. I was ready to drop.

But I also wanted to find out if any other exciting titbits had emerged from the men's gathering in the kitchen, and I knew if I let myself go to bed I'd be asleep by the time Alan came up. So if I wanted the latest before tomorrow morning, I had to gather it now. I trudged back down the stairs and joined Alan and Edwin and Sam.

Sam was just about to leave, appearing somewhat less anxious than before, though his weather-beaten face didn't reveal much at any time. 'Thank you, sir. I'm grateful for you taking it this way. I reckon I can wait till tomorrow to go to the police.'

'Sam, you've no need to go to the police at all! You didn't steal the dagger. No harm's been done. Ruth's going to be just fine, and though the aquamarine fell out again, it can be put back. I've nothing against you, and neither will the authorities.'

'They may think differently, sir, considering.'

'Considering *what*, for heaven's sake? There would be no reason for them to believe you involved in anything illegal.'

'Ah, you're forgetting, sir. They could think I had good reason to want you off the estate.'

Edwin just stared at him.

'And why would that be?' asked Alan gently.

'Oh. Well, maybe you never knew,' said Sam, sounding sad. 'I suppose your father never had reason to tell you. I was just Sam, the reliable worker who'd always helped with the garden and sometimes in the house. I've always lived on the estate, Mr Edwin, as did my father before me, and his father, back a good long while. My surname is Dunham.'

TWENTY-FOUR

For a moment I couldn't think why the name sounded familiar. Alan got it first.

'Dunham,' he said. 'As in Dunham Manor.'

'Good lord!' Edwin goggled like a fish, and stammered. 'I mean to say-you-good lord! You're . . . this house is—'

'Now don't get into a swivet, Mr Edwin. This house is your family home, and has been for a good many generations longer than it belonged to my family. Your ancestor bought it from mine, fair and square, nearly two hundred years ago, and that was when our family started calling ourselves Dunn, so as not to create awkwardness, like. I don't have the ghost of a claim on the estate, and I wouldn't want it, even if I had a right to it. You'll forgive me for speaking plain, sir. I've no wish to be saddled with the responsibility of an estate. That's for those who are born to it and have the money to do what's needed. Which I don't and never have.

'But that doesn't keep me from being proud of such a grand house, built by my ancestors. They lost it, gambling debts if the family legend's true. Maybe it was just bad management. Any road, it's your family that's kept it up all these years, and I'd be a fool to think otherwise. And I'd cut off my right hand sooner than see the land broken up into nasty little parcels with nasty little houses such as that "Mr Smith" wants to do.'

I could hear the quotation marks, and the scorn that went with them.

'But what I'm saying is,' Sam went on, 'the police might not see it that way. They might think I had a grudge against you and your family and took a crazy way to do Joseph out of what's his by right. The townspeople, now, they'd know better. I'm one of 'em, and they know me and what I'd do and wouldn't do. But the police aren't from here. That sergeant, he's from Lowestoft, and the inspector's from London, and like to go back there, from what I hear. Sharp man who came here because it was a promotion, and they say he'll go to the Met next. I don't say he's not a fair man, and good at his job, but what I do say is, they're both of them foreigners. They might not see it the right way. So the sooner I get to them and tell my story straight, the better, before they find out some other way and get to thinkin' things. I'll be off, if you'll excuse me, sirs, ma'am.'

'You'll do no such thing, Sam!' Edwin had recovered his composure. 'You're quite right. They might well not understand. I know you meant nothing underhanded, and I'll have no foreign policeman getting some damn fool idea about the matter.'

'Then how are you going to explain how the dagger got to where it was found? They don't walk much.'

That had been the question in my mind ever since Sam began to talk. It wasn't going to be easy to answer, especially since Billings was no fool, even if he was a 'foreigner' (which I took to mean someone not born within a mile or two of the estate).

'We'll deal with that when we must,' said Alan. 'We won't lie –' he gave me a pointed look – 'but we'll try to avoid details. Don't worry about it, Mr Dunham – er, Dunn. It was good of you to tell us the story, but we'll take it from here.'

A broad smile lit the weather-beaten face. 'No need to call me that, sir. It's plain Sam I've been these many years, and plain Sam I'll go on with. A good evening to you, sirs, ma'am.'

Dignity unimpaired, he sketched a bow to each of us and left quietly by the kitchen door.

'Well.' Edwin's comment seemed all there was to say. We sat there, unspeaking, too tired and confused to think. After a while we all went up to bed.

Tomorrow, as Scarlett famously said, is another day, but when Monday dawned, it felt to me like an exact repetition of the day before. Whatever was going to happen today, it was unlikely to be pleasant.

'Groundhog Day,' I said sleepily to Alan when I opened my eyes.

'Mmm?'

'Never mind. It isn't snowing, is it?'

He rolled out of bed and walked a bit stiffly to the window.

'No snow falling. Grey skies, though. My guess would be rain, later, but I'm no weather prophet.'

I closed my eyes. If I could have pushed a button at that moment and found myself back in my own bed in Sherebury, I would have done it. However . . . 'I suppose I have to get up.'

'I'll go down and get some coffee.'

Alan knows that coffee and/or chocolate can almost always brighten my mood.

I thought I'd get an extra forty winks while he ran his errand of mercy, but the squirrel in my mind started running around and I couldn't knock it off its wheel. What now?

That was the question. Would the police be back to question Edwin some more? Would they draw some conclusions about yesterday's dagger incident that would incriminate the poor man? I was convinced, and I was pretty sure Alan was convinced, that Edwin was innocent of Ms Wilson's death, but what did Billings et al. think about it?

There were no more answers to the questions than there had been yesterday. Drearily I got out of bed and into a few clothes. Maybe the police would magically find the solution this morning and Alan and I could go home.

Right. And I was likely to be at the top of the June Honours List.

'You're awake,' said Alan, entering with a tray (and trying not to sound surprised).

'Sort of.' I took the coffee he handed me and drank it with the fervour of an alcoholic downing his first drink of the day. When I had finished it and started on a second cup, I smiled at my husband. 'Good morning, dear. Thank you.'

'Welcome to the world, love. Better?'

'Much, thank you. Coffee will be made a controlled substance any time now, as soon as the government figures out how potent it is. Do we have an agenda for the day yet?'

'Not that I've heard. It's still early. Only the children are stirring. They're upset because their snowman is melting.'

'There's always something to worry about, isn't there? Even when you're only four.' I finished the second cup of coffee and put down the cup. 'No more, thank you, or I'll be flying around the room, and won't dare get more than a few feet from the bathroom. Sorry, loo.'

'I do understand American, love. Even speak it from time to time. Would you like this somewhat elderly scone? It was all I could find in the way of a snack.'

'No, thank you. Let's go down and see if anyone else is up and about. It's nearly nine, after all. The girls are going to want their breakfast, and they're not allowed to use the toaster.'

We were nearly finished with toast-making and egg-boiling when Judith walked in, Joseph in her arms and circles under her eyes. 'Good morning, and thank you. A fine hostess I am, letting you do all the work.'

'Oh, and making toast is such intense labour!' I fished an egg out of the pan and set it in an egg cup. 'Don't be silly. I think after the trauma of the past couple of days we've morphed into family, don't you? And besides, you look tired to death. Oh, I'm sorry, that's rude.'

'But true. I look like death warmed over, and that's pretty much the way I feel.'

'Did your little bundle of joy keep you awake last night?' The second egg went into a cup, and I put both in front of Cynthia and Ruth.

'No, more my big bundle of joy.' She looked at the girls and lowered her voice. 'He took an age to fall asleep, kept tossing and turning. And then when he finally settled down he had bad dreams and talked.'

Alan had been quietly distributing butter and marmalade, but he looked up, suddenly alert. 'What did he say?'

Judith shook her head. 'Nothing intelligible. Just muttering, and now and then a "No!" I kept prodding him, and finally he woke up enough to shake the dream and go back to sleep, real sleep. By that time it was nearly five, and this one woke up right on schedule.' She looked down at her sleeping son. '*Now* he sleeps!' But she smiled as she said it.

I was about to offer any help I could when the phone rang.

Alan queried Judith with a look, and at her nod he made for the library. He was gone only a minute or two. 'That was Murbles, Edwin's solicitor. He wants to call here this morning at about ten to talk to Edwin. I said I'd phone him back if that isn't convenient.'

'Oh, dear! Yes, I suppose if he must, he must, though I can't say I have any great confidence in him. Edwin told me a little about him last night. He sounded . . . oh, not exactly incompetent, but certainly not inspired. What do you think he wants, Alan?'

'Probably simply to hear Edwin's story in full, without a policeman present to hear every word.'

'My husband has nothing to hide!' Her voice had risen. Joseph opened his eyes and whimpered, and Ruth, in a small voice, said 'Mummy?'

'Sorry, darling. Don't worry! I'm a bit tired and cross, that's all.' She took a deep breath. 'Ruthie, how's your hand feeling this morning?'

'It hurts.' It was Cynthia who replied. 'She didn't want to tell you because she wants to play out in the snow before it's all gone.'

'It *doesn't* hurt!' said Ruth. Her tears were very near the surface. 'You promised not to tell!'

'Perhaps one of those pain pills?' I suggested quietly to Judith. 'Or half a one? And you could put a plastic bag over her bandage so it wouldn't get wet. It's going to rain soon, and by that time the pill will probably have made her sleepy, anyway.'

Judith nodded resignedly. 'You may go out for a few minutes, both of you. But there are rules. Ruth, I'm going to give you a pill to help with that pain you're not having. And I'm going to wrap the hand in plastic; it mustn't get wet.'

'But Mummy! Then I can't use it at all!' The tears were flowing now.

'That's the idea, darling. Those are the rules. Accept them or stay inside.' She gave her daughter the universal look of parental ultimatum. Ruth recognized the finality and conceded. She pouted, true, but there was no more whining.

'And there are rules for you, too, Cynthia. You are to keep an eye on your sister. Don't let her do anything foolish. You know how to do that without being bossy. Practice that art today. And, both of you, the final rule is: have as much fun as you can before the rain comes! Now for the waterproofing, Ruthie-Coothie.'

'Shall I go tell Edwin to get his skates on?' asked Alan. 'He doesn't have too much time if the chap's prompt.'

'Oh, yes, do, and I'll make you some proper breakfast.'

* * *

The doorbell rang in synch with the chime of the mantel clock. Evidently punctuality was one of the solicitor's virtues. Edwin showed him into the drawing room, where all the adults were sitting. 'Judith, Dorothy, my solicitor William Murbles. Sir, my wife Judith, and Dorothy Martin, Mr Nesbitt's wife.'

He bowed. 'Delighted to meet you, ladies. Now, Sir Edwin, where shall we have our consultation?'

'We'll be quite comfortable right here, I think,' said Edwin. 'Would you care for some coffee, or tea?'

'No. No, thank you. But I think it would be best if we—'

'I wish to be a part of this consultation, Mr Murbles,' said Judith firmly. 'So does Mrs Martin, who has been a great help to us throughout this crisis. And Mr Nesbitt is, as you know, a part of the investigation.'

'Unofficially, Mr Murbles. As I told you yesterday, I am no longer an active policeman. But as Sir Edwin has asked for my help, I have of course given it.'

Murbles cleared his throat. 'Er . . . I see. I had not planned a group discussion. As delightful as it is to visit with these orna-ments to their sex, they may find a business discussion somewhat taxing. It would be more appropriate at this point—'

'Both my wife and Mrs Martin are quite intelligent enough to follow a business discussion, as you call it, and we all want to hear what you have to say, Mr Murbles.' Edwin was displaying an unexpected stiffness of backbone. 'I think you'll find that a comfortable chair.'

The lawyer gave in with bad grace. Sitting bolt upright, he said, 'Very well. This is most irregular, but as you wish.' He cleared his throat and turned toward Edwin, as if pretending the rest of us didn't exist. 'As you know, Sir Edwin, I am not experienced in the practice of criminal law. Our firm has never dealt with that sort of thing.' He made the practice of defending the accused sound disreputable, if not downright disgraceful. 'I am not a barrister, nor, I may say, have I ever wished to expand my efforts in that direction. My practice has been limited to matters dealing with estates, wills, conveyancing, and similar civil matters.'

He cleared his throat again. 'I am, however, of course versed in certain legal matters beyond my usual scope. Having spoken with the . . . er . . . the officer in charge of your case—'

'Forgive me for interrupting, sir, but I'm not sure to which case you refer.' Alan could be every bit as stuffy as a lawyer when he wanted to be.

'I don't believe I understand your question, sir. I refer, of course, to the murder case in which my client is involved!'

'Ah. In that event, I'm not sure exactly what you mean by "involved". Sir Edwin has not, to my knowledge, been charged with any crime. His sole and extremely tangential connection has been the misidentification by the police of a dagger which slightly resembles one owned by Sir Edwin and his family. That matter has now been cleared up beyond all doubt by the rediscovery of the Montcalm dagger, which had unfortunately been misplaced. So I ask again: in what way do you believe Sir Edwin to be connected with this alleged murder?'

Murbles looked unhappy; he tried to hide his shaking hand in his pocket. 'I – I seem to have misunderstood. I was certainly under the impression that Sir Edwin was in grave danger of arrest for the murder of Ms Wilson. Was that not the reason you sent for me? After all, the woman was his mother, and . . .' He ran out of words, seeing no approval on the faces around him.

Alan shook his head. 'You've seen the results of DNA testing to prove that assertion? I would not have thought they could be accomplished so quickly.'

'I . . . no, I have not. It was my understanding that the woman herself informed Sir Edwin of the fact.'

Alan smiled. 'But as of course you know, that is hearsay evidence, as Ms Wilson cannot now confirm or deny it. And as such it is inadmissible in a court of law. The police could not use it against Sir Edwin, even if they wanted to. As a former policeman myself, I believe they have nothing at all with which to build a case against him.'

Murbles stood. He was trembling. 'I came here, Sir Edwin, because you asked me to do so, though I stressed to you that I had no expertise in criminal law. I wish that I had been properly briefed, but in the circumstances I must decline to act further. I very sincerely hope that Mr – this gentleman – is correct in his assessment of the situation. If he is not, you may stand to lose, not only your estate, but your liberty. If you wish to sell up and move away while you are free to do so, I will of course do anything I can to assist you. Ladies, I hope I haven't distressed you. I beg to be excused. No, no, I'll see myself out.'

TWENTY-FIVE

'And what was that all in aid of?' asked Judith, her words falling into the silence that succeeded the lawyer's departure. 'I must say I wasn't terribly impressed.'

'The man is an ass,' said Alan. 'I thought so yesterday; now I have no doubt. I do feel somewhat sorry for him. He's plainly in over his depth. What I do wonder, though, is why he seems to have changed his mind about the possibility of breaking the entail and selling the estate. Even he can't be stupid enough to believe that you're going to be sent to prison.'

Edwin shrugged. 'I've no idea. It's almost as if he *wants* me to be arrested. And that wouldn't seem to be typical behaviour for a solicitor.'

The phone rang. Judith sighed and stood. 'I suppose it's going to be like this all day.'

'That means the landline is back in service,' said Edwin. 'I think we should start letting it go to voice mail.'

'Not a good idea if it's the police ringing you,' said Alan. 'Which they will continue to do, you know. This isn't going to be over until they work out who really did kill Ms Wilson.'

'And why.' I ran a hand through my hair. 'That's what's getting to me. I keep asking myself, over and over, why would anybody want that poor woman dead?'

Alan sighed. 'And as *I've* said over and over, motive is not a principal concern of the police. It can lead them to possible suspects, but when it comes to proof, they need evidence that can stand up in court. A good lawyer can—'

'Praise be to God!' Judith came back into the room. 'That was Mrs Walker. She's coming back, just as I was wondering what on earth we'd do about meals. There's not a lot left in the larder, and I was groaning at the thought of relying on eggs again.'

'There aren't many eggs, either. Alan and I used up most of them for breakfast. So what prompted your cook to return?'

'She heard about the dagger. So she thinks the christening is on and she can finish her cake and start cooking for a party again. I was so glad to hear from her, I hadn't the heart to tell her we haven't actually got the dagger back or talked to Mr Prior. He's the rector,' she explained to Alan and me. 'I'll have to make arrangements with him before we re-invite everybody. Alan, have you any idea when the police might let us have the wretched thing?'

Alan shook his head. 'Not for some time, I would imagine. When this business actually comes to trial, it's possible they might want it for evidence. They'll have tested it for fingerprints and so on by now, though, so it's possible they might let you borrow it for a short time. Or might let *me* borrow it, as I'm presumably above suspicion.'

'Fingerprints. That means they'll find poor Sam's.' Judith shook her head sadly.

'Unless he polished the dagger,' I replied. 'Which he might well have done. He was repairing it, and he doesn't strike me as the sort who leaves a job half-finished. He would have wanted it to be all beautiful and shiny again before he returned it to you. And he'd wrapped it back in the velvet cloth. Did I say I left that back on the snow? I'm afraid, Edwin, that you'll have to find a new one.'

'Dorothy, you didn't save the cloth?' Alan sounded upset. 'I must say—'

'Yes, but don't. I didn't throw it away, though it's a revolting object. I certainly didn't want it in my pocket. I spread it neatly on the snow pile, and as far as I know it's there still. Oh!'

'Indeed,' said Judith. 'We don't want the girls finding it. I'd best—'

From upstairs we heard wails that were growing in frequency and intensity.

'Edwin, you go out. I'll see to our budding opera star.'

He certainly did have a good pair of lungs, and a sense of dramatic timing. Judith and Edwin hurried away while I apologized to Alan. 'I know, I know. I should have taken it inside and put it away safely, and I'm sorry I forgot. But I had a lot to think about, and . . . oh, well, I might as well admit it, I'm getting old, and I can't juggle as many duties as I useta' could. Am I forgiven?'

'Are you trying to win me over by speaking quaint American?'

'Yes. Did it work?'

His kiss might have been more satisfactory if Edwin hadn't come quietly back into the room.

'Oh, Lord, I'm sorry . . . I'll—'

'Sorry to embarrass you, Edwin, but we're well past the age of consent.' I straightened my hair. 'You found the thing?'

'Yes, just in time. The girls hadn't quite worked their way up to that snow pile yet, but they were headed that way.' He gave the thing in his hand a look of distaste. 'I don't quite see why you wanted it.'

'I don't, really,' said Alan, the same expression on his face. 'But I think it ought to be kept safe, just in case. There'll be plastic bags in the kitchen, yes?' He went to find one, brought it back, and then took the repellent object off somewhere.

'What's he going to do with it?' Edwin sounded as if he didn't much care.

'What he said – put it somewhere safe. Probably on a closet shelf where the girls won't come across it by accident.'

'Right.' Edwin flumped into a chair.

'You've given up, haven't you?' It was one of my best schoolteacher voices.

He straightened a little. 'Not at all, I'm just . . . tired of it all.'

'After – what is it, three days? Edwin Montcalm, it's a wonder to me you do so well in business, if you're ready to quit after three days.'

This time he sat up all the way, and glared at me. 'Business negotiations are an entirely different matter! This is personal. It involves my family, my very way of life! I can't look at it as calmly as if it were a business deal!'

'Can't you?'

I let the silence stretch out. Around us small sounds of the house grew loud. The ticking of the clock. The creaks of an old house as it stretched and grumbled. The shrieks of the little girls as they played outside. Footsteps overhead.

'I don't know what you want of me,' said Edwin finally. He still sounded petulant, but some part of him really wanted to know.

'I want you to consider this matter with your mind, not your emotions. Yes, I know!' I held up a hand. 'Edwin, I'm more than

twice your age. I know it isn't easy to step back from a situation
and look at it dispassionately. But over the years I've learned a
trick. Pretend it's happening to someone else. A friend, or if
that's still too hard, someone you don't know. You've read
about this whole mess in the newspaper. It has nothing to do
with you. Now how do you react?'

Edwin was not, I thought, a man of strong imagination. This
might not work.

But it did. I watched his face, watched the wheels turning,
and waited.

'I'd think the chap was being a bloody fool. Sorry, but
really! It's not the end of the world, after all. And he's done
nothing – I've done nothing – to deal with the problem, except
wallowing in misery and making everyone else miserable as
well. I owe you all an apology.'

'Apology accepted,' said Alan, walking back into the room.
'Now what are you going to do about it?'

'Think like a businessman,' I urged.

'Yes. Well . . .' He paused, looking straight ahead, but not, I
thought, at the fireplace. He was seeing a balance sheet (or
something of the sort – I know nothing about business).

'You know, this is very odd,' he said at last. 'Murbles has
suggested I ought to sell. A couple of years ago he told me that
I would have a great deal of difficulty breaking the entail, so
that, in effect, I could not sell. What has changed?'

I cleared my throat. 'I don't like to bring it up, Edwin, but
. . . there's the question of your ownership of the estate. If
Ms Wilson really is your mother . . .'

'Yes, of course I've thought of that. God, I've thought of
nothing else since the wretched woman showed up! But if I'm
not in fact the heir to the estate, if I don't own it legally, then I
can't sell it, can I? What is Murbles on about?'

'I have no idea,' said Alan. 'The laws regulating the matter
are complicated, I take it?'

'Extremely. I did try to do some research, that time when I
was thinking about breaking the entail, but I gave up after a few
minutes. I don't understand the terminology at all, and when I
looked up a word, the definition was written in more legalese.
That was when I got in touch with Murbles.'

'And he discouraged you from even trying,' I said. 'Interesting. You know, the more I learn about that man, the less I like him. At least, I suppose he's kind of sweet, in his doddering way, but I don't get the feeling that he's really competent to act in your interests.'

'Nor do I, but it would seem he was looking out for me, or at least my bank balance, when he counselled against the attempt before. He stood to make a good deal of money if the legal action dragged on.'

Alan and I looked at each other. I shrugged. 'So why is he singing a different tune now?'

Edwin had lost his apathetic look. He was leaning forward, actively engaged now in the brainstorming. 'When one party in business negotiations changes his position, it always, always means something has changed in his company's situation. Perhaps they're about to come out with a new product that they expect will dominate the market. Perhaps, on the other hand, the latest reports, when they are made public, will show devastating losses. It's never easy to get to the bottom of what's going on, but a good negotiator will spot the signs and start delving.'

'Aha!' Alan and I exclaimed in chorus. 'In short,' Alan went on, 'you have to become an investigator, a detective.'

'I suppose I do. I never thought of it that way, but yes, that's what it amounts to.'

'Then I suggest,' said Alan, 'you start looking into Mr Murbles' affairs. Or his firm's. I might be able to provide some help with that; I still have a few contacts.'

'Thank you,' said Edwin with his new-found dignity, 'but I think I can manage. I do know a lot of people in the City, and they know people at the Bar. Excuse me; I need to start phoning.'

I sat back, exhausted. I did have some experience in nudging a bright but reluctant student along, but it was years since I'd practised the art. I'd forgotten just how much energy it required.

'You look like something that's been left out in the rain,' said my loving husband with less than his usual tact.

'You do know how to make a girl feel good. In fact, that's pretty much how I feel. Limp dishrag.'

'But you brought Edwin up to the post, to complete the stew of metaphors. Bravo!'

'I just went into my schoolteacher act. It wasn't as hard all those years ago. I'm getting old.'

'Or it could be that you'd never had quite such a difficult pupil. Never mind. He's on the job now.'

'Who's on the job?' Judith walked in, Joseph cooing happily in her arms.

'Your lord and master has begun to unravel the puzzle. He's busy turning over every avenue and searching every stone. And I thought I was worn out, but that adorable child has given me new strength.' I held out my arms, and Joseph chuckled and reached out for me.

I felt as if I'd just won the lottery.

TWENTY-SIX

We played, all of us. I couldn't get down on the floor with him when he decided that was what he wanted to do, but I could play silly little games like peek-a-boo, and sing to him, and put out a toy for him to grab. And we talked. I'm not sure I made any more sense than he did, but we both enjoyed the conversation immensely.

The best part was when the girls came back in. The rain was just beginning, dooming their snow play, and they were delighted that Joseph was awake. And when Edwin eventually came back, he joined in the fun. It was the first time I'd seen him truly enjoying his family, and I rejoiced.

Of course Joseph tired soon, but instead of becoming whiny and cross, he just got quieter and quieter and finally fell asleep, right there on the floor. Edwin gently picked him up. 'You sit still,' he told Judith. 'It's my turn. Girls, want to come with me?'

Judith looked from Alan to me after they left the room. 'I would say he's made some progress. Don't you agree?'

I nodded. 'He's certainly in a far better mood. I'm dying to hear what he found out. He was looking into—'

The doorbell rang. 'Drat. I'll be right back.'

She returned almost immediately, her hands full of carrier bags. 'Mrs Walker went to Tesco on her way here, bless her. We're prepared for anything now.'

'I'll help with the bags,' said Alan, getting to his feet.

'No, don't. Mrs Walker would be highly offended if someone thought she couldn't manage. I only took these so she could go back for more. I'll just put them in the kitchen, and then I want to know what's been happening.'

With Mrs Walker busy in the kitchen, the sounds of cupboard doors opening and closing and pans rattling, the house lost its forlorn air and became a normal home. Judith sat down in the drawing room and heaved a great sigh. 'My word, I hadn't realized how much I depended on her. I feel like I've dropped a thousand-pound weight.'

'Everything's humming along again,' I said, smiling. 'I can feel that, too. But you, my dear, you had to keep everything together, not just meals, but Joseph and the girls, and Edwin, too. He's . . . um . . . not exactly a rock in a crisis, is he?'

Judith laughed a little. 'No, he panics easily, poor dear. At least on the domestic front. I've always been the sensible one when it comes to the house and the children. But you should see him when it's anything to do with money. He really is a financial genius, you know. I'm sure you're wondering how he's managed to hold down a job, and quite a good job, being so dithery. Believe me, when it's business, he's . . . all business.'

'Talking about me behind my back, are you, dear?' He came into the room, Ruth on his back, Cynthia dancing ahead.

'Daddy let me help,' she boasted. 'I got to powder Joseph's little bum!'

'But *I* kissed him goodnight!' Ruth slid down. Her head turned in the direction of the kitchen. 'Mummy! Is Mrs Walker back? Can we go talk to her?'

'"*May* we". I don't see why not. Don't get underfoot, now. And no begging for biscuits! It's nearly lunchtime.'

Edwin sat, raising his eyebrows at his wife.

'Yes, dear. I was telling them what a brilliant financier you are.'

'As opposed to my flimsy performance on the home front, I suppose.' But he was smiling. 'You're quite right. I fall utterly to bits when I'm out of my sphere. But I've just put in a little work in an area where I do know what I'm doing, and you may be surprised at what I've accomplished.'

'We're not going to beg, darling. Tell us.'

'It was Dorothy and Alan who put me on the right track. We were talking about Murbles and his change of attitude. You heard him. He was suggesting that I sell the estate, which would of course mean breaking the entail. And it wasn't too long ago that he told me that would be a difficult, complicated, and time-consuming endeavour. Time being, to a lawyer, money.

'So Alan suggested I delve into Murbles' financial position.'

'Ah.' Judith's monosyllable spoke volumes.

'"Ah" indeed. There wasn't time to get full information. But I talked to a few people I know, and they all said the same. It seems that the firm of Murbles, Rattisbon, and Blair has been the subject of a good deal of rumour of late. My sources think there's been some unwise speculation, and the firm may be in trouble. Nothing certain yet, mind you, but the tremors are growing stronger, strong enough to suggest a true earthquake in the not-too-distant future. One of the chaps I talked to strongly advised my taking my business elsewhere.'

'So that's why!' I slapped my knee with satisfaction. 'He wants to stick you for a huge bill for breaking the entail – and then another huge fee when he handles the sale of the estate. Lining his pockets at your expense.'

'I think so. I certainly think so. And I think my next move is to tell him I no longer require his services.' He pulled his phone out of his pocket.

Alan held up a hand. 'Perhaps. But in your case I'd wait a bit. If the man is indeed acting in bad faith, he won't be best pleased to think you've rumbled him. And he is acting for you in a police matter. Do you think he would shrink at a little misrepresentation that would get you into real trouble with Billings et al.?'

Edwin frowned. 'At this point I'm not certain he'd shrink at selling his grandmother. What do you suggest?'

'I'd give him a bit of rope. Tell him you've thought over his advice and would like to see him tomorrow. Meanwhile ring your friends back and ask them to look into the firm's dealings in earnest. Oh, and don't use your mobile. It might be best if he didn't have that number.'

A figure appeared in the doorway, looking so exactly like a cook that she might have come from Central Casting. 'Luncheon is ready, m'lady. Only a scratch meal, but you'll have a proper dinner.'

She clumped away, and Judith rose. 'She likes us to be prompt,' she said with a smile. 'And we'll be eating in the dining room, of course.'

Mrs Walker's 'scratch lunch' consisted of a heavenly cream of carrot soup, jacket potatoes with various toppings (cheese, bacon, vegetables), and an apple concoction that I couldn't put a name to, with delectable biscuits (in the English sense – i.e. cookies) that the miracle cook had somehow whipped up in no time at all. She allowed the girls to help serve and clear away. Judith nodded approvingly. 'She's letting them do more and more. It's very good for them. Makes them feel important, and trains them up for dealing with their own households later on.'

'Is she teaching them to cook, too? I should think she could start a Cordon Bleu school.'

'She's priceless. I don't know why she's willing to come all the way out here to us, but I just count my blessings. Yes, she's teaching the girls little things like organizing a kitchen. Later, when they can work safely around the Aga, I hope she'll teach them some tricks. I can cook a little—'

'Indeed you can!'

'—but not to her standard. I pray every day that she won't leave us.'

'If you ever have to leave here,' I said softly, one eye on the girls, 'what then?'

'I don't know. We could still afford a cook, I think, though in a smaller house I wouldn't need much other help. We would all miss Sam, but I know he'd never leave here. Even before he told us what he did, I could see he was attached to the estate by bonds of iron. Now I understand why.'

'Yes. The Montcalms have lived here for several generations, but the Dunhams have belonged to this land for hundreds of years. I envy the English that, you know. We don't have that kind of feeling in America. We're too young, and too restless.'

'Yes, it was that way in Ontario, too. That's one of the reasons, actually, why I married Edwin. I wanted a more stable life, especially when we had children. I wanted them to go to one school, get to know one set of friends, before they moved on to wider fields.'

I nodded. 'Yes, that stability is good for children. Perhaps, though . . . perhaps not so good for adults, not all the time. There's a fine line between stable and stodgy. "We've always done it that way" is great, as far as it goes, but sometimes that old way isn't the best way, and sometimes people find that hard to believe.'

Alan was shaking his head. 'Consistency, thy name is not woman. You've been telling me for years how much you love and admire English traditions, how you believe the Colonies made a big mistake all those years ago when you broke away from the Mother Country.'

The girls had been patiently waiting for a break in the conversation. While I framed my reply, Cynthia said, 'Mummy can we . . . may we please be excused?'

'Off you go. But not outside, not until the rain stops. Promise.'

Cynthia sighed and Ruth made a face, but they said in unison, 'We promise.'

'Will they nap?' I asked as they ran up the stairs.

'Probably. Ruth may well fall asleep on the rug in the playroom, with her new doll, and Cynthia on the couch with a book.'

'I feel guilty for not reading to them.'

'They'll live. But you were saying, about English traditions.'

'Not just English ones. I've seen a few examples of those over the past few months, and I'm sure there are many more I haven't seen, as well as the ceremonies and rituals cherished by the Welsh and the Scots and the Irish. And I have to say that I've been deeply moved by some of what I've seen. But . . . oh, all right, you can call me a crass American if you like. But some of the ancient traditions seem to me to be just plain silly. The whole Black Rod performance at the opening of Parliament, for example. I don't know how much that costs the taxpayers every year, but I can't see that it's worth it.'

'And there are a good many Brits who agree with you,' said Edwin. 'I'm sure you know that there's a spreading anti-monarchist movement in the country. They find the ceremonial silly and wasteful, and they deplore the vast expense it takes to keep the whole show going.'

I nodded again. 'Yes, I've seen their arguments. The antis claim the royals do nothing to earn their keep, they are *not* hard-working, in fact they hardly work at all, and so on and so on. And they have a point. But I think that perhaps they forget the enormous amount of money Liz and Co. bring into the coffers by way of the tourist trade. I wonder, for example, if anyone has tallied how much hotels and restaurants and souvenir shops and the railways and the airlines profited from Harry and Meghan's wedding. Not to mention milliners and dressmakers and tailors and the rest.'

'Or,' said Judith, 'the general boost to the spirits of people all over the world, and the general atmosphere of good will. You can't measure that sort of thing, or note it down on a balance sheet, but it's real, all the same.'

'It is. And I'll stand up firmly against anyone who wants to abolish the monarchy. But I have to repeat, at the risk of being rude – well, there's a lot of silliness in these traditions, all the same. Okay, I know about the House of Commons maintaining their precious independence, and I suppose Black Rod's role in that is harmless. But somebody in Scotland having to wash the monarch's hands, which certainly don't need it, just in order to keep the estate somebody gave them eons ago?'

'Or, you are about to say,' said Edwin, 'a christening at which a useless ceremonial dagger must be present in order to ratify the child's inheritance?'

I swallowed. 'You said it. I didn't.'

'But you were about to.' His voice was not exactly cold, but not totally friendly, either.

'Okay, I was thinking it, anyway. And I do find the connection between the dagger and the inheritance to be incomprehensible. All right. I can see why the dagger is an important part of your family history. It was presented as a reward for valour. It serves as a reminder of a glorious incident in your heritage. It deserves to be kept and preserved and the story handed down. I just can't understand what it has to do with the sacrament of baptism, or with your son's inheritance.'

Silence. We could hear Mrs Walker working in the kitchen, humming snatches of hymns as she stacked plates in the dishwasher and got food out of the refrigerator in preparation for dinner.

At last Alan spoke. He spoke gently. 'My dear, we were talking the other day about Julie Andrews and how much we both admired her. I'm sure you remember her in *Camelot*.'

'Yes, but what—'

'And you must remember the ending, the melancholy song King Arthur sings to the page boy, or whoever it was.'

'Of course. "Don't let it be forgot that once there was a spot, for one brief shining moment . . .". Oh.' I felt my face grow red.

'Exactly. He wanted the story to be handed down, wanted the

future world to remember the failed, but glorious, experiment that was Camelot. Don't you think that's the case here? The king who gave Edwin's ancestor the dagger wanted Montcalm's descendants to remember his bravery. The king whose hands were washed in Scotland wanted the gracious, courteous act to be remembered. Memory works better when it's renewed periodically, and that can be assured if there's a ceremony involved.'

'As for the connection with baptism,' said Judith, 'I have a theory about that. I'm not much of a church-goer, but isn't baptism supposed to wash away one's sins, or something like that?'

'That's part of it, certainly,' I replied.

'Not that I think a baby has many sins to be washed away, mind you. But mightn't a dagger be regarded as, sort of, cutting evil away? Maybe even . . . um . . . stabbing the devil? Oh, it sounds so silly when I put it into words, but you see what I mean, don't you?'

If I hadn't been so abashed myself, I'd have smiled at Judith's embarrassment. So many people can't talk about religion, even obliquely, without discomfort. I pulled myself together. 'I do see exactly what you mean, and I think you're exactly right, and I apologize all over the place. Witness Dorothy attempting to remove foot from mouth. Next time I'll try to think before I speak.'

There was another silent moment. Everyone seemed to want to say something, but couldn't think what to say. And then Judith stood. 'I'm going to check on the girls, though I'm sure they're asleep, and then on the son and heir who's been the centre of so much consternation, bless him. Do you think, darling, that while you're making all those phone calls you could phone the police and ask when we might have the dagger back? I need to speak to the vicar.'

TWENTY-SEVEN

I finally remembered to call Jane and tell her we wouldn't be back for at least another day or two. I explained the problem briefly, and she brushed off the nuisance. 'No worry. Happy to do it.' And it was true, I knew. Jane is one of those people who will do anything for a friend and count it a privilege.

The rest of the day we played a waiting game. Wait for Edwin's friends to report back about Murbles and his firm. Wait for the police to respond about the dagger. Wait for anyone to come up with any more bright ideas.

The rain kept on raining. The girls woke up from their naps feeling somewhat fractious. I read about the rhinoceros getting his skin and the leopard his spots, but we were all tired of it by the time I closed the book. Cynthia kept getting up and looking out the window, hoping the rain had stopped, or preferably turned to snow. It hadn't. Their snow woman was only a memory and a little heap of buttons, scarf and hat.

Judith came in and started a rowdy game of Snap, a card game I didn't know. It seemed to require very little in the way of skill, only speed and a loud voice. When the girls began to quarrel over who won, we went down to tea and then sat in front of the fire for a while, the girls nursing their dolls, the adults reading or making desultory conversation. When Joseph began to get lively, Judith brought him down to be with the rest of the family and decided it might be time to start him on a little cereal. That proved to be excellent entertainment. He was curious about this new, funny-tasting stuff with the strange texture, but of course he hadn't the slightest idea what to do about a spoon.

'Years ago when my sister's children were babies, she fed them cereal from a bottle with an extra-large hole in the nipple. Of course they were bottle-fed from the start; breast-feeding hadn't yet come back into fashion.'

'My paediatrician said they'd adapt better if I used a spoon to begin. I'm afraid it's terribly messy at first.'

That was when Joseph caught the spoon with a waving fist and sent cereal flying over himself, Judith, and the kitchen counter. Mrs Walker, amazingly, was tolerant. 'They're all the same, aren't they? Can't expect old ways from young ones; he'll learn soon enough. Go on, now, you clean up the babe and yourself and I'll clean up in here and finish dinner. Cynthia, Ruth, I'll want your help.' She herded the giggling girls toward the refrigerator, and the rest of us obediently went to the drawing room for drinks.

We were a more relaxed group than we had been. The air had been cleared. Though no one said so, we all felt our ordeal was nearly at an end. The police would discover how Ms Wilson had died, and who used the dagger so ineffectually, and why. Edwin's friends would uncover any shady dealings that Murbles might have engaged in, and Edwin would find a new solicitor if it seemed advisable. (I would have fired him on the spot, but it wasn't for me to say.) Soon, now, the Montcalms would be allowed to go on with their lives.

The next morning those illusions were shattered.

We were allowed to eat our excellent breakfast in peace. Mrs Walker had given us kedgeree, a dish I had heard of but never tasted. I loved it; so did the children, to my surprise. At their age I wouldn't have touched a mixture of fish and rice, flavoured with curry – but then I had lived only in Indiana at that point, a place which, as I had shown the children a day or two ago, was very far removed from India. The Montcalm girls were far more sophisticated.

Judith continued in her efforts with Joseph and cereal. This time he got a bit more into him than distributed over the kitchen and his attendant humans, but a general clean-up was still in order. It was when Judith brought him back downstairs, all dressed for the second time, that the phone rang in the library.

Edwin answered it eagerly. 'This'll be Jack Hounslow with something he's dug up. A fast worker, is Jack.'

He came back with a frown on his face. 'It wasn't Jack. It was Inspector Billings. He's on his way, without his sergeant this time.'

'Just as well,' I put in. 'That man is useless.'

Edwin ignored the interruption. 'Says he has a few more questions.'

'Why?' I was frowning now, too. 'That sounds ominous.'

'Not necessarily.' Alan sounded soothing. 'Probably something has come up that requires an explanation. Or, since the sergeant isn't to be here as witness, the inspector may have some new information for you.'

'Then this will simply be yet another interview?'

'Almost certainly. If he were planning to charge you with anything, he'd have brought the sergeant along, or asked you to come to the station. There are ways that these things are done, you know.'

'I don't know. But you do, and I'm so happy you're here to guide me through the maze.'

Judith had put Joseph's blanket on the floor, near the fire, but not too near. 'When he starts crawling I'll have to put him in a playpen, but for now he can roll around as he likes.'

'The police are coming, darling. Do you think . . .?'

'I'll take him away if anything becomes intense, but meanwhile he's been alone too much of late. And who knows? The Law may melt at the sight of that adorable face.'

'I don't know about the Law,' I said, 'but I melt every time I see him. Is it all right if I hold him for a little?'

She smiled and handed him to me, and we had a fine conversation until the doorbell rang. I must have stiffened at the sound, because the baby made a little sound of distress, and I handed him back to his mother.

'I want to be in on this,' I said to Judith, 'if it's all right with you.'

'It's fine. Edwin will take them into the library, and I'll stay here with Joseph. If things sound like they're getting heated, I'll remove him from the battlefield.'

'Anyway I'm glad the girls are upstairs playing. They would understand too much.'

I joined the men in the library. They were being cool, but courteous. Handshakes all around. Seats taken. Tea and coffee offered; refused. I stayed in the background trying to be invisible. Alan knew I was there, of course, but he said nothing.

'Sir Edwin,' said Inspector Billings, 'I'm sorry to disturb you again, but we've had rather a disturbing conversation with your solicitor.'

I sat up, all attention.

'He came to us this morning, saying he had some information he felt he must pass along to us.'

'An odd attitude on the part of a solicitor,' Alan commented. 'When I was a working policeman, I found solicitors to be sparing of information, if not downright miserly. I don't think I can recall a single instance of a solicitor voluntarily parting with information that might be material.'

'That's rather what we thought,' said Billings, spreading his hands. 'However. He came to us, as I said, and said some remarkable things about your financial position, Sir Edwin. I wonder if you can confirm his statement.'

'I have no idea what you're talking about,' said Edwin, shaking his head as if to clear it. 'In the first place, the state of my finances is confidential information, and no one has the right to disclose the details without my permission. I can't imagine why Murbles . . . but tell me what he said.'

'He said quite a lot. For one thing, he told us that some years ago you consulted him about breaking the entail on this estate.'

'That's perfectly true, but it had nothing to do with money. It was before Joseph was born, and I was worried about what would become of the estate if we never had a son. My income was substantial, but it would not, then, have run to purchasing a home like this one, with all the land. So, if I died, my family was left out in the cold. I was concerned to assure their safety and comfort.'

'And did Mr Murbles take any further steps in the matter?'

'No. He told me that, as the law stood at that time, the procedure would take a long time and could be very expensive.'

'Yes, that agrees with what he told us.' Billings paused. 'Now, of course, with the inheritance in question for a different reason, Murbles told us he had suggested that you would be well advised to reconsider the matter.'

Edwin sighed. 'He refers to a matter which is no longer any secret to anyone, the fact that Ms Wilson claimed to be my mother and therefore I was – am – illegitimate.'

'Yes. And you might have hoped, Sir Edwin, that Ms Wilson's death would keep that secret.'

'I am not a stupid man, Inspector.' His voice was tight; the temper was rising. 'Nor have I lived on another planet for the past twenty or thirty years. I am aware of the use of DNA testing to determine ancestry. I am also aware that when someone is killed, his or her background is often the key to the murder. If I had considered murdering Ms Wilson – which I did not – I would have known that it was a futile exercise.'

'And yet you did not tell anyone about Ms Wilson's claims.'

'No, I did not proclaim to the world that I was a bastard!' The temper finally slipped the leash. 'Would you have done, Inspector? Would you have told your wife that she was married to a lie? That she had no security for the future?'

'I'm not sure I would, sir. But I wonder what you had planned to do about the question of the estate, the inheritance?'

Edwin took a deep breath, then another, and regained some measure of control. 'First, I intend to verify my parentage. That should be fairly simple. I understand that Ms Wilson's body was not badly burned. It is, I take it, possible to obtain a sample for testing?'

'That should not be a problem, sir. And if you find that she was telling the truth?'

'Then I will try to discover who is the true owner of the estate and, if at all possible, buy it from him.'

'Ah.' Billings was a master of the neutral monosyllable. 'Mr Murbles gave us to understand that you might have difficulty with that transaction.'

'Inspector, I'm getting tired of hints. If Murbles was talking about the entail, that would no longer apply if I'm not the owner of the property.'

'No, sir. He was talking about your greatly diminished income.'

'My *what*?'

'According to him, sir, some of your investments have not yielded the return that you, and he, had anticipated, and that your short-term liquidity is therefore compromised.'

'And what the bl— what would he know about that?'

'I understand that he handles your financial transactions.'

'Minor ones, yes. He pays my bills. I handle such things as stock transfers and so on myself. I remind you that I am a financier. Murbles has never had anything to do with my investments. Nor will be, from now on, have anything to do with any of my dealings. As of this moment, he is no longer my solicitor. And anything he has told you about my financial status is a flat lie. Now, if there's nothing else—'

'Just one more thing, sir. I'm still not quite clear in my mind how it was that you came to find the dagger. The "real" dagger, so to speak.'

'As you will recall,' he said, 'I did not in fact find it. It was found by my daughter and my house guest, Mrs Martin.'

The inspector looked at me. So much for my invisibility cloak.

'Yes, Mrs Martin. I wonder if you'll tell us again what happened.'

'You know about little Ruth's injury, when she and her sister were playing in the snow. I thought it would be a good idea to find what had cut Ruth so badly. Dangerous objects should not be left lying around. So Cynthia and I went to the pile of snow where Ruth had been digging. I rooted around and found the thing. I suppose I should have left it where it was, but I didn't think of that at the time. I was more concerned with putting it where it could do no more harm to anyone.'

'Understandable, though it would have been useful to see exactly where it had been. Did you find anything else in that location?'

'A good deal of dirt, clumps of grass, that sort of thing. Also a rather foul and dirty rag. Oh, and eventually, after a little more digging, a small jewel that had come loose from the hilt. An aquamarine, I think. But you'd know; you have it.'

'Yes. How did you conclude that it came from the dagger?'

Oh, for heaven's sake. I hope my sigh wasn't audible. 'Cynthia pointed out that there was a gap where a stone was missing. The prongs that should have held it had bent. We searched carefully and found it. Of course I can't prove it is the missing stone, but it's the same colour and it fits in the gap and what else could it be?'

'I agree. However, what I don't quite understand is how the dagger came to be where you found it.'

Uh-oh. I hadn't yet worked out a believable story. Alan had forbidden me to lie. 'I don't quite understand that myself,' I said in what I hoped was a convincing tone. 'I can only imagine that it was somehow turned up from underground when the drive was ploughed earlier that day. You'll remember that the snow was very heavy, and as the plough was horse-driven, it probably couldn't be steered, or regulated, or whatever the word is, as efficiently as a motor-driven one.'

Alan's eyes bored into mine. He didn't do anything as obvious as shaking his head, but I got his meaning. I was talking too much. Shut up.

I shut, but the inspector didn't let me stay shut. 'So you believe the dagger was buried somewhere, and the plough dug it up?'

'I really don't know.' I was tempted to amplify, but I was getting the message that silence was golden.

'If that was the case, it couldn't have been buried very deeply, one wouldn't think,' he persisted.

I shrugged and spread my hands.

'And why would anyone have buried it? A thief would surely have taken it away with him, or her, don't you think?'

'I haven't had much experience with thieves,' I said. I thought that was rather clever until I saw the expression on Alan's face.

'No, probably not.' He changed tack. 'I believe you and Mr Nesbitt are old friends of Sir Edwin's.'

Alan picked up on the comment. 'That's not quite correct, sir. Sir Edwin's uncle was a very great friend many years ago when we were in the Penzance police together. I met his brother, Sir Edwin's father, on only a few occasions, the last one being at the time of young Edwin's christening. I had not seen Edwin since that time until we encountered one another in London, and he asked me and my wife to stand godparents to his infant son. My wife has no connection with the family at all.'

I wondered why he was being so stuffy about it. I was soon to learn.

'I see,' said the inspector. 'So it seems that neither of you would have had any reason to hide the dagger. Sir Edwin, on the other hand . . .'

'Oh, for—!' Edwin pounded his fist on the arm of the chair. 'This has gone far enough. I don't know why you thought I might hide my own dagger, but the facts are these.' He repeated the story Sam had told us. 'I should have told you as soon as I knew, and I may say that Sam was all for going straight to you, but I was hoping to save him some unpleasantness.'

'And why would you have expected any . . . er . . . unpleasantness, sir?'

'Because Sam is a Dunham. You probably knew that, but I didn't, or at least if I did, I'd forgotten. He thought that you might think he had eyes on the estate. Which he emphatically does not.'

'That is what he told you.' Billings made the statement with no inflection whatever.

Edwin was growing angry. 'Yes, and I believe him! I've known the man all my life, man. He was more of a father to me than my own father. There's not a dishonest bone in his body!'

'And yet he took the dagger, without your knowledge, and kept it for some little time, and told you his story only when the weapon was found.'

'I object to the word weapon! Yes, I suppose it might once have been, though even that seems improbable. Now it's nothing more than a ceremonial object, an artefact, if you will.'

'An artefact sharp enough to injure your daughter rather badly.' Billings stood. 'I believe that's all, sir. For now. I will of course verify the story about the dagger with Mr Dunham. And no, before you upset yourself, I have no suspicions of the man. He has an excellent reputation locally.

'I also need to verify your statement about your finances. I could, of course, get a court order, but I would rather approach it in a less formal way. Would you object to my checking with your bank?'

'I would object very strongly. A man's bank accounts are his own business. But I have nothing to hide, and I won't stand in your way, if that's what you mean.'

Edwin was clearly furious by now. He had raised his voice; I could hear wails from the drawing room, getting louder by the second. We'd upset Joseph, and now Judith would have to take him upstairs.

'Again, I'm sorry to have disturbed you, Sir Edwin. I'll take my leave. Mr Nesbitt, Mrs Martin.'

'One moment, sir,' said Alan. 'Since the "real" dagger seems to have nothing to do with the crime, would it be possible for the Montcalms to have it back? Regardless of the inheritance question, they are very anxious to see little Joseph properly christened.'

'You're certain that the gardener's story is true, are you, sir?'

'I am. Utterly. He is not the sort of man who tells lies.'

'And you've certainly learned to identify that sort over the course of your career, I'll warrant. Furthermore, I agree with your assessment. Very well. You may come to the station and pick it up any time you want.'

'And the aquamarine,' I added.

'And the aquamarine,' he said. 'I'll ask you, Sir Edwin, to let me know if you plan to leave the area.'

'My business will require me to leave the country soon after Christmas,' he replied. 'I trust this matter will be cleared up by then, Inspector.'

'We certainly hope so, sir.' He made a little bow to us all and quietly vanished.

TWENTY-EIGHT

Awkward silences were becoming commonplace in this house. Into this one slipped Judith, quietly taking Edwin's arm. He put his hand over hers.

Alan spoke. 'This is the sort of case that used to make me tear my hair out when I was a working detective. Lots of hints of all sorts of things, but no real proof of anything at all.'

'Except that my solicitor is a damned liar! Sorry, ladies. But he is. And I don't know about anyone else, but I could use a drink.'

'I think we all could.' Alan looked at Judith. 'I don't suppose . . .?'

'I'm going to stretch a point this time, and have a small sherry. His lordship has just been fed, and he's begun the transition to solid food, anyway – and I pumped some milk for his next cereal. Let joy be unconfined.'

We repaired to the drawing room and more-or-less fell into the comfortable, squashy chairs, glasses in hand.

Alan raised his glass in a toast. 'Confusion to our enemies!'

'It would be nice,' I said, after the chorus of responses, 'to know who our enemies are.'

'Well, we know one of them,' said Alan comfortingly.

'Will you let me sack him, now that I have something concrete against him?'

'I think it would be advisable to wait a bit longer, Edwin. Perhaps you could simply phone anyone with whom he might have dealings on your behalf, and tell them to ignore him?'

'Oh, well, I have to talk to my bank manager in any case, give him permission to allow the police the freedom of my accounts. There was a time,' Edwin added bitterly, 'when a gentleman had a few privileges!'

'Longer ago than you might think,' Alan responded. 'And even when we police had to approach the nobility with kid gloves, we got there in the end. You might be surprised at how many peers of the realm found themselves, over the centuries, in a spot of trouble.'

Edwin muttered something and left the room, presumably to telephone various people involved in his financial affairs.

Judith rose with a sigh. 'I'd better see what the girls are up to. They should be awake by now, and Joseph probably is, too. If he wants to be fed, it'll have to be a bottle, I'm afraid, or cereal.' She lifted her sherry glass, looking surprised to find it empty. 'And I don't regret it a bit. This has been rather a trying afternoon.'

That English habit of understatement again! Judith was going native.

I sat and mused, my forgotten glass in my hand. Why had Murbles lied so egregiously? That he had lied, I had no doubt. Edwin would not have insisted that the police get a court order to examine his accounts, if he hadn't been positive they were in good order. Murbles wasn't terribly bright, but surely even he could see that a lie would be found out almost immediately. Why, in fact, would he blurt out something confidential to the police, who had no right to know? Something that would seem quite damaging to his client's interests.

Because, said the calm voice of reason I often ignore, *he wanted to damage his client's interests. Because the only interests he cares about are his own. Because he's hoping for Edwin to be arrested for murder.*

And how would Edwin's arrest benefit Murbles?

I sometimes think out loud, and I must have voiced that last question, because Alan smiled. 'My guess, and it's only a guess, is that Murbles would like his client out of his hair for the moment. It's possible that the man has been embezzling. Since he pays Edwin's bills, he could have created some false accounts and then paid himself. We don't know that, of course, but the police soon will, one assumes. Or it could be that he's up to some other nefarious activity, and Edwin in jail wouldn't be in as good a position to check up on him. Or, of course, if he succeeded only in scaring Edwin into breaking the entail and selling the estate, that would also bring him a good deal of business.'

'But none of it really makes sense. The man can't believe he'd really get by with it, any of it: embezzling, lying, spreading rumours. It's all just so . . . so silly, especially when he's dealing with a man like Edwin. Our host may not be the most sensible man on the planet, but he knows about money.'

'And we're forgetting what started all the trouble to begin with: poor Ms Wilson with that absurd dagger in her back.'

'Which didn't kill her.'

'Exactly.'

I sat and finished my bourbon and thought about pouring a little more. I desisted. Alcohol wouldn't help me untangle this mess, if indeed there was a way to do that. So far I hadn't been able to find even a loose end that would give me a place to start.

When Edwin came back into the room, he was accompanied by the rest of the family. The girls were rosy and energetic after their nap; Joseph was feeling sociable and active. Their presence put a brake on our discussions, and I thought that was probably a good thing. My head felt stuffed with cotton, hay and rags, as Henry Higgins claimed was the case with all women. Playing with three lively children was an ideal antidote, even if one of the children was too small to contribute much except noise, and I was too old and stiff for much except cheering them on.

While I watched Joseph roll around on the floor, though, and listened to the girls converse with their dolls, I was thinking about a dagger. A cheap dagger with paste 'jewels' that had been used, apparently, to try to kill someone.

('You know, I think he's going to crawl very early. Six months, they say, and that's about when the girls started. He's only a little over five, but look at him scooting about.'

'I think you're right. He wants to go places!')

I heard the others talk, and responded now and then, but my mind was on the puzzle. Why, why, why would someone go to all that trouble to kill – or try to kill – an inoffensive woman like Angela Wilson?

Why did I think her inoffensive? She posed a very great threat to Edwin and his family, if her story was true. With one DNA test she could destroy Edwin's claim to the estate. But killing her wouldn't change that. Maybe whoever had started the fire had hoped she would be burned so thoroughly that no usable DNA could be found. That, presumably, would erase the problem

for the Montcalms. But so consuming a fire was very unlikely
in a pub which, presumably, had smoke detectors in every room,
and probably sprinklers or some other fire-suppression system.
Of course a very old building, dry timbers . . .

'Edwin, is the Swan an old, picturesque place?' I asked,
interrupting some remark he was about to make.

'What? No, quite the reverse. It's rather ugly, in fact. A sort
of concrete box built sometime in the fifties on the site of one
that was bombed in the war. They have good beer, though. Why?'

'Just wondered.' So no dry timbers.

Mrs Walker brought in a sumptuous tea, presumably in our
honour. At least they couldn't have meals like this very often, or
Judith wouldn't have been able to keep her lovely figure.
Delectable little sandwiches, scones, what looked like shortbread,
rich, dense fruitcake – nothing was missing. I dislike fruitcake,
but even I could see that this was a prime specimen. And everything else looked and smelled scrumptious. I took the cup of tea
Judith poured for me and a sandwich when the plate was passed,
and fell back into my reverie.

Who wanted to harm Edwin, I had asked earlier, and had found
no very satisfactory answer. But now I wondered . . .

'Alan, would the police have tried to trace the dagger? The
fake one, I mean?' I spoke quietly, and the girls, concentrating
on their tea and the dolls that were sharing it, paid me no
attention.

Alan, who had probably been following my thoughts all this
time, smiled. 'Yes, of course, love. A weapon in a crime is always
traced. Or we try. It's not always easy. This one was clearly old,
though not really valuable enough to be classified as an antique.
You'd be surprised at the number of "junk" shops there are in
this country. And then there are the pawn shops. Pictures will
have gone out to every police station – the Internet has made
some kinds of searches much easier – and eventually the thing
will be traced. It all takes time.'

'And they're looking into our non-esteemed solicitor's affairs?'

'After this afternoon's disclosures, you may be sure they're
looking into them, if they weren't before. Carefully. And I'm
sure Edwin's pals in the City are chasing down all the rumours
they can. But again, it takes time. And you know, just confirming

that Murbles is in deep money trouble, if he is, won't quite explain why he seems to have turned traitor to Edwin. If he hopes to bail himself out with money from handling transactions like the entail business and then the sale of the estate, he'd want to keep on Edwin's good side. And if he's been robbing him blind, that's an even better reason to stay on good terms with him. Now all he's done is to alienate him completely and ensure a searching investigation.'

'Hmph! Whatever he's done, he's one of the bad guys in my book, and I hope he's done something he can be nailed for.'

My voice had risen a little, and Alan glanced over at the girls and then looked at me reprovingly.

'Oh, I know, not a nice sentiment, and all that.' I moderated my tone. 'All right, I'll be quiet about it. But really, the man is a menace. I don't know anyone who's made me so cross, at least not for ages.'

We finished our tea, and the girls wanted me to read to them, but I wasn't in the mood. Kipling was all very well, but I didn't want to be soothed just now. I wanted action. Judith saw me struggling with what to say, and told her daughters that I wasn't feeling very well. 'Perhaps after dinner,' she said. 'Run away now and play with your lovely dolls.'

Cynthia looked at me with a sharp eye, not believing a word of it, but she and Ruth went away as bidden. Judith took Joseph to the kitchen for another messy session with cereal, and Edwin gave us a grim smile.

'I have some quite interesting news,' he said. 'Murbles is very nearly bankrupt.'

'Well, well, well,' said Alan softly. 'Not entirely unexpected, but still . . .'

'Has he been stealing from you?' That, to me, was the critical question.

'Not that I can determine. You understand, it's all quite complicated. I'm going to have to call in an auditor to look at all my holdings. But my bank accounts, at least, are intact.'

I let out a gusty sigh. 'So that worry, at least, is set aside for the moment.'

'Yes,' said Alan. 'And of course it explains now why he was so anxious to persuade you to sell the estate.'

I nodded. 'His fees. But he certainly went about it the wrong way. How could he possibly think that you, a finance professional, would believe you were broke?'

'I imagine, Dorothy, that he hoped the distress and confusion of recent events would cloud Edwin's reasoning faculties somewhat.'

'And it almost worked,' said Edwin. His smile became warm. 'If it hadn't been for you propping me up, Dorothy, I might have fallen apart completely.'

I muttered something, and Alan went on. 'And had you done that, the plan, while you weren't thinking too clearly, would have been to make the fiction a reality.'

'You mean, embezzle for real?' I put in.

'Just that,' said Edwin. 'I'll wager you're right, Alan. He certainly knows how to do it. According to my source, he's been pilfering from his firm for years, in a relatively small way. The other two partners let him get by with it because they didn't want the reputation of the firm sullied, but now they've called in the police. He'll probably be arrested tomorrow, if not tonight.'

'And none too soon!' I said with heat. 'But I still think his chief liability is stupidity. This whole plot is simply cockeyed. And it's getting to me – paths that lead nowhere, ideas that end up meaning nothing – I'm going quietly out of my mind!'

'And not so quietly,' Alan murmured, as Judith came back into the room.

'We're all a bit out of sorts, I think,' she said in a soothing voice. 'And I just had a lovely idea. Do either of you know Maltings?'

I looked blank. 'It sounds sort of familiar, but . . . does it have something to do with making whisky? Or beer?'

Alan grinned, and Judith laughed out loud. 'Sorry. You didn't hear the capital letter. The Maltings, I should have said. Yes, Dorothy, malting is a part of the brewing or distilling process, and maltings – small m – were big shed-like places where the grain used to be malted. Nowadays they do it differently, and most of the old malt houses have been put to other uses. The local one, Snape Maltings, has been made into a concert hall. I don't know if you're interested in music, but Benjamin Britten—'

'Oh, of course! Aldeburgh, the music festival he founded. I remember hearing that it was at a place called The Maltings, only I didn't know what that meant, or where it was. But the festival is in summer, isn't it? I've wanted for years to go, but the timing was never right.'

'Oh, there are things going on all year round. And the point is, right now they're doing the *Nutcracker*, for Christmas, you know. And if I'm right, there's a matinée tomorrow. If we can get tickets, how would you like to go? The girls would love it, and I can get a friend to look after my little ball and chain for a couple of hours. I think it might be just the thing to cheer us all up.'

'Just the thought of it cheers me up! I've always loved Tchaikovsky, and there's nothing quite as Christmassy as *Nutcracker*. Let's do it!'

TWENTY-NINE

The girls were ecstatic about *Nutcracker*. Cynthia had reached the ballet-mad stage that strikes most little girls eventually, and Ruth followed in big sister's train. My mind was eased enough by the prospect of a respite that I was able to help Judith with some Christmas preparations, after she had phoned to secure tickets to the ballet and a sitter for Joseph. The men closeted themselves in the library and did whatever men do when they can get away from their womenfolk. They may have talked about the murder – or about cabbages and kings, so far as I knew. Mrs Walker whiled away the afternoon by making dozens of mince pies and then prepared a light supper before taking herself home. After that huge tea, none of us needed a lot to eat, and the girls were too excited to be hungry, anyway.

Just after we finished supper, and the girls had helped clear away (under protest; they felt much too festive to take to everyday chores), one of Inspector Billings' minions delivered the dagger. He didn't even come in; Edwin took it from him at the door and laid it on the hall table. I happened to be going through the hall at the time, and saw him put it carelessly aside.

I sighed. What an anti-climax. That frivolous object had been the centre of his world a few days ago, the focus of all our anxieties. Now he didn't spare it a thought. I popped back into the kitchen where Judith was feeding Joseph and supervising the girls, and told her the dagger was back. She wasn't very interested, either.

'Um . . . shall I put it away for you? Only I don't know where it goes.'

'No, don't bother. I'll deal with it later.'

I counted to ten. 'Then I'll read to the girls, shall I?'

'Oh, do. They'll never get to sleep without a cool-down.'

So we went up to the nursery, and I rummaged in their bookcase and found, against all odds, a copy of a picture book called *A Very Young Dancer*. The pictures are beautiful photographs by

Jill Krementz of a girl named Stephanie and the exciting true story of her dancing the starring child's role in a New York City Ballet production of *Nutcracker*. I knew the book in America, where it was published over forty years ago, and I couldn't imagine what it was doing at Dunham Manor, but I knew the girls would love it – and they did. I sat on a chair in their bedroom and let them sit on the floor for a little while, the better to see the pictures, but when Ruth's eyelids began to droop, I made both girls get into their beds. I read and read more and more slowly, in the most soothing voice I could muster, with fewer displays of the pictures, until they slept. Was there ever, I wondered, a time when I could sleep so soundly, so utterly relaxed?

Probably when I was their age, I thought with a sigh, and went down to the drawing room for some sleep-inducement of an adult variety.

We both slept late in the morning. I don't know what Alan's excuse was, but I knew that I, cravenly, simply didn't want to face the day. We were to leave for Maltings soon after lunch, but the fewer hours of morning I had to face, the happier I'd be.

It wasn't that I expected anything spectacularly awful to happen. I was sure it would just be another dreary morning of worrying and wondering and speculating about what might have happened, what was going to happen. Who killed that poor woman? Was she really his mother? If so, what would happen about the estate? What would happen to Murbles?

And a hundred other questions for which I had no answers.

I turned over and pulled the covers over my head.

My intentions were doomed, of course. No matter how hard I tried to stay asleep, I couldn't ignore the urgent bathroom call. And once I was out of bed, there seemed no point in climbing back in to seek sleep again. I knew it wouldn't come. So, resentfully, I showered and dressed, and by that time Alan was awake (and also grumbling), so we went down to breakfast together. Though by this time it was almost lunch.

To my surprise, the rest of the household was bright-eyed and bushy-tailed. Certainly the weather was as dreary as I had feared, but Mrs Walker was singing as she worked in the kitchen – rather

tunelessly, but cheerfully. She did not, by either word or implica-
tion, chide us for our tardiness, but simply set coffee before us
at the kitchen table, and waited for us to ingest some of the
life-giving caffeine before asking what we'd like to eat.

While we were crumbling toast, Edwin came in, exuding
affable goodwill. 'Good morning! Beautiful morning.'

I glanced at the grey clouds looming over the outbuildings.

'Oh, I know, but they say it isn't actually going to rain. Or
snow.' He laughed.

I drank more coffee.

'You see,' he said, pulling out a chair, 'I've had calls this
morning from a number of people. First, my broker reassured
me that all my accounts are perfectly in order, the investments
doing nicely. That's what I was told yesterday, but it's nice to
have it confirmed. Secondly, I've had reports from a friend and
from our beloved Inspector Billings. Murbles is under arrest.
He's in the local lock-up for now, until some further evidence
can be garnered and a trial date set.'

'Hmph.' With Kipling's stories fresh in my mind, I realized I
was in a camelious mood. 'I'd think, if your friends knew about
his peculations, they might have warned you against continuing
to do business with them.'

'They may have tried, but I'm not good at picking up hints.
My family has been doing business with the firm for generations.
One doesn't easily flout that sort of tradition. Although it's true
that Murbles – the current Murbles – has been with them only
a few years. I believe he's some sort of cousin of the original
partner, the direct line having died out. At any rate I'm out from
under now, though I'm casting about for someone else to handle
my affairs.'

I thought they could certainly do with some competent
handling, but I held my peace.

'And finally, the vicar has agreed to baptize Joseph right after
Christmas. We'll have the christening party later, when . . .' He
faltered for a moment. 'When the question of my birth is settled,
and the death of my . . . of Ms Wilson is explained. So if you
can stay until then and stand godparents, Judith and I will be
most grateful.'

'Certainly we will serve as Joseph's godparents,' said Alan

heartily, 'but I'm afraid we can't stay on for the occasion. We'd best go home and come back.'

'Christmas, you know,' I murmured. This would be the time to say how lovely the visit had been and how much we regretted the necessity of going home. I couldn't quite bring myself to speak the words.

Edwin took pity on me. 'I know it hasn't been the happiest of visits, and I'm truly sorry. If you can bear to return once more, after the christening, we'd all love to have you here for the party, but we'll understand if you only want to see the back of the place.'

'We'll see, shall we,' said Alan, and changed the subject. 'When do we need to leave for The Maltings?'

So we went to the ballet, which was superbly done, and went back to Dunham Manor, to watch the girls trying to accomplish pliés and arabesques and other ballet moves at which they were, of course, hopeless. They could barely be coerced into sitting down for dinner, which we ate to the accompaniment of pleas for ballet lessons, preferably beginning tomorrow.

After dinner they needed some calming down before they could possibly sleep, so I went up with them. They wanted me to finish the book about ballet that I'd begun, but I thought that topic was too exciting for them just now and firmly said that we would tell stories, instead. 'I'll begin. I used to tell stories to my schoolchildren, and sometimes they would help. One of their favourites was about a pig. I read that story to them, but I don't have the book here, so I'll tell you about him. He was named Freddy.'

'Silly name for a pig!' Ruth was scornful. 'Sounds like a little boy.'

'Oh, but Freddy was no ordinary pig. He could talk, and read and write – sort of. And when there was some trouble at the farm where he lived, he became a detective.'

'A detective! A pig?' That was Cynthia.

'Yes, indeed. Any farmer will tell you that pigs are very intelligent, the smartest animal on the farm. Well, Freddy was extra-smart, but of course he was also lazy. He was a pig, after all.' And I launched into what I could remember of the wonderful book by Walter Brooks. When my memory failed me I asked the children to help decide what happened next.

'I know! I know!' Ruth was excited, which was exactly the opposite of the effect I had hoped to produce. Oh, dear.

'Yes, love, what do you think happened?' I asked in the quietest, calmest voice I could muster.

'Freddy heard two men talking. They were talking about a tail. One of the men said they were going to take it. Freddy was afraid it was his tail they wanted. They were going to build some dolls' houses, but they had to get permission to plant flowers for the houses.'

'But that doesn't have anything to do with the story,' Cynthia objected.

'I don't care! It's what I heard. There really were two men, and one of them was that nasty man who made Daddy shout, the one who wants to buy our house. I told you before, but you never believe me!' She dissolved in the sobs of an overtired child.

'Oh, Ruthie, it's okay. Don't cry. I believe you, I really do.' Cynthia jumped out of bed to hug her sister. 'Don't cry. I have a chocolate biscuit.' She gave me a sideways glance as she produced her illicit treasure from a hidden stash in a small drawer. 'Here. It's all for you. Don't cry!'

She managed to stem the tide, and when she had crawled into bed with Ruth I tucked them both in and kissed them goodnight, and went off shaking my head over my well-meant attempts. Soothe the girls, right! I might as well have set off firecrackers in their room. Just as well that I was leaving tomorrow, and Judith could take over mothering duties. I hadn't the necessary experience.

We didn't talk much on the way home next day. The weather continued gloomy; the rain started just as we neared London, the worst part of the journey. Alan concentrated on getting us through the frantic Christmas traffic, and I ignored his sometimes pungent comments about the other drivers. Not until he had negotiated the last roundabout and we were on the home stretch did I open my mouth.

'Not very satisfactory,' I said cautiously.

'No.'

'No completion. No "closure" as they say.'

'No.'

He said no more, and I shut up. He'd talk about it when he was ready.

Our pets greeted us according to their temperaments. Watson nearly turned himself inside out in his frenzied rapture, trying to lick every part of both of us at once, and shouting his joy to the skies. The cats let us know that we were in disgrace, having abandoned them to the cold world, and they didn't intend to let us forget our sins any time soon.

Meanwhile Christmas was ahead, with very little time, now, to be ready for it.

Christmas was as joyful, and as hectic, as it always is. Whatever I missed out on by not having children, I recouped in full with Alan's grandchildren. On Christmas Day they were all with us, active and noisy and delightful, and the next day Nigel and Inga brought their two, and Jane came over with Walter and Sue and their baby, little Bill, and we had it all over again, presents and too much food and too much excitement for the children, who nevertheless enjoyed it thoroughly.

I slept badly that night, a combination of indigestion and exhaustion. Getting up for the third time in the night, I tried to hold onto the rags of my dream, the better to get back to sleep again, but it fled. It hadn't, I thought vaguely, been an especially pleasant dream anyway. Something about dollhouses and a frightened pig.

When I finally staggered out of bed in the morning, though, the dream came back. Pigs. Dollhouses. What could they have to do with each other?

'Alan,' I asked after my second cup of coffee, 'what do you call the places where pigs live on a farm?'

'Pigsties. What do you call them?'

'The same. I thought . . . you so often have different words for things, different from American English, I mean. Sties wouldn't ever be called dollhouses, would they? Or dolls' houses?'

'Not that I've ever heard, though heaven knows what the Irish might call them. Or the Welsh, or the Scots.'

'You're a linguistic snob, Alan Nesbitt. I've always suspected it. I could ask Nigel what the Welsh call them, I suppose, though he's never actually lived in Wales.' Nigel was the son of a Welsh father and an English mother, but his father had never played much of a role in his life.

'What put this bee in your bonnet, anyway? Too much Christmas pudding?'

'No, it was something Ruth said, the night before we left. I was telling them a story about Freddy the pig, and Ruth started talking about a conversation she said she overheard, about pigs' tails and dolls' houses and planting flowers. It was a mishmash of nonsense, but she insisted she'd heard it, and broke down in tears when Cynthia didn't believe her.'

'Hmm. Ruth can be a handful, but she's a truthful child, as a rule.'

'Yes. I suppose that's why her story lodged in my mind. I had a dream about it last night. My brain trying to make sense of it?'

'Where did she hear all this?'

'She didn't say. Oh, but she did say – I forgot – she did say that one of the men – there were two men talking – one of them was the man who wanted to buy the house. "Mr Smith", I suppose. You remember she'd overheard him earlier, when he came to the house.'

'Dorothy, this could be important. Tell me again what she said, in exactly her words, if you can remember.'

'Alan, it was BC! Before Christmas! My memory banks are all but wiped out, but I'll do the best I can. I know it was all mixed up with the Freddy story. The men were talking about a tail, she said, and she mixed that up with Freddy and thought it was a pig's tail. Someone was going to take it. Then there was something about dolls' houses, and planting flowers or something. Oh, getting permission to plant the flowers, that was it.'

'Take a tail. Dolls' houses. Permission to plant.'

I repeated it in my mind and got an idea. 'Alan, could it have been permission to plan? Or planning permission?'

'Certainly it could! And her dolls' houses could have been small houses. That sounds alike. But taking a tail?'

'Take a tail. A tail. Alan, an entail!'

'I think you've got it, love! "Mr Smith" was talking to someone about his plans to break the entail, purchase the house – no, the estate – "take" – and turn it into small houses if he could get planning permission!'

'What if we run that by Ruth? We're going there next week anyway. Will she have forgotten by then?'

'Children that age have pretty good memories. Their minds aren't cluttered with years of garbage like ours.'

'Right. So we'll wait till then. But meanwhile I'm going to call Judith and see if she has any idea when Ruth might have heard what she did. It had to be somewhere besides the house.'

'I agree. And you might ask Judith if she has any idea who the second man was. Because that's critical!'

Judith, deep in preparations for the christening, had no idea where Ruth might have overheard the conversation. 'She'll be able to tell you, of course. Meanwhile, we've had some news. I was going to wait to tell you after the christening. You see, in a way it isn't going to matter. I mean, as religious rite, of course it matters. But there is no question now of inheritance. We got the results of the DNA testing, and Ms Wilson was quite definitely Edwin's mother. So . . .'

'Oh, *dear*! Is he really despondent about it?'

'Not as much as I would have thought. I think he knew it was coming. So we're going to have our party as originally planned. We won't mention the skeleton in the closet to our guests. And after the party Edwin's going to get into the legal question and try to find out who really owns the estate, and if he can perhaps buy it. I care about that for the children's sake more than my own. I do love this house, but I could be happy almost anywhere with my family. The children would really miss the freedom they have here, living in a safe place, with lots of room to run and play and . . . and build snowmen, and—' Her voice broke.

'They're young and resilient. They'll adapt. And maybe it won't be necessary, if Edwin can work out the legal tangle. Look, we'll be there in just a few days; we can talk then.'

THIRTY

The bombshell came the day before we were to return to Dunham Manor. Alan got a call from Inspector Billings, and put it on speakerphone for me to hear.

'There has been a development, Mr Nesbitt, and I thought you would be interested. It's all due to excellent work by Sergeant Lewis, so I'll let him tell you.'

Goodness, was I about to learn that the man could actually talk?

His voice was actually quite pleasant. 'Good morning, Mr Nesbitt.'

'Good morning, Sergeant. If you don't mind, I'd like my wife to hear this, as well.'

'Certainly, sir. Good morning, Mrs Martin.' He cleared his throat. 'I should explain that I was assigned to do some investigating in Grantham, especially at the Swan. We'd asked all the usual questions, so I thought it might be worth an evening of talking to the regulars over a pint or two. I'm not married,' he added, in what might not have been a non sequitur. 'I . . . well, I've not been on the force all that long, so they – the regulars, I mean – don't think of me first as a policeman, but just as somebody who stands them a round now and then when I'm in funds.'

'And someone more or less negligible,' put in Billings. He must be on speakerphone, too. 'That wet-behind-the ears look is very valuable at times. Sorry, Jon.'

Sergeant Lewis cleared his throat. 'Er . . . yes. So I went in, got my beer, threw a dart or two, and waited. Sure enough, the talk got round to poor Ms Wilson. I got let in for some ribbing because we haven't solved the crime, so I blustered a bit. How did they expect us to solve it when nobody would talk to us, that sort of thing. Hoping someone would take the bait, you know. And sure enough, one of the darts players said he'd been sitting out that night, had a sprained wrist or something.'

'What night?' asked Alan, intently.

'The night she died.' The sergeant paused for further questions and then went ahead. 'He said he saw her, sitting alone, eating her bangers and mash and nursing a half.'

'He's sure it was Ms Wilson? She wasn't an especially notice-able person, as I understand it. Sorry to keep interrupting.'

'He's quite sure, because he'd seen her before. She'd stayed at the Swan once before, he said. We knew that, of course. It was the first time she visited Sir Edwin. Actually, the only time. And she'd signed for her meal, and Ron – that's the chap who talked to me – had happened to see the chit when the waiter brought it up to the bar. So he knew who she was. Not to mention that he knew almost everyone else in the place, so she stood out as a stranger, or not a local, anyway.'

'So he saw her eating,' prompted Alan.

'Yes, and then he saw a man come and sit down with her.'

We both held our breath.

'It wasn't the usual pick-up, though, Ron said. For one thing, the woman wasn't that sort. For another, neither was the man. Very respectable he looked, Ron said. Looked like he just wanted a place to eat his fish and chips, and there wasn't an empty table. He hardly said a word to Ms Wilson, but he was nervous. Or clumsy. Kept dropping things, finally knocked over the lady's beer.

'Now from here on it's guesswork, because Ron wasn't close enough to hear what the man said. The place was pretty noisy, probably. But the man stood up, said something to Ms Wilson, and took her glass. She shook her head and said something, but the man went to the bar and got her another half.

'And this is the best bit. Ron swears he saw the man put something in her beer.'

Alan was on it like a trout taking a fly. 'Did anyone else see this?' he asked.

'Ron doesn't see how they could. Ms Wilson didn't, for sure. She was sitting with her back to the bar. And what made Ron notice, the man was sneaky about it. Reached in his pocket and took something out, and then looked around, cautious-like, before he dropped it in the glass.'

'And how did Ron see it, if the man was so careful not to be seen?'

'Have you ever been in the Swan, sir?'

'No.'

'The darts board is off in an alcove, near the bar. Ron was sitting facing the board, so he could watch, but because he was in a corner he could see most of the room from there. Couldn't see the far end of the bar very well, when customers were crowded round, but he had a perfect view of the near end. He said he wouldn't have noticed especially if the man hadn't been so furtive about it.'

'Hoist with his own petard,' I remarked. 'And does anyone know what was in the beer?'

'As it happens, we do,' said Billings. 'After we heard Lewis's report we put pressure on the forensics people to speed up the autopsy. Early this morning we had the result. Ms Wilson died of smoke inhalation, as suspected. As we also knew, the dagger wound was negligible. It was deflected by a rib and touched nothing vital. She would have had a pretty fierce backache, had she lived, but that's all. The stomach contents, however, were revelatory. She'd taken a fairly potent dose of chloral hydrate.'

'Good heavens! A Mickey Finn!' I exclaimed.

Alan looked amused. 'And where did a respectable lady like you learn about Mickey Finns?'

'You know perfectly well. I read mysteries. Long before other drugs found their way into the hands of fictional villains, they would slip some chloral hydrate into someone's drink, and combined with the alcohol, the drug put the victim out of business for long enough to do what they wanted. It isn't usually fatal, though, is it, inspector?'

'Not unless taken at a very high dosage – which would be unlikely, considering its bitter taste. However, beer is bitter enough on its own to disguise the taste somewhat.'

'So.' I looked into the distance, seeing a scene in the bedroom at the pub. 'So he dumps some of the stuff into her beer. She drinks it and trots off to bed, where she falls heavily asleep, heavily enough that she doesn't hear X coming in and stabbing her in the back. Wouldn't that have waked her, though?'

'Perhaps, but she would have been disoriented and would probably have fallen asleep again immediately.'

I shuddered. 'And then . . . and then what? Did he start the fire to disguise the murder?'

'We thought that at first,' said Billings, 'and I don't mind telling you I shuddered at the thought. A fire in an inn, where people were sleeping? That argued a man with no conscience whatever.'

'There are not, God be thanked, many of those about,' said Alan, 'even among the criminal fraternity. And this matter has borne, all along, the marks of the amateur.'

'Besides,' I went on, 'we've thought all along that the whole point of the dagger was to point the finger at Edwin. And even that was done amateurishly, with a weapon that bore only a superficial resemblance to the real one. So the fire . . .?'

'The arson team has been at work, of course,' said Billings, 'and they have concluded that the fire was almost certainly started accidentally. They say it started in the waste-paper basket, where somebody dropped a cigarette. The filters don't burn well, you know. They tend to melt, instead, and unless a fire is very hot, they may remain. In this case, as the fire was contained very soon, the filter was found.'

'I meant to ask about that. Sprinkler system, I assume?'

'Indeed. And of course a smoke alarm. We think, though we can't prove, that our villain – X is as good as any term, I suppose – either stayed in the room for some reason, or returned to take care of some real or imagined mistake, something left behind, perhaps, and lit a cigarette to calm his nerves. Then he saw the smoke alarm and panicked, dropped the cigarette, and fled.'

'Leaving his victim, alone and helpless.' Alan's voice was very dry indeed.

'You must remember that he thought she was dead, or dying.'

'I take it,' said Alan, clearing his throat, 'that you have no clue to the identity of X. Your informant didn't recognize him?'

'Unfortunately, no. Said he'd never seen him before. However, we do in fact have an idea. And that's actually why we've called. You have a reputation, sir, for being able to handle delicate situations with a minimum of repercussions. I hope you can help us with this one. Our suspect – I'd rather not mention names over the telephone – has a certain amount of influence. It's necessary that we be very sure of our ground before we accuse him.'

'Inspector Billings,' I said hotly, 'you're not saying you suspect Sir Edwin again!'

'No, Mrs Martin, I am not, but I'd really rather wait and talk to you both in person. You'll be at the christening tomorrow, of course?'

'We will.'

After Alan ended the call, I slapped my forehead. 'We should have told him about what Ruth overheard!'

But Alan shook his head. 'Much too tenuous as yet. Let's wait and hear what the child has to say about our reconstruction. We could be all wet.'

'But you don't think we are.'

Alan just shook his head.

The next day, two days into the New Year, was one of those blindingly sunny winter days that looks warm until you get out in it. The air was, in fact, bitingly cold. There had been fog in the night and when the temperature plummeted it was transformed into hoar frost, covering every bare twig, every blade of sere winter grass, every die-hard weed with diamonds. It was gorgeous, and my spirits rose.

We got to Dunham Manor well ahead of the time for the ceremony. Judith and all her household help were bustling about with final arrangements. The cake, on display in the drawing room, was truly magnificent. 'And make sure you greet the man of the hour,' said Edwin proudly, leading me to the library. There, ensconced in a large playpen, Joseph was happily crawling around the perimeter. True, as yet he could crawl only backwards, but that didn't seem to bother him.

'Goodness, and it's only been – what – three weeks since we saw him?'

'He's clever, isn't he?' Cynthia was clearly as proud of him as was his father. 'Ruthie couldn't crawl until she was *much* older.'

Ruthie, perhaps fortunately, wasn't around to dispute that titbit of information. Where, in fact, was she? I would have expected her to be in the thick of the action.

Deciding that my presence was not essential to the preparations, that I was indeed in the way, I went upstairs. And there, in the playroom, I found Ruth. She was sitting on the floor with the doll we'd given her, and she was in a snit.

'Hello, Ruth,' I said cautiously.

She muttered something. I sat down and began talking to her doll. 'You're looking very pretty today, Belinda. Is that a new dress?'

'Sarah,' said Ruth, glowering at the floor.

'Oh, Sarah, I'm so sorry. I forgot your name. I used to have a doll very much like you, and I named her Belinda. That's how I came to make the mistake. Did Ruth give you a new dress for the party today?'

'Mummy says she can't go.' Ruth at last addressed me. 'It's not fair!'

I honestly couldn't understand why Judith had issued that order. Perhaps if the ceremony had been in the church . . . but it was to be held here, because of the dagger. However, I had to uphold parental authority. 'Oh, dear, what a shame. But there'll be a terrible crush of people. I expect Sarah would enjoy the party more if she looked on from the hallway. There's a very good view between the railings, isn't there?'

'Only of the front hall. The christening's in the drawing room.'

'But all the people will be coming in through the front door. She can see them all if she sits right by the stairway.'

'I have to go downstairs. There wouldn't be anybody to look after her.'

'Hmm. Well, how would this be? I could take her downstairs until it's time for me to do my thing at the christening, and then I could hand her to you. Mummy wouldn't mind that, I'm sure.' Mummy would, at least, not make a fuss in the middle of the ceremony, and I could take my scolding later.

Ruth's scowl changed to a brilliant smile. 'We'll fool Mummy, won't we? She'll be really cross.' She was delighted at the prospect.

'Oh, I don't think she'll mind very much. Now, we have some time before we both have to go downstairs, and there's something I want to talk to you about.'

She was ready to cooperate with anyone who was conspiring with her. She took Sarah onto her lap, smoothed her dress, and beamed at me.

'It's like this, Ruth. Do you remember that time you heard the two men talking? About a tail, and dolls' houses?'

'I *did* hear them!'

'I know you did, and I'd like to know where you were when you heard them. It wasn't here at home, was it?'

'Of course not! I was with Mummy in Grantham. We were Christmas shopping, and Cynthi couldn't come because we were buying some of her presents.'

'I see. Very sensible. So you were in a shop?'

'No, we'd finished shopping, and I was tired, so we went to a café where Mummy could get coffee and I could have cocoa. With whipped cream on top!'

'Yum! I like it that way, too. Nice and warm on a cold day.'

'And then Mummy went to the counter to get us some biscuits, and that's when I heard the men. They were sitting pretty close to us, so I could hear them, even though they weren't talking very loud.'

'Oh, you have a wonderful memory! Now I want to tell you what I think they said, and you tell me if my memory is any good. Did they say something about an entail? Breaking an entail, maybe? Could that have been the "tail" you heard?'

'Maybe.' She looked at the floor. I thought she was seeing the café and the two men. 'There was something before "tail" every time they said it, and they said it a lot. And I thought I heard "take" but maybe it was "break". There were lots of other people talking, too.'

'Yes, of course, and it's always hard to hear when there's a lot of noise. And when they were talking about "planting", could that have been "planning"? They sound very much alike.'

'Maybe. I don't know. Let's go downstairs now. Sarah wants to see what's happening.'

Well, she hadn't actually rejected the interpretation. I could pursue the issue later, but I wasn't sure I wanted to. If I started putting ideas in her head, she'd be compromised as a witness – if it ever came to that.

I rejoined Alan, who glanced at the doll in my arms, but made no comment. Ruth stayed glued to my side until we assembled in the drawing room around the silver punch bowl that was to serve as a font. Then Alan and I took our places as godparents and Ruth went to stand with the rest of her family, Sarah clutched firmly in her arms. Judith gave me a questioning look, I raised my eyes to the ceiling, and she shrugged.

The baptism went off without a hitch, as they almost always do. Nobody dropped the baby, nobody made the wrong responses, and Joseph, the star of the show, slept through the whole thing. Edwin held the dagger in prominent display as Alan and I vowed on Joseph's behalf to renounce the devil and all his works, the vain pomp and glory of the world, and all the rest, and on our own part to make sure he learned the Creed and the Lord's Prayer and the Ten Commandments. Then the vicar poured the water on his head, not waking him even then, there were a few prayers, and the ceremony was over. No mention was made about questions of inheritance. That would come later, but for now, nothing was allowed to cloud the occasion.

We were escorted to the head of the buffet line, along with the vicar and the little girls. As we filled our plates, I managed to give Alan the gist of my conversation with Ruth. He sighed. 'Better than nothing.'

'Yes. But not much.'

And then Ruth needed some help keeping the cake on her plate, and we sat down wherever we could find chairs, and there was no more opportunity to talk.

THIRTY-ONE

As things were winding down, I took the opportunity to slip into the kitchen. I didn't intend to stay and get in the way, but I wanted to congratulate Mrs Walker on her superb party food and especially the gorgeous cake, a triumph of marzipan trellis-work and pulled-sugar roses.

She was taking the opportunity to sit and rest for a bit. Her work was nearly done. The clean-up would be handled by a crew of dailies, and supper, for anyone who wanted it, would consist of the plethora of leftovers.

She greeted me with weary courtesy. 'Was there something, Mrs Martin?' She started to push her chair back.

'No, please don't get up. I just wanted to compliment you on your splendid work. Everything was wonderful, but that cake! I've never seen anything so beautiful, truly. Not to mention that it even tasted good!'

She laughed at that. 'I'm not one to sacrifice taste to beauty. You can have both, if you've a mind to.' There was a rap at the kitchen door. 'Drat! Who'd that be, now, coming here just when there's only the washing-up left to do?'

'I'll get it. You're tired, and every right to be.'

I opened the door to Inspector Billings.

'I didn't want to interrupt the festivities,' he explained. 'I was hoping the guests might be gone, but when I saw cars in the drive, I thought I'd come in the back way.'

'You know,' I said, gesturing him in, 'Americans think English police are wonderful, and we're right. Even if I didn't love my husband, I'd marvel at the courtesy of the force. I can't imagine that most American cops would bother about using the back door so as to be less conspicuous.'

'Yes, well.' He was embarrassed by the compliment. Also typical.

'Almost everyone's gone,' I went on, 'but there are always a few who take half an hour to say thank-you-for-a-lovely-party. Shall I go get Alan and bring him in here?'

'I don't want to interfere with Mrs Walker and her minions. Would there perhaps be a room tucked away somewhere, a place where we wouldn't be in the way?'

'And where you could be private,' said Mrs Walker, not fooled for a moment. 'If you go up the back stairs, there's a spare bedroom, first door on the right. It's never used, and you'd be comfortable and quiet there.'

'Right. You'll be up shortly with your husband, Mrs Martin?'

'As soon as I can get him away without making a fuss.'

Alan and I eased away, and quietly climbed the back stairs, feeling like conspirators. We found Billings easily, in a room that one could easily see was never occupied. It was spotlessly clean, and that was part of the air of desolation. No room that people live in is ever quite free of dust, or lint, or the tiny bits of almost invisible detritus that human beings leave behind them. This attractive room was totally empty, sterile. I shivered as I went in.

'Cold, love?'

'Not that way.'

We sat.

'There have been further developments since I spoke to you yesterday,' said the inspector, 'and I may not need your help, after all. I know now, almost to a certainty, who our murderer is.'

If he was waiting for us to guess, he was disappointed. We simply waited.

'Sergeant Lewis has been at work diligently, and he has managed to trace the dagger. Not the "real" one, but the one used in the crime.'

'That young man has a career ahead of him,' Alan commented.

'Indeed. I've recommended him for promotion, and I expect he'll finish up with the Met. He's invaluable to me, and I'll hate to lose him, but I don't want to stand in his way.'

He'll need to learn to talk, I thought, but didn't say. 'So he traced the dagger. And?'

'It was purchased at an antiques shop in Broadway, by a man who paid cash and gave a false name and address. However, Lewis had the forethought, when he went to interview the proprietor, to take along photos of several of the people involved in the matter.'

'And the man identified "John Smith",' I said, unable to keep mum.

'No.' Billings let the pause draw out. 'He identified William Murbles.'

'But-but . . . we knew he was a scoundrel, but a murderer! The antiques man made a mistake.'

'No mistake, Mrs Martin. Faced with that damning piece of evidence, Murbles confessed.'

I gasped.

'You may well exclaim, Mrs Martin. I call it a confession, although technically it's really not. Murbles did break down and told us the whole thing – or almost the whole thing. As we suspected, his motive was to discredit Sir Edwin so he would sell the house. He bought the dagger, thinking it was enough like the real one to fool us.'

'Speaking of fools,' I muttered, but I don't think Billings heard me.

'Then he managed to encounter the poor woman at the Swan and put the drug in her drink. He claims that he never meant to kill her, only to implicate Edwin in an attempted murder. The stabbing, he says, was deliberately superficial. The fire was not an accident, but he never meant it to get as far as it did. It was intended to call attention to the stabbing, after he was well away, but it smouldered much longer than he had anticipated – long enough to kill Ms Wilson. Our pathologist says her drugged condition could have made her extra-sensitive to the smoke. At any rate, she died, and there was Murbles with a murder on his hands. An unintentional murder, so he says.'

'So all along we were trying to figure out who benefitted from her death – and the answer is, no one did. There was no motive for killing her.'

'No, the motive for the whole series of events was greed. Murbles wanted the fees for handling the sale of this estate. And of course, if Edwin could be convicted of a crime, Murbles might work out a way to taking the whole profit. He is, after all, a gifted embezzler.'

'Not yet,' Alan reminded him. 'Innocent until proven guilty, don't forget.'

'Indeed. But he will be proven guilty. The evidence there is plain for anyone to see. Anyone with an eye to finance, that is. His mistake was going just those few steps too far – greed again.

If he'd been content with a few takings here and there, his partners would have let it slide. If he hadn't gone out of his way to
frame Edwin with an elaborate scheme, he might well have
succeeded in getting that fat commission—'

'Wait!' I cried. The men looked up in surprise. 'Wait! I've
been thinking – who is "John Smith"?'

'The man who wants to buy the house,' said Alan indulgently.

'Do you mean, who is he really? I'm not sure that's important—'

'No. I don't care who he is. He's just a figurehead anyway.
He's an agent for someone else. Someone with whom he was
seen talking, not too long ago, talking about entail and planning
permission for small houses. I'll explain later, Inspector, but that
conversation did take place, and it took place in a café in
Grantham, and Ruth Montcalm overheard it. And what I would
like to propose is that Ruth be shown that photo of Murbles,
and see if she recognizes him. Because if he was the man behind
John Smith, he stood to get a lot more from the sale of the estate
than transaction fees. He could have manipulated the sale price,
being the negotiator at both ends, and when all was said and
done, he'd have an enormously valuable piece of real estate,
acquired from a desperate man at a bargain price, that he could
sell to developers, and make a fortune!'

'And that would finally make sense of all the persecution
Edwin's had to suffer.' Billings slapped his knee. 'As it happens,
I have that photo with me. Is little Ruth still up, or is it past her
bedtime?'

'It's certainly past her naptime, and she'll be cranky, but
she wasn't about to miss a single moment of the party. Come
with me.'

The next day, Sunday, we all went to St Matthew's. The
Montcalms were not regular churchgoers, but they felt they had
good reason for giving thanks. The girls thought it was all about
Joseph's new status as a member of the church. And that was
certainly part of it.

They used the lovely old service, modified only slightly from
the original Book of Common Prayer, whose language I so love.
All right, it's archaic. All right, some of it needs to be explained
to a modern congregation. (I had to translate a couple of times

for the girls, who were sitting on either side of me.) But it's the language of Shakespeare, and it's poetry, and to me it's perfectly fitting for the worship of God, the creator of beauty.

The post-communion prayer always seems to me to be especially meaningful, with its assurance that we are 'heirs through hope of thy everlasting kingdom' and its plea for grace to 'do all such good works as thou hast prepared for us to walk in'. Not the way we would phrase it today, but completely understandable, and necessary.

I thought over those phrases on the short drive back to the manor. Heirs through hope. Do all such good works. When we got to the house I asked Edwin, 'Do you happen to have a copy of the document establishing the terms of the entail?'

'Yes,' he said, sounding surprised. 'It's just a modern transcript, so if you were wanting to see the ancient original, you'd have to wait until tomorrow. It's at the bank.'

'Good. I'm glad it isn't in the clutches of that ersatz solicitor of yours.'

'He wanted it,' said Edwin. 'To keep it safe, he said. I said nothing doing; it stayed with the family. At least, I don't know if I . . . anyway, come to the library and I'll try to find it for you. I haven't actually looked at it in years.'

It was a ponderous document, several pages of typescript, closely-spaced and in a very small font.

'Oh, dear. Unless there's a magnifying glass around somewhere, you're going to have to help me. I want to read the passage where it says who may and who may not inherit.'

'Oh, I think I can find that.' He turned over a few pages. 'Here it is. "Male heirs of the body, who shall have been christened in the presence of the Montcalm Dagger, and no one who shall not have been so christened may be deemed an heir of the Montcalm Estate."'

'And that's all? No mention of any other stipulation?'

'Isn't that enough?' He put the sheaf of paper down, sounding bitter.

'Oh, yes, it's enough, it's plenty, it's wonderful! Edwin, unless you've missed something, it doesn't say one word about *legitimate* heirs of the body. And there has never been any question that you are Louis Montcalm's son, even if on the wrong side of the blanket.

You are his "heir of the body". And therefore heir to the estate – which one day will pass on to your heir, Joseph.'

He looked at me for a long moment, his mouth gaping, and then picked up the papers and ran from the room. 'Judith! *Judith*!'

He nearly ploughed into Cynthia, who was standing just outside the door. 'Daddy!' she said severely. 'Mummy sent me to call you to dinner. It's getting cold. And you've frightened Joseph. Do quiet down!'